ALSO BY CASSIE EDWARDS

Winter Raven

Sun Hawk

Thunder Heart

Silver Wing

Lone Eagle

Bold Wolf

Flaming Arrow

White Fire

Rolling Thunder

Wild Whispers

Wild Thunder

Wild Bliss

Wild Abandon

Wild Desire

Wild Splendor

Wild Embrace

Wild Rapture

Wild Ecstasy

MIDNIGHT FALCON

Cassie Edwards

A SIGNET BOOK

SIGNET
Published by New American Library, a division of
Penguin Putnam Inc., 375 Hudson Street,
New York, New York 10014, U.S.A.
Penguin Books Ltd, 27 Wrights Lane,
London W8 5TZ, England
Penguin Books Australia Ltd, Ringwood
Victoria, Australia
Penguin Books Canada Ltd, 10 Alcorn Avenue,
Toronto, Ontario, Canada M4V 3B2
Penguin Books (N.Z.) Ltd, 182–190 Wairau Road,
Auckland 10, New Zealand

Penguin Books Ltd, Registered Offices:
Harmondsworth, Middlesex, England

First published by Signet, an imprint of New American Library,
a division of Penguin Putnam Inc.

ISBN: 0-7394-1749-5

PUBLISHER'S NOTE
This is a work of fiction. Names, characters, places, and incidents either are
the product of the author's imagination or are used fictitiously, and any resemblance to actual persons, living or dead, business establishments, events,
or locales is entirely coincidental.

In friendship, I dedicate *Midnight Falcon*
to two special readers who became dear friends—
Jan Bussell, from the entrancing state of Washington,
and Diana Overy, from my own beloved
state of Illinois!

—*Cassie*

They are a beautiful people with their
    raven hair and dusky skin.
They fought for home, and fought for kin.
Through hardships and heartache,
    they stood as one,
From dawn until the setting sun.
We, the white man, were full of greed,
They, the red man, killed for need.
We took their lands, their lives, their hides.
But through it all they kept their pride.
I've felt a connection to the past, and their
    plight.
Had I been there, I'd have joined their fight.
Time can't erase the wrongs or the pain.
The great Nations have suffered since
The ships came from Spain.
Once this land was as open as the clear blue sky,
You raced your ponies across prairies,
Held your heads high.
Forgive me, Great Spirit, for being pale of face,
I wish I was born from your Strong race.

—Lisa Marie Jones

1

There is a lady sweet and kind,
Was never face so pleased my mind,
I did but see her passing by,
And yet I love her till I die.
—ANONYMOUS

Virginia—1700

The moon was high and full in the sky. With an almost unreal white light, it shone down upon a lone figure.

The young, copper-skinned girl was standing outside a handsome, two-storied stone house the color of melted butter. Little Snow Feather peered into the room that lay beyond the sparkling clean pane-glass window.

A Powhatan Indian, her life was vastly different from that of the white people who lived in this mansion, and she could not help but marvel over their riches.

The room that she gazed at now was huge and airy with high ceilings and mahogany-paneled walls. The furniture was plush and grand. A large stone fireplace sat at one end, a fire blazing on the grate.

Dressed in a short, apron-like garment of dressed skins that was fringed at the lower edges, and soft buckskin moccasins, Little Snow Feather

smiled as she watched a girl sit down in a chair
before the fire. Shannon was the same age as her,
ten changes of leaves.

They had met in secret many times. Because
Little Snow Feather could speak English fluently
enough—her people had learned it long ago in
the time of Pocahontas and her father, Chief
Powhatan—she and Shannon had been able to
converse openly with one another.

They had quickly become best friends. While
they were together, it didn't matter to them that
they were of different cultures and skin colors.
They proudly taught one another their various
customs.

Little Snow Feather had even shared something
with her white friend that she had never shared
with anyone whose skin was not of her own color.
She had told Shannon all about Pocahontas!

Most white people knew that Pocahontas had
made friends with the whites against her father's
wishes, and that Pocahontas had even married a
white man. But they didn't know Pocahontas's secret Indian name.

How eagerly Shannon had listened when Little Snow Feather had told her that Pocahontas's
secret Indian name was Little Snow Feather's very
own name, and that Pocahontas had been her distant ancestor.

As soft music began to drift through the window, Little Snow Feather's thoughts turned away
from Pocahontas toward the woman who was sit-

ting at a musical box, which Shannon had told her was called a harpsichord.

The music the woman was playing was beautiful and serene, yet hidden somewhere in it was the sadness that she knew the woman must be experiencing by the expression on her face.

Little Snow Feather felt bad for the woman of the house. Her name was Chandra and she was Shannon's aunt. The color of the dress that she wore tonight was black, a sign of mourning, similar to how the Powhatan painted their faces black, and sometimes their bodies, when a loved one died.

Chandra was mourning the death of her husband.

Little Snow Feather had often come to watch how her friend and her family lived, and now she studied Chandra more closely. She saw, as she always had before, that Chandra's face was young and beautiful. She was petite, and the color of her hair was reddish-gold, like the splash of the sunset on a brilliant summer's eve. Chandra was five changes of leaves younger than Little Snow Feather's chieftain brother, Midnight Falcon, who was twenty-five changes of leaves.

Little Snow Feather again looked at Shannon. She, too, had lost a loved one. Her mother.

Although friendships between the Powhatan and the whites were discouraged, Little Snow Feather ignored the warnings of her brother and her people, especially since Shannon had told her that her friendship had helped ease the pain she felt over her mother's and uncle's deaths.

Little Snow Feather had as many friends as she desired in her Powhatan village, since she was the sister of her people's *weroance*, or chief, and her people's princess. But she felt that it was right to hunger for knowledge of white people, believing that this knowledge would benefit her and her people one day.

There was no denying that some day in the future white people would more than likely outnumber red-skinned people, for each year brought more settlers to this Virginia valley.

She had to admit that it was not only a desire for knowledge that drew her into a friendship with Shannon, however. Most of all, it was because she had found how fun it was to be the recipient of the pretty white girl's smiles and hugs.

Little Snow Feather was enjoying their secret friendship very much!

Suddenly Little Snow Feather felt a hand on her shoulder.

Before she could even wonder whose it was, she was spun around and found herself face-to-face with Midnight Falcon.

Her heart skipped a beat and she swallowed hard. The glow from the lamp through the window behind her splashed onto her brother and revealed too well his angry dark eyes. He glared down at her from his six-foot-four height, a man of much agility and strength.

His thick, black, waist-length hair was pulled back from his sculpted face with a buckskin headband. He wore a buckskin breechclout, decorated with little bones and shell beads, and moccasins made of a single piece of buckskin with a flap sewn down around the opening and tied tightly around the ankle with a drawstring.

"Little sister, you continue to be just as precocious as your distant ancestor Pocahontas was," Midnight Falcon said just loud enough for his sister to hear.

He never enjoyed scolding her, for she was dear to his heart. She was admired by all who knew her, not only for her honesty and determination, but also because of her sheer beauty at such a young age. With her full seductive lips and beautiful dark eyes, she was going to grow up to be a voluptuous Powhatan maiden.

But he wished now that their parents had not named her after Pocahontas, who was also called Little Wanton and Mischievous One by her people.

"Did not Pocahontas die too young because of her alliance with whites, venturing far from her homeland and customs with her white husband?" Midnight Falcon asked. "Do you want the same for yourself? To become caught up in the ways of the white world and live a short, uneventful life among them?"

Little Snow Feather proudly lifted her chin and gazed, undaunted, back into her brother's eyes. "Big brother, although I carry her secret name, that does not make me Pocahontas," she said in a manner much too defiant to address the chief of her people.

But she continued anyhow, for she *was* how her brother described her—precocious and stubborn.

"Nor does behaving like her mean that my fate will be the same as hers," Little Snow Feather added.

She reached for Midnight Falcon's hand and gently lifted it off her shoulder.

"Please do not be angry at me for making friends with the white girl who only recently moved here," she said softly. "Shannon is interesting and fun. She rides an animal called a horse and has a dog that is a friend to her instead of a work animal."

She clasped her hands together excitedly. "The dog is so friendly and sweet compared to Powhatan dogs. It allows me to pet and hug it." Her eyes were wide with wonder. "So do you not see why I am so interested? There is so much about the white girl and her customs that I want to learn."

She grabbed him by a hand and urged him to move closer to the window. "Brother, look through the window at the woman," she said. Chandra still sat at the harpsichord, singing along with the music that she was creating on the keys. Her reddish-gold hair hung down her back, contrasting with the solemn black of her dress. "Her name is Chandra. Is not she as beautiful as her name?"

Little Snow Feather looked up at her brother, whose eyes were on Chandra, watching her. "But look how sad Chandra is. She has lost a husband. The man who lives in the house with them is Shannon's father, Chandra's brother."

Midnight Falcon did see the sadness in Chandra's green eyes and could even hear it in her voice as she sang. He was already aware of who she was. He had seen her more than once. Only today he had seen her riding a white steed beside the river, her long hair fluttering in the wind.

But this afternoon she had not worn black. Her outfit had been the color of grass and fit her body snugly, revealing her enticing curves.

Midnight Falcon was intrigued by her. He stepped closer to the window, entranced by her voice, which was soft and sweet to his ears. As before, he admired her loveliness. There was no denying how beautiful she was.

But he quickly reminded himself how wrong it was to be there, even if it was only to get his sister. Watching a tall, stout man enter the room, sit down in a chair close to the musical machine, and light a pipe, Midnight Falcon realized just how risky it was to be on the white people's property, spying on them through the window.

He spun around and swept Little Snow Feather up into his arms and slung her body across his shoulder. He broke into a hard run toward their village, upriver on the James.

Little Snow Feather kicked and squealed as she

tried to get free of her brother's grip, her head bobbing as he ran even faster. Now that they were beside the shine of the river, they were far enough from the house for Little Snow Feather to openly object to how her brother was treating her.

"Set me down on my own feet!" she cried. She squirmed and yanked at his arm in an effort to get free. "Please? I'll be good. I'll run home with you. Please? I'm sorry for displeasing you. But you also seemed to enjoy looking through the window. Is not the woman with hair of sunshine beautiful? Is not the house and everything in it interesting?"

Midnight Falcon ignored her and continued running in the moonlight, but he did understand his sister's feelings. He, too, was interested, but only in one thing that he had seen tonight.

The woman!

He could not help but remember how she looked today as she rode the impressive animal.

He also could not forget how she looked at the harpsichord, the sadness in her eyes and the sweetness of her voice.

He did not want to be so taken by her, yet he had never seen anyone as intriguingly beautiful as the woman who was called Chandra. Not even his wife had made his heart stop in quite this way.

Would not Chandra make a beautiful queen for his people?

But it was Chandra's sadness that moved him almost as much as her loveliness. Having experienced the deep pain of losing his wife, who had died in an attack on his people's village some time ago, he understood the white woman's grief. It was something that one did not get over very quickly, if at all.

Midnight Falcon had had his people to help him accept his loss. He had been named chief after his father died in the same raid as his wife.

All of his immediate family, except for his beloved sister, had died at the hands of the murderous Pocoughtaonacks tribe on that horrendous day. Midnight Falcon had valiantly fought back, helping his warriors chase the cannibals back to Canada.

He was disappointed, though, that Chief Black Rock, the Canadian chief who led the attack, had escaped the battle unharmed.

Midnight Falcon hoped to come face-to-face with him again and avenge his people.

He would head to Canada right now to find Black Rock, but his devotion to his tribe, especially his sister, kept him home.

But one day . . . !

2

Oh, what a dear ravishing thing is
the beginning of an Amour!
—APHRA BEHN

The music of the harpsichord always filled her with an inner peace that was especially welcome now, at a time of her life when things had not worked out as planned. Chandra played and sang a while longer, then sat down before the roaring fire in the parlor.

Jan-Michael Neal gazed at his sister as Katie, their black maid, dressed in a black dress and white ruffled apron, poured Chandra a cup of tea. Katie refilled his own cup with the hot brew, and he nodded a thank-you to her before she left the room.

"Chandra, your playin' gets better each day," Jan-Michael said in his thick Liverpool accent.

He laid his pipe aside and smiled at his daughter as she took a chess board out of a cupboard. Shannon arranged it on the table, then sat down at the table, facing him.

"It's good that you decided to take lessons," he said to Chandra. "It helps to lift some sadness from your heart, don't it now?"

Watching the flames lap at the logs on the grate,

Chandra only nodded slightly. "Yes, I guess it helps me, somewhat," she said. Her voice was more cultured than her brother's. Jan-Michael, five years older than Chandra, had spent long hours on his fishing boat earning a living to help put food on the family's table after their father had abandoned them, but Chandra had been able to squeeze in enough time from helping her mama with chores to become somewhat educated. She felt learned enough now to mix with most classes of people.

Chandra took a sip of tea, then glanced over at her brother. She laughed softly. "But I have a way to go before mastering that instrument. My fingers are much too short. One must have long, slim fingers to truly play it well."

"I don't think you even know how far you've come," Jan-Michael said. He placed the chess pieces on the board, one at a time, as Shannon waited eagerly. They played most evenings before the fire, something they had begun back in England as early as Shannon was old enough to know the rules of the game.

"I shall continue trying," Chandra said, setting her half-empty cup on a table beside her. Idly, she ran her hands over her lap. "Thank you for encouraging me although you know that I have never truly aspired to play. But for now it is something, a diversion, to help occupy my mind . . . and time."

"I saw you ride out today on White Iris," Jan-

Michael said, changing the subject. "Don't you think it's a bit disrespectful to be out ridin' so soon after your husband's death? Today you even wore your green ridin' suit instead of your black dress. Just because he was buried at sea on our voyage to America don't mean Lawrence has been erased from havin' ever existed."

"I—" Chandra began, but sighed as her outspoken brother interrupted. She had learned long ago how to only half listen as he voiced his strong opinions on one thing or another, and she nodded and only half listened now. She would have her say, but she always allowed him to finish his speech before telling him how things would be, and more often than not it would not be his way. She was as willful and determined as he, and he knew it.

She had wondered many times why he wasted his breath on lecturing her, but she guessed he felt that, as her big brother, he should at least try.

She had decided long ago that no one would order her around. She had seen her mother shy and cower away from her father, whose loud voice almost shook the rafters of their tiny little shanty in Liverpool.

Often Chandra had silently prayed that her brother would not walk in their father's shadow and be like him. But as each year passed, her brother became more and more overbearing.

Chandra tried to tolerate his occasional rudeness toward her. He was her only brother and very dear to her heart, despite his faults.

Her gaze swept over him. He was tall, heavy-set but muscled, with bright red hair, golden-hued eyes, and freckles across the bridge of his wide nose. Today he wore a dark suit that fit him well, emphasizing his brawn.

But his confidence in himself had been shaken due to a boating accident back in England.

"Chandra, have you heard a word I've been sayin'?" Jan-Michael asked loudly, bringing Chandra out of her deep thoughts. "Why must you sit there and daydream while I'm tryin' hard at makin' a point? You'd best heed my advice, little sister, for I not only feel it's disrespectful to go ridin' so soon after your husband's untimely death, I also think it's dangerous to ride on unfamiliar land unescorted."

"Please, Jan-Michael, don't lecture me again about doing what I love—what I must do—to try and make sense of why I am in America." Chandra sighed heavily. "I should never have listened to anyone but myself when coming here was mentioned that very first time. I—I should not have even married—"

"Chandra," Jan-Michael interrupted again. "Will you just listen to my warnings? I know how much you love ridin' and how much you resent havin' been encouraged to come to America. I can imagine how hard it is to be widowed at such a young age. But you must be more careful about ridin' alone. That Indian village isn't far from our home. You know that the redskins don't just stay on their land. While you are alone on your horse, a warrior could jump out at you at any moment, and I don't have to spell out what Indians are known to do to ladies."

He lifted a hand away from the chess pieces and nervously kneaded his brow. "How can you forget how my own wife was captured by Indians when the ship we traveled on broke down at sea?" He took a deep breath, remembering. "While we were stranded on land near the Canadian border, awaitin' the ship's repair, a band of wild Indians came from out of nowhere and killed several passengers. They dragged more than one lady away to their canoes. Those damn savages stole my wife! When we found my Priscilla, she was . . . dead. She had been raped. Lord have mercy, I hate to think of what she suffered before she took her last, dyin' breath."

He made a fist and pressed it hard against his thigh. "Damn it all to hell, Chandra, you'd better hear me. Although we've been told that the Powhatan Indians in this area are peaceful enough, who is to say what their true feelings are toward whites? Surely a defenseless woman ridin' a horse would be a temptin' target. You should never ride alone again." He looked over at his daughter as if just remembering she was there. "Nor, daughter of mine, should *you* be out there so footloose and free."

Jan-Michael sighed heavily and raked his fingers through his thick red hair. "But it's like talkin' to a wall when I try and tell you two anything."

Shannon, quite independent in her own way, sat quietly listening, knowing how upset her father would be if he found out about her friendship with one of the Powhatan Indian girls.

How she enjoyed being with Little Snow Feather, laughing and playing, but Shannon knew that if her father ever found out, he would forbid her from seeing Little Snow Feather again.

Shannon knew that Chandra felt kindly toward Indians, though.

And by the way Chandra's eyes suddenly flashed as she glared at her brother, Shannon knew that Chandra was about to defend the Powhatan.

"Just listen to yourself," Chandra said, rising from her chair. She went and stood over her brother, her hands on her hips. "From the very beginning of the white man's contact with the red man, whites have physically abused and shamefully used the Indians. I know how the colonists of this new world took advantage of the Indians as sources of information and as providers of needed foodstuffs when they were too lazy, or too unskilled with firearms, to go out and kill food for themselves. The Indians have good cause to resent whites."

She swallowed hard and turned with a swish of skirts to stand before the fire and again watch the flames dancing on the logs. "And as for my husband, I shall never forget Lawrence," she murmured, suddenly consumed by memories of how it had begun between them, and how it had ended so tragically at sea.

Her husband, Sir Lawrence O'Banyon, had been a gentleman, kind and soft-spoken. An Oxford-educated minister, he had been appointed the Rector of the James City Parish Church in Jamestown.

Lawrence had inherited his wealth from his aristocratic family and had been raised in opulence in a castle in England.

For some time it had been his desire to settle in the New World, and after he had, with his position in the church and a beautiful mansion on the James River, he went back to England long enough to find a wife.

He had told Chandra more than once that when he had first seen her, while she was shopping in the street market in Liverpool, he became lost to her, heart and soul.

It had not mattered to him that she was dirt poor and so young, nineteen to his own age of fifty-five.

He had also told Chandra that although it had been her beauty that had first attracted him to her, after knowing her, he discovered her sincere sweetness. He could not help but ask her to marry him, even though he was old enough to be her father.

Chandra had been stunned by the offer of marriage, and even somewhat frightened by the prospect of being married to a much older, wealthier man, yet she had hungered to go to the New World after hearing such wondrous things about it.

When Lawrence offered to take Chandra's brother, his wife and child, and even Chandra's mother, so that they could all live as one big happy family in America, Chandra could not say no.

But her mother had no desire to leave Liverpool, even if it meant turning down a life of luxury in America. She was afraid that due to her poor health, she would not survive the long voyage to the New World. Her mother's refusal caused Chandra to back down from going herself, and to decline the offer of marriage.

It was her brother who persuaded her to go to America, after all, by making her realize that it would be selfish of her to say no and deny her brother and his entire family the opportunity to better themselves.

A fisherman by trade, Jan-Michael had run into bad luck after his one and only fishing boat had sunk, and with it his equipment and a good number of his crew.

Blaming himself for the loss of so many of his friends, he seemed despondent. The offer to go to America was a chance to start all over again, especially since Lawrence said that he would set him up in a new fishing business there.

Loving her brother so much, no matter how overbearing he could be at times, and wanting the

best for his wife and child, Chandra had recon-
sidered.

She had been longing to experience something
new in her life, and was truly taken by the kind
gentleman who offered her more excitement
than she could have ever dreamed of. Her mother
didn't want to leave England, but she sincerely
wished for Chandra to marry this man who could
give her so much.

Chandra had married Lawrence two months before setting sail for America. He had purchased
Chandra's mother a new home and filled it with
more comforts than her mother knew existed, and
Chandra was moved by his generosity. In the short
time she knew him before he died from a heart
attack, Chandra had learned to love Lawrence, but
not the way a woman should love a husband. She
loved and admired him for being the generous
person that he was.

Although they had been intimate, Lawrence
had sped through lovemaking so quickly that
Chandra had never felt much of anything.

He had been gentle enough and never hurt her,
and for that she was glad. When he took her to
bed he had fulfilled his needs almost the minute
he stretched out on top of her. He would then roll
away, without even a kiss, and fall asleep as
quickly as he had achieved sexual gratification.

And now Chandra secretly feared that she
might be with child. On the very morning of the

day that her husband had died, she had realized that her monthly flow was late.

And that had been weeks ago.

If she was pregnant, though, it would still be some time before her body would show it. She was saddened by the thought of having a baby without a husband with whom to share the miracle. She would be alone.

"Chandra, you have more than yourself to consider when you are foolishly ridin' alone on your horse," Jan-Michael went on, bringing Chandra's thoughts back to the issue at hand. "You have Shannon. You are now like a mother to your niece."

Chandra went to Shannon and ran her fingers through the girl's long auburn hair. "I love you as though you were my own daughter," she said to her. "And I will always be here for you . . . always."

Full of determination, Chandra turned back to her brother. "But Jan-Michael, *you* are not *my* father, so please stop acting as though you are. You will not dictate to me what I can or cannot do. You will not treat me like an imbecile who cannot think for herself. And as for riding White Iris, you can't tell me when, or when not, to ride her."

She slid a hand over her abdomen reflexively. "And as for Lawrence," she continued, "a part of him will always be with me."

Thinking about the boat she had purchased for

Jan-Michael that now rested in the river down the long, sloping lawn from the house, Chandra decided to try a new tactic. "Jan-Michael, if you would set your mind on more important things, like hiring men and starting your fishing business, you wouldn't be worrying so much about me, or Shannon. You should be more concerned about yourself and what you are doing with your life. You need to be working, not sitting around devising ways to argue with me and your daughter."

She started for the door but turned to look back at her brother. "It's not healthy brooding so long on the fishing accident," she said quietly, her eyes wavering. "You will never be happy until you are out on the water bringing in big catches of fish. Fishing might even help you get past your own mourning."

Chandra saw an instant pain enter his eyes. Jan-Michael hung his head to hide his emotions. She knew he felt responsible for the loss of so many lives, perhaps even for the death of his own wife. Realizing just how hard it was for him to set foot on another fishing boat, Chandra turned and left the room.

She paused in the spacious entrance hall, with its shining oak floors and lacy plasterwork. She now owned a home filled with plush furnishings covered in richly colored fabrics, with beautifully designed wallpaper and expensive paintings on the walls. English china gleamed on the mahogany dining table beneath a sparkling crystal chandelier.

The opulence of her surroundings was always a reminder of the wealth her marriage had brought into her life. She had more now than she could have ever dreamed, yet she was not happy. A big part of her heart was empty.

Oh, how she hated the title of widow!

Sighing, she climbed the spiral staircase to the second floor. Too restless to ready herself for bed, she went to a small, narrow staircase at the far end of the corridor and climbed up to a room where a cupola looked out upon everything.

She stepped to one of the windows and gazed out.

From this height, the black sky stretched wide above her, and down below she could see the reflection of the moon on the James River.

A sensual shiver ran through her as she recalled her ride along the river that afternoon. She had noticed a handsome Indian warrior watching her today from a bluff. She smiled as she shamelessly thought about what he had worn—the briefest of breechclouts!

But she remembered one special moment, when their eyes met and held. A combination of feelings—of being afraid, yet fascinated—had made her look quickly away. When she had looked at the bluff again, he was gone.

"He had to have been Powhatan," she whispered to herself, for he was on foot.

There were other tribes in the area, but the Powhatan was the only one in walking distance of Jamestown. She knew little about the Powhatan, only what had been explained to her shortly after her arrival in Virginia.

Among the chiefdoms formed by various Algonquian-speaking Indians along the Atlantic coast, the Powhatan empire of Eastern Virginia was by far the largest.

She was at ease living so close to these Indians, because there were peaceful relations between them and whites.

"I wonder if I will ever see that warrior again?" she whispered as she turned away from the window and left the room.

She closed her bedroom door behind her. She had lit candles in the room before she had ventured downstairs to join her brother and niece in the parlor, and they were only half burned down now, giving off enough light for her to see the loveliness of the room. As with the rest of the house, only the finest furniture filled the room, yet she still felt lonely. Back in Liverpool, where they had only two rooms for the entire family, no one was ever alone. She missed that closeness. She missed her mama!

Shaking the thought from her mind, Chandra went to the wardrobe and opened its door to gaze at her clothes, which hung neatly inside. For some reason an image of the Indian came to her again.

"Should I even want to see him again?" she

wondered as she eyed her clothes, aching to wear something besides the drab black things. Today it had felt so good to wear her riding attire.

She ran her fingers over the various silk blouses and dresses, then shrugged and went over to the window.

She drew back the sheer white curtain and sighed. It was such a beautiful night. Everything was bathed in moonlight, and the breeze still held some of the day's warmth. It would be a wonderful night to take a stroll beside the river.

She was still too restless to go to bed, and a walk would do her good. The fresh air alone would be welcome after such a long evening beside the fireplace.

She grabbed a shawl and started to leave, then turned back and went to the wardrobe again. A beautiful pink silk dress caught her eye, and it was at this moment that she decided it was time to live again and look to the future.

Chandra hoped that none of them would ever have reason to wear black again.

She would leave her mourning behind her. Perhaps by doing so, it might even help alleviate her brother's grief and give him the strength to go on with his life.

And it would set a good example for Shannon, whose own grief had been overwhelming at times.

But Chandra had noticed, of late, how Shannon's eyes were again filled with the warmth and excitement of a ten-year-old girl.

Chandra had understood why Shannon had not wanted to wear black, and in that, Jan-Michael had agreed. Tonight, Shannon had looked sweet and happy in her lacy pink dress, although she usually wore something more casual that gave her more freedom to ride her pony and explore.

As Chandra dressed, she wondered just what was putting the skip in her niece's step again. Perhaps while on an outing she had found a friend. She would have to ask Shannon about it soon.

Not wanting her brother to catch her going out alone at night, having been lectured enough for one evening, Chandra took the rear staircase and went out into the moonlight.

She was careful to stay on her own property, so that she could scream and alert Jan-Michael that she was in trouble if necessary.

Yet, she felt safe enough.

Standing on the riverbank in the shadow of her brother's new fishing vessel, she gazed at it. It shimmered and swayed as the waves lapped against its wooden hull. Only recently had she begun to fully understand how tragedy had put the fear of water into Jan-Michael's heart. She had seen him panic on the journey to America when a sudden squall hit.

Often, Chandra would watch from her bedroom window as Jan-Michael came to the river and sat for hours staring at the new vessel.

But courage failed him—he hadn't once boarded the boat.

Chandra was beginning to think that he never would.

Wanting to ease this worry from her mind, she walked away from the boat and sat down on the riverbank. She began to hum a soft, sweet song.

She enjoyed the quiet serenity of night and the beautiful river, and for the moment she was able to forget everything else.

3

A lady's imagination is very rapid; it
jumps from admiration to love, from
love to matrimony in a moment.
—JANE AUSTEN

Having made certain that his sister was sleeping
safely in her blankets, Midnight Falcon could not
help but be lured back to the white woman's land.

He ran along the moonlit path, his eyes set
straight ahead for the first sight of the large home,
where he had gazed in near rapture at the woman
whose name he now knew.

He didn't plan to stare in the windows again.
He would only look at the house and try to un-
ravel the mystery of why she intrigued him so
much, when no other white woman had. Even
women of his own tribe had not made him feel
as Chandra had.

There was something about the softness of her
face, the gentleness of her movements, that captivated him.

He had watched her draw a tight rein on her
horse and climb down effortlessly, as though she
were no more than the weight of a feather. She
had delicately walked along the river, her hands
holding the reins.

In her eyes, so green they seemed luminous, he

had glimpsed more than sadness. He had seen that she was lonely, but she seemed at peace with the world and her loneliness, for there was no anxiousness in her eyes or in her smile.

She had turned to her steed and run a gloved hand along its mane, and Midnight Falcon was surprised to see Chandra actually talking to the horse, as though it might be a friend, not an animal just there to do its duty to its master.

Then, when she had looked up and had seen him standing on the bluff, how his heart had seemed to leap from his chest. She did not show any fear of being watched by a man with red skin, even though he would have thought a lone white woman would become instantly afraid.

He knew that there were tales of atrocities committed by the red man against white women, although he also knew that white men could be as cruel. He had heard of white men who raped women, then abandoned them, and he became angry at the thought.

It thrilled Midnight Falcon to know that Chandra trusted enough not to scream and flee at the first sight of a red man. Yet he also was uneasy to see her so trusting of any man, knowing that she could be taken advantage of by those whose hearts were dark and filled with evil.

He had thought about that more than once since their eyes had met that day, and he felt a desire to be the one to always protect her from those who might mean her harm.

"I am filling my heart and mind with too much fantasy," he whispered to himself, and the words made him stop abruptly. Frustrated, he ran a hand through his hair, then turned to head back toward his home. Yet he could not will his feet to take him there even though he knew it was where he belonged. Chandra might have gazed trustingly into his eyes, but inside her heart, she must have seen him as loathsome, the way most white women saw all Indians.

And was not she one of the wealthy white people? Would she not consider the Powhatan poor because they lived in bark-covered houses instead of those made of stone? Could she understand that wealth among the Powhatan was in their foodstuffs and hides, and, especially, in their precious children?

"I must return home," he said aloud, sad at the thought of turning away from moments that could thrill his very being. He had hoped to see her again, even her shadow through a window. Yet he knew he must not give in to such desires.

He had thought to make an effort to know Chandra after she shed her black mourning attire, even though he had discouraged his sister from making friends with the white girl her age.

So far, that friendship had brought no harm to his sister, and he wished it would be all right for him to make friends with the woman. But he knew that such relationships were forbidden. Still, it was not as though it had never happened . . . a Powhatan and a white becoming close.

Had not Pocahontas married a white man?

He frowned when he remembered his own words about how Pocahontas had died far too young after marrying John Rolfe. Many Powhatan blamed her death on the marriage, although, in truth, she had died from a disease anyone—red or white—could have fallen victim to.

His mind made up, Midnight Falcon turned back in the direction of the woman's home and started running along the riverbank.

After just a short distance, he became aware of a sound so sweet his breath caught in his throat. He recognized it. He had heard the same sort of sound only a short while ago as Chandra had sat singing at the harpsichord.

He heard a woman now, but instead of singing, she was humming a soft and beautiful song.

And she was near!

He knew that it couldn't be just any woman calling to his heart with her music.

It had to be Chandra!

He crept closer to the sound until he saw what seemed to be a vision sitting beside the river. It *was* Chandra, with her hair the color of sunshine shimmering in the soft breeze of night.

And she was no longer wearing the color of mourning!

Did that mean that her grief was behind her now? He reminded himself of how she was dressed while riding. Perhaps she would be wearing black again the next time he saw her.

As the moon bathed her in its satiny sheen, Midnight Falcon continued to gaze at her in awe, stirred by awakenings he had never felt before.

The feelings were so intense, it seemed as though he had known this woman, somehow, forever.

Until now, there had been only one special woman in his life. As were so many marriages among his people, his had been arranged by his wife's father and his own. Midnight Falcon and his wife had been so young, *too* young, to know the true meaning of love.

He knew that he must fight his feelings tonight as never before.

He started to leave, but as he turned, he stepped on a brittle twig, which snapped loudly as it broke.

He stiffened and his heart seemed to freeze inside his chest as he waited for Chandra to scream from fright. When she didn't, he held his breath and turned slowly to see that she was still there, standing now instead of sitting on the riverbank.

Her eyes were on him.

To his relief, to his utter fascination, he once again saw no fear in how Chandra looked at him.

Instead, her expression was one of wonder.

When Chandra had heard the twig snap, she knew that she was no longer alone, and she was afraid.

Her first instinct was to scream, but she was so

glad that she had looked to see who her intruder was before she did.

Chandra could not believe that Midnight Falcon was there, so close, and that she felt no fear in his presence. If he had come to harm or abduct her, he could have done so already. This had to mean that he was there for another reason.

Again she recalled that brief moment when their eyes had met while she had been out horseback riding. His curiosity about her must have brought him this close to her home, and he had found her sitting there, strangely enough, at the very moment she had been thinking of him.

It was as though her thoughts had drawn him to her.

That made goosebumps suddenly rise on her flesh.

They both stood still, seemingly spellbound at having discovered each other.

Her pulse raced at his handsomeness, at his tall, muscled body that she knew must be strong.

His hair shone like a raven's wing in the moonlight, waving slightly in the gentle breeze. She could not help but stare at his full, seductive lips, and at his eyes that were as dark as all midnight skies.

Up this close she could see exactly what his breechclout was made of. It was made of buckskin, but what fascinated her were the pelts of animals, their heads and tails still intact, that were fastened to a belt around his waist.

Her gaze shifted to his fancy moccasins, and then lingered on his body. As before, when she had seen him on the bluff, she stared at him shamelessly.

Afraid that she had studied him for much too long, and not wanting him to realize the extent of her fascination with him, she made a daring first move by taking a step toward him.

"My name is Chandra," she said, lifting a hand toward him. She knew that the Powhatan understood English well enough.

Seeing her gesture of friendship, Midnight Falcon relaxed. He was so glad that she still seemed to trust him. He knew that she could have been prejudiced or afraid.

He stepped closer and took her hand, surprised at the instant electricity of their touch. He jumped with alarm and pulled back his hand.

He knew that she felt it as well, by how she gasped and moved away from him. He watched as she ran that hand nervously down the side of her dress.

"I am called Midnight Falcon," he said. "I am chief of the nearby Powhatan village. For the most part my people are friendly with whites. I accept your offer of friendship."

She had heard the name of the Powhatan chief, but no one had said how young he was.

She was in awe that the very warrior she had seen on the bluff was not only standing in front of her, but also was a powerful chief.

He was so young, surely not much older than herself, and he was breathtakingly handsome.

And he actually wanted to be her friend!

When she had thought about coming to America, she had wondered about Indians, and whether or not she might meet one face-to-face.

She had imagined Indians would be civil and peace-loving. But when her brother's wife had been abducted and killed, she learned that, like white people, Indians were a mixture of bad and good.

She was glad to discover the good this time, for in Midnight Falcon, she sensed much kindness, much goodness.

"I do wish to be a friend," Chandra said. She wanted to offer her hand again, yet she was still stunned by how something magical had seemed to flow between them.

"I haven't been in the area for long," she added. "I live with my family."

"I have seen your family—a man and young girl."

It was so easy to talk to this woman, he thought, to be with her. Maybe anything was possible.

He gazed down at her hands, which she now clasped before her. He wished to reach out and hold one of them again, but he realized that what he had said about her family seemed to shock her.

Not wanting her to know that he knew even more about her, especially not wanting her to know just yet that his sister was friends with her niece, he tried to act innocent.

"What are the man and girl to you?" he asked.

"I have seen you wearing black," he said, not giving her a chance to answer his question. It was not something he had planned to say. "Black is the color of mourning." His gaze swept slowly over her. "You no longer wear black. Does that mean that you are no longer in mourning?"

Chandra was stunned by how observant he was.

He must have seen her more than that once, because she had worn her riding outfit then, which was green, not black.

He must have gone out of his way to see her, for she had not left her house many times lately except to ride. Knowing that he *had* noticed her before did not frighten her.

"I *have* been in mourning," she found herself saying, comfortable enough to tell him the truth. "It was for my husband. He died at sea, on our way from England to America. But now I wish to move forward with my life."

She hung her head and took a deep breath, then looked up again into Midnight Falcon's dark, almost mystical, eyes. "I will always be sad about my husband's death," she said softly. "But I am young and must enjoy life, for too often lives are cut short by circumstances beyond control."

Talking about her husband made her think

about her missed monthly flow. If she was pregnant, she must live for her baby!

And there was sweet Shannon. Shannon needed a mother, and Chandra was and would always be there for her.

Did that leave anything for anyone else?

Was there truly time in her life now for a man?

Chandra slid a hand over her belly and wondered if any man would see her as desirable if he knew she was with child, if she *was* with child.

No, this would be her secret, for as long as possible.

She was stunned by where her thoughts had taken her, that she was actually thinking about this Powhatan warrior, who had his own heavy responsibilities to consider, in such a way.

It was ridiculous to even consider this chance meeting as anything but that. And it was foolish for her to ever think there could be anything more between them.

"I, too, have known such loss," Midnight Falcon said.

Her words inspired him to open up to her. He could feel a special bond already forming between them and wondered if she felt it, also.

"I once had a wife. She died during a raid on my village by an enemy tribe."

"I'm so sorry," Chandra murmured, feeling his sadness as he spoke of his loss.

"Did . . . did you have children before she died?"

She was amazed that she had asked him such a personal question, yet she badly wanted to know everything about him.

"No, no children," he said, shaking his head. "But there is my young sister. I look to her as a daughter, for she is my responsibility now as though she were."

She caught herself before asking why.

Afraid that she had been gone for too long, Chandra took a step away. She did not want Jan-Michael to discover her room empty and begin looking for her.

"I must return home," she said.

They gazed at one another for a long moment.

"I do hope, though, that we can meet and talk again," Chandra added.

"We shall."

Stunned by the meeting and the feelings this woman had awakened in him, Midnight Falcon watched Chandra run off in the direction of her house. He wondered how they could meet without others knowing, at least for now.

He set off toward his village, already certain with every beat of his heart that he wanted this woman with hair the color of the sun.

Ah, yes! He wanted to make her his queen.

4

How much better is thy love than wine?
—SONG OF SOLOMON 4:10

Shannon was like her Aunt Chandra in that it was hard to keep her inside the house. She often strayed from their property to explore this new, wonderful land of wide spaces and clear, blue skies.

Today was another day of adventure. Having heard about purple pearls, she was now knee-deep in the James River, searching with her bare toes in the rocky bottom for mussels in which she hoped to find a rare pearl.

She still couldn't believe the fresh air of Virginia. Back in England, it seemed to be gray and rainy every day, and smoke from so many home fires lay thick over the city.

She stopped to gaze heavenward. It was a beautiful, carefree day, and fluffy white clouds scudded across a wondrously blue sky.

Shannon inhaled deeply, the tall spruce and pine trees beside the river giving off a heady fragrance that she could never get enough of.

A bark and a splash drew her eyes to the shore,

where her Scottish Terrier had just leaped into the water. He was swimming toward her.

"Oh, Scottie, you love it, too, don't you?" Shannon said, hurrying to meet him.

When she reached him, she bent low in the water and swept him against her. Her terrier had quickly grown from a puppy into a stout, fat thing with black, curly fur.

Its large, dark eyes gazed up at Shannon adoringly. Up until only a few weeks ago, she had been able to carry Scottie around, but now, with the dog's added weight, she almost toppled backwards when she tried to lift him.

"Sweetie, you are going to have to be happy with only hugs and kisses now," Shannon murmured, running her fingers through her dog's wet fur. She smiled as Scottie nuzzled her hand with his shiny, black nose. "It's a wonder you don't sink, you are so fat and lazy now."

Shannon felt a presence and looked up. Little Snow Feather approached the river. Her face was radiant with a smile and her long black hair fluttered in the breeze.

"Hello, there!" Shannon cried, waving at her newly found friend. She giggled as Scottie broke loose and swam back to shore, knowing that once her dog was on dry land, her friend would get a shower.

Shannon had found it hard to believe that the Powhatan used dogs for labor, not fun and hugs.

The animals didn't even bark. They howled like their ancestors, the wolves!

With mischief in her eyes, Shannon watched as Little Snow Feather, unaware of what was about to happen, innocently bent to a knee and reached her arms out for the dog.

"I do so love your dog," Little Snow Feather said. She squealed and closed her eyes as Scottie shook himself and sprayed water all over her beautifully fringed blouse and skirt.

"That wasn't fair of me. I should have warned you," Shannon said, giggling again as she came out of the water.

She knelt beside Little Snow Feather and gently wiped the river water from her face with the sleeve of her cotton dress. "I'm sorry. Look at your dress. Look at your hair. I had no idea Scottie would spray *this* much water on you."

As Scottie lay down, resting his chin on his paws, Little Snow Feather hugged Shannon. "It's all right," she said. "I enjoyed it. I do love your Scottie so much. It makes me wish that I could tame one of the newborn pups in our village to be so sweet and friendly."

Little Snow Feather looked at Shannon questioningly as they both rose to their feet. "Why were you in the river?" she asked, glancing at Shannon's discarded patent-leather shoes.

She studied Shannon's dress, wet only up to her knees. As usual, Little Snow Feather admired her friend's attire, which differed so much from her own. The dress was fully gathered at the waist and its puffy sleeves were rolled up to Shannon's elbows. The collar, trimmed in white lace, accented her friend's delicate, long neck.

Like her Aunt Chandra, Shannon was petite, but there was a difference. Shannon's pink, soft face was round, and she had blue eyes and deep dimples.

Little Snow Feather would never forget how open Shannon had been with her that first time they had met beside the river. Shannon had explained why they were in America, and how her mother had been abducted by Indians in Canada and killed. It had touched Little Snow Feather's heart that Shannon would trust her, an Indian, after losing her mother in such a terrible way.

But Shannon *had* trusted Little Snow Feather, and they had talked of everything that day, of mothers and fathers, aunts and uncles, and of how Shannon had refused to wear black.

Shannon had explained to Little Snow Feather that she would never wear black, as was the custom, because to her, her mother was still very much alive. She would be alive, forever, inside her heart!

"Don't you remember telling me about the purple pearls that could be found in the James River?" Shannon said, eager to go back into the water. "Today I am searching for mussels. Maybe I'll find one with a purple pearl inside."

Little Snow Feather giggled, realizing that Shannon thought purple pearls were found already that color.

"Come and sit with me," Little Snow Feather said.

She grabbed one of Shannon's hands and led her closer to the water. They sat down on the riverbank, their eyes locked.

"I guess I did not explain things well enough to you before about the pearls," Little Snow Feather said.

"What else is there to know?" Shannon asked. She smiled as Scottie squeezed between them and stretched out on his side, soon contentedly asleep.

"The pearls don't start out purple," Little Snow Feather said. She enjoyed running her hand down the dog's fur. "White pearls, *special* white ones, sometimes can be found in mussel shells. It's cooking the mussels that turns them purple."

"Really? Then it is white pearls I should be looking for? Not purple?"

"They are always white first, then purple," Little Snow Feather said, nodding. "I love how we often use both white and purple pearls on clothes for special occasions. They are made into designs of flowers on skirts and dresses."

"That sounds so beautiful," Shannon said, sighing.

"I will make you a beautiful bracelet of pearls one day," Little Snow Feather said, her eyes dancing. "But that will have to wait. If I were to give you a special bracelet now and you wore it, it would raise too many questions about where you got it. Later, after we are no longer forced to keep our friendship a secret, I will give a bracelet to you."

"And I will take you for a ride on my horse with me," Shannon said, even now envisioning them together on her pony, riding and laughing into the wind.

"I would like that." She, too, could picture how fun it would be to ride on the four-legged animal with her friend.

"But for now, I think we've sat out in the open long enough," Shannon said. She grabbed Little Snow Feather by a hand and encouraged her to her feet. "Let's go to our secret hiding place before someone sees us. There we can talk for as long as we wish about everything that we wish. I love hearing about you and your people."

"Me too."

Shannon picked up her shoes, and with Scottie following behind them, panting, they ran together until they reached their secret nook beneath a bluff farther upriver.

They dangled their legs over an outcrop of rock that looked down on the blue water of the James. Flying squirrels, woodchucks, beavers, and lizards came to see them, then would run back into the forest as Scottie playfully chased them away. A pair of eagles soared overhead, their eyes watching the two little girls now busy talking and sharing.

"I have a secret to tell you," Little Snow Feather said. She moved to her knees and turned to face Shannon. "Do you want to hear my secret? Do you?"

"Always," Shannon said, scrambling to her knees to face Little Snow Feather. "I do love secrets, especially yours."

"Promise you will not tell a soul?" Little Snow Feather asked, her eyes imploring Shannon.

"A secret between us remains a secret for as long as breath is in my lungs." Shannon leaned her face closer to Little Snow Feather's. "Oh, please, Little Snow Feather, don't wait another minute. Please, please tell me!"

"You know of Pocahontas," Little Snow Feather said, watching Shannon's eyes widen as she eagerly nodded. "You know that she is my distant relative?"

Again Shannon nodded, her eyes even wider than moments before.

"Well, the ghost-spirit of Pocahontas comes to me sometimes." Little Snow Feather blurted it out, as though it was a relief to finally be able to tell someone. "I even laugh and talk with Pocahontas. Before you came to America, she was my best friend."

Shannon's breath caught in her throat. In awe of what she had just heard, she stared for a moment at Little Snow Feather. Then, caught up in the intrigue of the moment, she moved even closer to her friend. "Can I see Pocahontas, too?" she asked. "Can I actually talk to her?"

Little Snow Feather looked past Shannon at the river, then gazed into her friend's eyes once again. "No," she said, her voice gentle.

Her eyes pleaded with Shannon. "Please understand? It is not because I do not want to share her with you. It is just that only I can see and talk with her, because we are bonded by name and family ties."

"Oh, I see," Shannon said. She tried to hide her disappointment, because she didn't want to give her friend any reason not to confide in her again. "Yes, I understand."

But how she wished she could see Pocahontas's ghost! Everyone knew the story of Pocahontas. If it was ever possible to be visited by a spirit, would not that be the most wonderful thing ever? She hoped there might be some way for Little Snow Feather to make that happen some time. She truly believed her friend had seen Pocahontas and could not envision her making up such a story.

Shannon and Little Snow Feather moved to the rock's edge again and dangled their feet over the side.

Shannon reached out for Scottie and pulled him closer as he plopped down on his belly.

"My brother caught me peeking in your window last night," Little Snow Feather said suddenly. "For a moment he also watched your family."

"You were there? When? You were watching?" Shannon said, her eyes widening. "And your brother, too?"

"You are not angry, are you?"

"No. If I were given the chance, I would watch you through your window. I'd love to see where you live, but I do not dare wander that far from home. My father would tie me to my bed and leave me there for a full week!"

"What?" Little Snow Feather gasped. "He would do that?"

Shannon laughed. "No, my father wouldn't do that," she said. "He is strict, but usually his bark is worse than his bite."

Shannon saw some color drain from her friend's face at that statement and had to explain what it meant. "What did your brother say when he caught you?"

"At first he was angry, but after he took the time to look, I saw his anger fade into wonder," Little Snow Feather said. "His eyes never left your beautiful aunt, and as he watched her, I saw how interested he was."

"Truly?" Shannon said, caught up in the excitement of what it could mean to her and Little Snow Feather if Midnight Falcon and Chandra actually met and fell in love! That would bring the two families together. That would mean that Shannon and Little Snow Feather wouldn't have to keep their friendship a secret.

The possibilities of how much fun they could have if they didn't have to hide were endless!

"What can we do to get Midnight Falcon and Chandra together?" Shannon asked. She turned to Little Snow Feather and grabbed both of her hands. "Let's arrange a meeting between them, one that they will think happened by chance. Just think of it, Little Snow Feather. Would not it be wonderful if your brother and my aunt fell in love? We would no longer have to hide our friendship. We would no longer have to sneak around. We could finally go horseback riding together!"

"That is something I have dreamed of," Little Snow Feather said, sighing. "You see, the only hoofed animals I ever saw before you came were white-tailed deer." She giggled. "One never tries to ride on the back of a deer."

"No, I don't think so," Shannon said, giggling herself.

Then they got serious. They put their heads together and sorted through plans, smiling when they came up with one that they both agreed on and felt was easy enough to arrange.

"I can hardly wait," Shannon said, quickly hugging Little Snow Feather. "Oh, won't it be such fun to watch?"

5

The look of love alarms
Because 'tis fill'd with fire;
But the look of soft deceit
Shall win the lover's hire.
—WILLIAM BLAKE

Of all of the magnificent rooms in the twelve-room mansion, Chandra liked the breakfast room the best. It had windows from floor to ceiling, giving the sun freedom to fill every corner with its glorious warmth and light.

Chandra and her brother and niece would sit at the table, Scottie resting beneath it on one of Shannon's feet, and they would have a good view of the river that lay down the slope of green lawn away from the house.

Today, Chandra sat with them and ate fried mush and eggs, a steaming cup of tea at hand. In the morning sunlight, she gazed down at the river where Jan-Michael's fishing boat sat, empty and unused.

This was another reason Chandra liked this room and its view. She had made sure the new boat was where Jan-Michael could see it at every meal. It was always there, beckoning to him.

She hoped that if Jan-Michael glimpsed the boat now and then, he might feel the urge to board it and finally begin his fishing business again. That would mean he had left his bad memories behind.

Chandra looked over at her brother, his face hidden behind a newspaper. His red hair was slicked back from his rugged, square face, and he still dressed in his dark suit of mourning. "Today would be a perfect day for you to go on your boat and see how nice it is," she said. She lifted her white linen napkin from her lap and delicately dabbed her lips. "It's such a beautiful day, Jan-Michael. How can you stand *not* going aboard the boat and taking it out for a trial run?"

Jan-Michael lowered the newspaper and gave Chandra an annoyed glance.

"I know that I should appreciate what you are tryin' to do, Chandra, but I don't," he growled. "Just because you took it upon yourself to purchase that boat, don't mean that I have to board it now, or ever. Just mind your business, little sister."

He looked more closely at her.

"I noticed yesterday, and now this mornin', that you have chosen to shed your mourning," he said. "I still think it's a wee premature."

"And now who is minding whose business?" Chandra said. She sighed heavily, for she had been waiting for him to comment on her change of attire.

Jan-Michael glanced down at his own black suit. He ran a hand over the wool fabric of a trouser leg, then smiled awkwardly at Chandra. "I, too, am bone-tired of wearin' black," he said. He also sighed. "I would change into something more comfortable, but it's just that—"

"Chandra, I know a place where a person can find purple pearls," Shannon blurted out, purposely interrupting her father. She knew where the conversation was leading, and she didn't want to hear any more talk about what happened to her mother. It pained her so much to think about it, much less talk about it, or hear her father tell how he couldn't save his own wife that day.

"Purple pearls?" Chandra said, her eyes widening in wonder. "Why, I have never heard of such a thing. Are there really some in the area?"

Shannon had sat quietly at the table eating her mush and patiently waiting for a break in the conversation, and now she was eager to get the plan into motion that she had put together with Little Snow Feather. Especially now that Chandra had put her black clothes of mourning in a trunk.

Shannon hoped that neither Chandra nor her father could read the deception in her eyes, or hear it in her voice, as she encouraged her aunt to go and see the purple pearls.

She would explain later that the pearls were really white. The main thing was to get her aunt to the river at the private spot where the "chance" meeting would take place.

"Yes, there are purple pearls, but they are very rare. That's what makes it so exciting," Shannon said, avoiding her father's questioning stare.

"Would you like to go with me and dig for mussels to try and find one?"

"It's such a beautiful day, and I can think of no better way to spend it than that," Chandra said, already pushing her chair back from the table.

"Then we can go now?" Shannon asked, trying not to sound too eager. It was getting close to the time that she and Little Snow Feather had arranged.

Shannon hoped that Little Snow Feather could persuade Midnight Falcon to go along with her. He *was* a chief, who had duties of his people to tend to.

He might not believe whatever reason Little Snow Feather used to lead him to the rendezvous spot.

"Please consider going into town today and posting a notice for fishermen," Chandra said to her brother. "Please do something, Jan-Michael, besides sitting around this house and brooding. You are going to make yourself into an old man before your time."

"You two go on and search for your pearls," he grumbled, not bothering to even look at his sister.

Chandra sighed, gazed at him for a moment longer, then left the house with Shannon.

As they walked down the slope of green grass toward the river, Scottie ran after them, attempting to keep up.

Chandra gave her niece a questioning look.

"Don't we need something to dig with?" she asked.

"Just your toes," Shannon said, giggling. Even though that was true, she knew no one would be digging for anything today. By the time she brought Chandra to the meeting spot, someone else would be arriving there.

And when Chandra saw Midnight Falcon, and he saw her, all thoughts of pearls, and whatever else might be on their minds, would be forgotten! She hoped they would be pleased with the scheming of two ten-year-old girls!

"Toes?" Chandra repeated, stopping to stare at Shannon. "What do you mean?"

"You remove your shoes and go into the river almost knee-deep, and then you use your toes to dig around the rocks and mud at the bottom until you find the mussels," Shannon said, watching Chandra's eyes widen in wonder.

"I'd best go and change from my silk dress then," Chandra said, turning to go back to the house.

Shannon grabbed her hand. "I shall do all the digging," she said. "You can watch. And when I find the shells, you can pry them open. I want you to be the one to find the purple pearl."

"But isn't most of the fun in the digging?" Chandra asked, raising an eyebrow.

"I don't think so," Shannon said. "I still have mud beneath my toenails from yesterday's search."

Chandra looked alarmed, then laughed. Hand in hand, they resumed walking toward the river.

"This time you can dig, but the next time, when I don't have on one of my best dresses, I shall be the one to go into the water and find the mussels," she said. "A wee bit of mud beneath one's toes can't be all that bad, not when it has gotten there by finding rare pearls."

"Yes, the next time I shall watch while you dig." Shannon was relieved that Chandra had not gone back to the house to change, especially when she looked so pretty in her fancy dress, for that would take away precious time.

Chandra and Midnight Falcon must arrive there at the exact same moment, or all would be spoiled!

"You do like America, don't you?" Chandra asked, affectionately squeezing Shannon's hand.

"More and more every day," Shannon said. "I never want to return to England. I have found much happiness here."

"And friends? Have you managed to find anyone to play with while you have been out each day exploring on foot, or riding your pony?"

Shannon gave her aunt a sidewise glance. "Yes, I have found a friend," she admitted, as Scottie stopped and lay down, apparently deciding to wait there for their return. "One who is becoming more special to me every day."

"You must bring her to our house for tea soon. Also her mother. I think I would be happier if I made a good friend, too."

Shannon's eyes wavered. "Her . . . her mother is dead," she said, her voice breaking.

"Oh, how horrible!" Chandra looked quickly over at Shannon. "But perhaps that is what has made your friendship so special . . . in that neither of you has a mother."

"Yes, perhaps." Shannon hoped that Chandra didn't pursue questioning her about her friend much longer, because she didn't think it was quite the time to reveal that her new best friend was an Indian!

But after Chandra met Midnight Falcon, it would be different. They would surely become friends, and hopefully more than that, and then Shannon could tell Chandra everything about Little Snow Feather. It was something that she would love to share with Chandra.

"How much farther do we have to go before stopping to dig for the mussels?" Chandra asked, although she did not care. She was enjoying the wonderful fresh air, the soft breeze, and the birds and animals around them.

"Just a little farther."

Shannon and Little Snow Feather had calculated how long it would take for each of them to get Midnight Falcon and Chandra to the rendezvous spot, and Shannon expected that Little Snow Feather might at this very moment be setting out. They had less distance to travel, for Shannon had thought it was wise to get Chandra as far as she could from their home, so that Jan-

Michael might not happen along and catch the meeting taking place.

This way, if Chandra and Midnight Falcon enjoyed meeting one another, they would have their privacy to continue talking.

"Purple pearls," Chandra said. She envisioned wearing a full necklace of them, although she knew the chances were slim of finding even one.

It was just good to go along with Shannon.

Her niece seemed to have accepted the loss of her mother well enough, but one could never tell when a child her age might be hiding her true feelings.

"I have yet to see one," Shannon said, trying to make sure Chandra wouldn't be disappointed. "But it will be fun trying."

"Yes, much fun," Chandra agreed and smiled.

Still holding hands, laughing and talking, they continued on their way along the river.

Soon Shannon's heart began to beat more quickly. It couldn't be long now before she found out whether their plan worked, or backfired!

6

Keep me as the apple of the eye,
hide me under the shadow of thy wings.
—PSALMS 17:8

So pleased that thus far the plan was working, Little Snow Feather anxiously clutched her brother's hand as they walked beside the James River. While they had been eating their early-morning meal, Little Snow Feather had told Midnight Falcon how she had recently found a place in the river filled with many mussels.

She had said that she wanted to dig for more, that it had been her dream to find a mussel with a pearl inside.

She explained that it was especially important to find one of those special mussels now, since she would like to make a bracelet out of purple pearls for a friend.

She had asked Midnight Falcon if he had the time to help her dig the mussels.

He had said how sweet and generous she was to want to make a bracelet for a friend, and Midnight Falcon had agreed to go with her to the river.

As they walked beside the shine of the river, Little Snow Feather could not help but feel torn.

A part of her was excited about getting her brother to come with her. Yet another part of her felt guilty for having told him a non-truth, for she was not bringing him to the river to dig mussels as she had said.

She was bringing him there to meet a lovely lady who was as lonesome as he was. She had no husband, as Midnight Falcon had no wife. They had at least that in common—having lost a spouse at a young age.

Little Snow Feather's heart beat rapidly at the thought of how her brother and Chandra might react when they realized they had been duped by two young girls. They could be angry, or they might seize the opportunity to get to know one another better.

Little Snow Feather had seen her brother's interest in Chandra, and she could not imagine how Chandra could be anything but taken by the handsome Powhatan chief, whose midnight eyes and friendly smile filled hearts with trust and warmth.

"You are so quiet now. Only a short while ago you chattered endlessly about mussels and purple pearls," Midnight Falcon said.

He realized how tightly his sister clutched his hand. It was as though she wasn't going to allow him to slip away from her, no matter what.

It seemed strange for her to be this anxious over making a bracelet for a friend. And for her to plan to make this bracelet out of something as rare as purple pearls made him even more intrigued.

"I did not realize that I was so quiet," Little Snow Feather said.

She looked at her brother quickly, then giggled.

"But if I am," she said, "I would think you would be glad of it. You often complain about my habit of going on and on about things."

"Yes, I guess I do," Midnight Falcon said, chuckling.

He could not help but enjoy this little outing with his sister. It was a vibrant, beautiful day of sunshine and bird song.

He only now realized how infrequently, of late, he had taken an opportunity to walk with her beside the river away from their village.

Duties to his people too often kept him away from his duties as a brother, which also had become duties of a father when their parents died during the Pocoughtaonacks raid.

Although precocious, and too often opinionated about things, his sister was the sort of child who could find countless ways to fill her day.

He frowned when he recalled Little Snow Feather peering through the window of the white people's house, and how fascinated she was by their culture.

It was not the culture he had found fascinating.

Remembering the brief moments with Chandra beneath the moonlight brought a smile to his lips. He had been filled with awe of her ever since and had tried to come up with a way to be with her again.

He had thought to wait for her to go horseback riding again. He would not stand in hiding, watching. He would step out into the open and hope that she would stop and talk with him again, if only for a minute.

He felt guilty for having thought so much about Chandra since their meeting.

Had she thought of him?

He knew that something had begun to develop between them in the short time they were together. He wanted to build on that and see how far they could go.

He wondered if she was the sort of person who could dismiss the prejudices that most white people felt for an Indian and allow herself to feel something for him.

"Midnight Falcon, now it is you who is suddenly so quiet," Little Snow Feather said.

She could see much going on behind his eyes. It was as though his mind was actively thinking of something that pleased him.

Or could he be thinking of someone? Did he notice how beautiful Chandra was as she sat at the harpsichord, singing?

Or was it only wishful thinking on her part that he might be daydreaming about Chandra now, when, in truth, they were moments away from becoming acquainted?

"Do you forget that your brother often is filled

with thoughts instead of talk?" Midnight Falcon said, trying to justify why he had been so deep in thought.

Chandra was so far removed from his life, and her own customs and duties to family probably kept her inside most days.

He wondered how long it would be before he saw her again on her mighty horse.

Today?

Tomorrow?

Or perhaps never?"

The breeze ruffled his breechclout against his bare, bronzed thighs. His chest was warm with sunshine and his feet were comfortable in new buckskin moccasins. His long black hair was shining from his early-morning swim in the river. His eyes were filled with the wonders of a new day, for he never took a day for granted. He knew how quickly one's life could be snuffed out. He had lost too many loved ones ever to forget.

Each day was a blessing, especially a day shared with his precious sister.

"This friend you are anxious to make a bracelet for," Midnight Falcon said, assessing his sister's reaction. "You never told me her name. Who could be this special to you?"

The question and the way her brother looked at her as he awaited an answer made Little Snow Feather's heart skip a beat. Yes, she did hope to make Shannon such a bracelet one day, but it was not her plan to tell her brother about Shannon today. How could she tell her brother that? He would then know that this had all been a ploy.

"Little Snow Feather, why do you not answer me?" Midnight Falcon asked, stopping. He placed his hands on his sister's shoulders and turned her to face him. "Why is it so hard for you to answer such a simple question?"

Little Snow Feather felt suddenly dwarfed by his height and questioning eyes.

She swallowed hard, looked quickly past him for signs of Shannon approaching in the distance with her aunt, then gazed up at her brother again.

"Well?" Midnight Falcon said, raising an eyebrow.

And then it came to him just who the friend might be that his sister was so hesitant to mention.

He dropped his hands away from her shoulders. "Are you digging mussels to make the white girl a bracelet?"

He was torn over how he should feel about it if that were true. He had warned her about such a friendship and the taboo aspects of it. Yet he had not heeded his own warnings, for he was intrigued by someone with white skin himself.

He could not find it in his heart to scold her, and he most certainly did not intend to force answers out of her.

"You need not answer," he said, taking her by a hand again. "Come. I will help you dig the mussels. You can make a bracelet for whomever you wish. It is not your brother's right to interfere where your heart is concerned. If you have found a friend you think this much of, and she is worthy of such a gift, then I will only ask that I have the opportunity to meet her one day, face-to-face."

"Bringing you two together would please me so much," Little Snow Feather said, surprised that Midnight Falcon would so quickly drop his line of questioning.

She could tell by his attitude that he knew her special friend was Shannon.

In a sense, he had practically approved!

This made the next few moments even more thrilling.

Deep down, she felt almost certain that he truly wished to know the white woman, which made her heart soar.

But now that they were so close to the rendezvous point, Little Snow Feather's heart began pounding furiously with a mixture of excitement and fear that her brother might become angry at her for plotting to get him together with Chandra.

She took comfort from knowing that, as always, if he got angry, he would get over it. He never stayed angry at his sister for long!

7

Still holding Chandra's hand, Shannon felt her heart race. She was nearing the place of the planned rendezvous and was feeling somewhat guilty. She had never played tricks on her aunt. Today's scheme included a man! And not an ordinary man—this was an Indian who was a powerful chief!

But even though Midnight Falcon was an Indian, Shannon believed that he was perfect for Chandra. Little Snow Feather had talked endlessly about how handsome he was, and how kind and big-hearted.

From the very beginning, after having heard Midnight Falcon described in such a positive way, Shannon had felt that this sort of man would be good to Chandra and could help her forget the tragedy that she had suffered when her husband had died so suddenly.

A man like Midnight Falcon might put the soft, sweet light back in Chandra's eyes, and the music back in her heart.

"I'm so glad you encouraged me to come with you today," Chandra said, interrupting Shannon's thoughts. "I haven't been out of the house enough since our arrival."

She held her head back and shook her hair so that it shimmered in waves down her back. She continued to walk alongside the river with her niece, watching everything around her.

"Yes, I've gone riding," Chandra said. "But other than that, I have for the most part sat like the spinster I might become, embroidering and knitting my life away beside the fire."

"There is so much to see here," Shannon said. She kept an eye out for Little Snow Feather in the distance, no longer willing to consider that Midnight Falcon might not have agreed to come.

Shannon stopped suddenly and squealed, grabbing her hand away from Chandra's and pointing. "Did you see?" she cried, eyes wide. "I think a long-tailed weasel just ran into those bushes over there."

"Or a very large, fat rat," Chandra said teasingly, knowing how much Shannon hated them back in England.

"Heaven forbid!" Shannon looked so pale that Chandra immediately regretted having teased her about something as loathsome as a rat. "Oh, what if some boarded the same ship that brought us here?"

"My dear, I was only jesting," Chandra said, again taking Shannon's hand. "That surely was a weasel."

For a while, they walked in silence, observing

the grandeur of the land that stretched away from the James River. The area that was not forested was still picturesque, with deep, cool valleys, the vibrant greens more intense in the gentle sunshine that pulsed across the heights and hollows.

Chandra loved all of the animals that she had seen while riding White Iris, but had puzzled over how few wolves there were, especially after having been told that wolves freely roamed across American land, their eyes like red fire in the darkness of night.

When Chandra had mentioned this to her brother, Jan-Michael had questioned the shop owners in Jamestown about the lack of wolves in the area.

They had shrugged and explained that there were hardly any wolves left. English hunters, as well as the Indians, had almost exterminated the animals for one reason or another. On nights when a distant howling could be heard, it was more than likely the dogs owned by the Powhatan.

Jan-Michael had said that the Indian dogs had good reason to complain by howling, for they were not considered pets, but treated like work animals instead.

Chandra's thoughts went to Scottie, and how lazily he lay around, soaking up sun beside a window.

She smiled, for she couldn't envision Scottie laboring over anything but a dish full of baked chicken, his favorite meal.

Hearing Shannon gasp loudly, Chandra looked quickly over at her, wondering what the girl had seen this time.

Shannon was staring at the bend in the river where Little Snow Feather was supposed to come with her brother. Shannon could see them now, just walking around the bend.

She could tell that Little Snow Feather had just spotted her and Chandra. The moment Little Snow Feather and Midnight Falcon arrived at the designated meeting place, Little Snow Feather ran to the left toward the shadows of the forest and left her brother there, alone.

Shannon followed her lead and released her aunt's hand and headed in the same direction toward the dark, dense hardwood forest.

Chandra was taken aback by her niece's sudden departure and watched her for a moment, puzzled. She saw an Indian girl running toward the same place in the trees.

And then Chandra's pulse quickened and her knees grew weak. Farther off to the right, she saw Midnight Falcon standing beside the river, his own eyes watching the flight of the young girls.

Then he, too, shifted his eyes and saw Chandra.

They gazed at one another in wonder both quickly realizing that they had been tricked into this meeting by the girls.

Chandra felt it almost impossible to breathe, much less move. She found it hard to believe that Shannon could be so scheming, that she had had a part in this meeting with the handsome Powhatan chief.

Midnight Falcon was stunned by what his devious and foolhardy sister had done, even after he had taken pains to warn her about becoming too involved with the white people. He continued to stare at Chandra, speechless.

Since their chance meeting beneath the moonlight, he had thought more seriously about a relationship with her. He was chief! What would his people think about him being involved with a white woman? Would they resent him if he were to bring this woman into their lives?

He felt torn. His heart was telling him one thing, and his head was warning him about another.

It was one thing for two young girls to become friends, but another for a grown man, a chief, to be infatuated with a white woman. And it was obvious that the two little girls wanted more than friendship between him and Chandra.

Chandra blushed, becoming timid. She wasn't sure what to do next. It was clear that her niece and the lovely Indian girl were close friends and surely had been for some time. And it was clear what they wanted to happen.

And, oh, how Chandra wanted the same. She was totally in awe of Midnight Falcon. Yet she was hesitant to allow things to go any further between them.

How could she expect an Indian chief to even consider caring about a white woman, let alone one who might be with child. Surely Midnight Falcon's people would be horrified by the very idea of it.

Midnight Falcon tried to read Chandra's expression, but he was unsure of how she felt about this planned meeting. She seemed to be as stunned about the rendezvous as he was.

But the more he thought about what his sister and the pretty white girl had done, the more he realized the irony of it. The two girls had planned for Midnight Falcon and Chandra to meet like this, not knowing that they had already met and had become enamored with one another. Midnight Falcon smiled at the thought and quickly forgot his concerns when he saw that Chandra was returning his smile.

Suddenly they both laughed, their laughter filling the air.

The two wide-eyed girls watched from the bushes, puzzled by Midnight Falcon and Chandra's reaction. They gasped when they saw Chandra and Midnight Falcon run to one another and hug, still laughing.

Midnight Falcon and Chandra both seemed to immediately realize what they had done, and they stepped quickly away from each other as Shannon and Little Snow Feather came out of hiding.

"How long have you known one another?" Little Snow Feather asked, peering up at her brother with wonder.

Midnight Falcon wasn't sure how to answer her,

how open he should be about having already met Chandra.

And there was that hug.

It had happened so quickly and naturally. How could he explain that away, not only to his sister, but also to himself?

For the moment he was given a reprieve, as Chandra questioned her niece, bringing all eyes to Shannon.

"How long have you been friends with the Indian girl?" Chandra asked. "Why didn't you feel free to talk to me about it, or introduce her to me? Surely you know that I would not be against such a friendship."

Shannon momentarily lowered her eyes, feeling guilty about keeping so much from her aunt. "I was mainly worried about father knowing, not you."

Shannon reached out for Little Snow Feather, and the girls clasped hands.

"Chandra, this is Little Snow Feather," Shannon said proudly. "She's Midnight Falcon's sister. We met the day after I arrived. I was taking a ride on my pony. When I saw Little Snow Feather watching me, I stopped. We have been close friends ever since."

"She is your sister?" Chandra asked Midnight Falcon. Then she smiled. "Oh, she is such a lovely child."

Midnight Falcon's heart soared on hearing Chandra approve of his sister so quickly, seeing no trace of prejudice toward the girls being friends. This proved the kind of woman she was, and his feelings for her could not help but deepen.

"And this is your niece," Midnight Falcon said, reaching out his hand.

Seeing his offer of friendship, and so happy at how things were developing, Shannon smiled widely and took Midnight Falcon's hand. "Your sister has told me so much about you," she said, looking into Midnight Falcon's mesmerizing eyes. "I am happy to meet you, sir."

Chandra smiled at her niece's words. She was so pleased by the way things had worked out, by the warmth she felt around her. Yet a part of her could not help but be afraid. She did not want to think about what Jan-Michael's reaction might be if he found out about this meeting.

The girls ran off hand in hand, squealing and giggling over their successful venture, leaving Chandra alone with Midnight Falcon. She quickly forgot about Jan-Michael.

Chandra looked up at Midnight Falcon slowly and awaited his next move, his next words.

One thing was for certain—they wouldn't be digging for any mussels or purple pearls today!

8

Only I discern
Infinite passion, and the pain
Of finite hearts that yearn.
—ELIZABETH BARRETT BROWNING

"They seem so much alike," Midnight Falcon said, breaking the awkward silence that had fallen between him and Chandra. "It seems only right that they have become friends, although I . . ."

He stopped short of telling her how he had discouraged the friendship when he first found out about it. Now, after seeing them together, laughing and holding hands, he realized that there was nothing wrong about their friendship. It had grown so deep that they had even felt comfortable enough to plan this meeting, which could have pulled them apart had it gone awry.

And if it wasn't for the girls' friendship, he would not have been lured to this place and would not be standing in front of this beautiful woman right now. He had been searching for a way to see her again, to find out exactly how she felt about him.

He hoped to discover that today.

"You were about to say?" Chandra prompted, having noticed Midnight Falcon's hesitation.

She wondered if he had been about to tell her

that he did not approve of the relationship that had developed between the two mischievous girls.

"My sister has been precocious since she was old enough to realize that she could be," Midnight Falcon said, chuckling.

"So has my niece," Chandra said.

She was glad that they had found something safe to talk about. She was not going to allow her suspicions of being pregnant, or anything else, to stand in the way of becoming closer to Midnight Falcon. The more she was with him, the more her heart belonged to him.

"Shannon often makes her father want to pull his hair out," Chandra added, laughing at Midnight Falcon's reaction. She realized how what she had said must have sounded strange to him. Even though he was a powerful chief, he did not know when she was or was not being serious.

"I don't mean that Jan-Michael would actually pull his hair out," she explained. "It is only a way of describing his frustrations with his daughter."

"I see," Midnight Falcon said, pondering her different way to describe things.

Chandra's breath caught in her throat when a red bird flew past her head and perched in a tree only a few feet away. She was awestruck by the bird's bright color, its black beak, and its melodious song that seemed to echo another bird somewhere deep in the forest.

"I have never seen such a bird before. There is no such bird in England," Chandra said. "It is so beautiful. And . . . and listen to its song. It's even more beautiful than music played on a harp."

"This bird is called a cardinal by the whites," Midnight Falcon said, taken by her sincere fascination. That meant that she, too, must love nature and its creatures. It was good to have something as wonderful as this in common with her.

"A cardinal," Chandra repeated, not daring to move, for she wanted to watch the bird and listen to its song for as long as possible.

She could tell that Midnight Falcon was pleased about her interest in birds.

"In the winter, when the ground is blanketed with snow, the cardinals look like red roses," Midnight Falcon said. He was disappointed when the cardinal suddenly took flight and disappeared in the trees.

Chandra looked at Midnight Falcon. "There is another kind of bird here in America that is new to me," she said. "I have learned that it is called a parakeet. As they streak through the air with their colored wings, they resemble a rainbow."

"Yes, there are many parakeets that fill the air with their color," Midnight Falcon said. "But their song is not as pleasant as the cardinal's. In fact, they own no song at all. They chatter and squawk."

"I know," Chandra said, laughing. "I have one. I caught it and put it in a cage. I wish to tame it for a pet. But I doubt that can happen. The bird is constantly fussing at me."

"It is trying to tell you that it wants to be set free." Midnight Falcon placed a hand on her shoulder. "I encourage you to do that. Nothing should be caged."

Seeing his seriousness, she nodded. "Yes, I shall set it free as soon as I return home today."

She was extremely aware of his hand on her shoulder, the feel of his warm flesh making her tingle from head to toe.

When he removed his hand, a part of her wished that he would caress her face and touch her lips, which burned for his kiss.

But another part of her cried out to run from him while she still could.

"That is good of you," Midnight Falcon said. He gestured toward the river. "Do you have time to sit and talk some more? Or do your duties beckon you home?"

Her heart raced at his suggestion.

She had few duties. Before her husband had found a wife to bring back home to America with him, he had hired maids, cooks, and servants to see to the running of the household.

Not used to such pampering, one by one Chandra had let them go, all but one maid, cook, and stable boy, who was the maid's son. There was not much for Chandra to do throughout the day around the house, except knit and read.

It was a life vastly different from that which she had lived. She could still feel the callouses from washing and scrubbing the floor of their shanty in Liverpool, and from cleaning in private homes. She did not miss the work, but she did miss the more simple life.

She doubted that she would ever get used to her huge home and the wealth within its walls, especially the clothes that were too fancy for her liking. She had silently admired Little Snow Feather's buckskin skirt and blouse, imagining how wonderfully soft they must feel. She could almost envision herself wearing the same sort of attire and living in a wigwam as a Powhatan wife.

"Will you walk with me?" Midnight Falcon asked, jarring Chandra's thoughts back to the present. He wondered what had made her so lost in thought. "Or *do* you need to return to your home to your chores?"

"I would like nothing more than to walk with you, or sit with you and talk," Chandra said.

She did not reveal to him that she was a lady of leisure, which he might think was wasteful and frivolous. She imagined that Powhatan women wasted not one minute of their day.

But she did worry that spending more time with Midnight Falcon might make her brother suspicious. Should he wonder why it was taking so long for her and Shannon to dig for mussels, as they were supposed to be doing, he might come looking for them. If he found either her with Midnight Falcon, or Shannon with Little Snow Feather, there would be no end to his ranting and raving.

"I believe it is best that we walk and talk elsewhere," Chandra said. She pointed to the bluff a short distance away, the very bluff that had given her her first view of this wonderful Powhatan chief. "I enjoy the bluff that overlooks the river. It is amazing how far one can see from there. Perhaps we can go there?"

"Come then. I, too, enjoy sitting there." Midnight Falcon began walking away from the river with Chandra. "It is a place of wondrous peace and beauty. I often commune with the Great Spirit there."

"I have felt the same peace there," Chandra said. "I find myself thinking of being there even when I am not."

"I, too, have had such moments as that," Midnight Falcon said. He stepped aside as he allowed Chandra to begin the slow climb to the butte ahead of him.

He started to reach out and place an arm around her waist to assist her, but had second thoughts. He had seen her tense reaction to his hand on her shoulder.

When they finally reached the butte, Chandra smoothed the skirt of her dress out beneath her as she sat down on a thick bed of moss. Midnight Falcon sat down beside her.

"From here I feel as though I can see foreverland," Chandra said. "I am so proud to be in America."

She made a wide sweep with her hand and her

gaze moved with it. "America is so beautiful," she said, sighing.

"This land is rich in animals and plants," Midnight Falcon said. "There are many flowering plants used by the Powhatan, as well as those that are edible."

"Please tell me about them. So that when I am walking or riding in the forest, I will know what your people know about them."

"It pleases me that you ask." Midnight Falcon enjoyed Chandra's eagerness to learn and knew it was not pretended. "Edible roots are produced by the bugleweed, the toothwart, the downy yellow violet, the trout lily, and the Indian cucumber root."

He paused, then added more at her encouraging nod. "The berries and the leaves of the chokeberry are eaten, as well as the sunflower and trout lily," he said, smiling.

"I'm amazed to know that so many plants can be useful as food," Chandra said, truly marveling over it. "I know so few of those that you mentioned. As we take future walks, will you point them out to me? Plants here differ so much from those in England."

"Our dyes are also made from plants, from goldenseal and wild indigo as well as bloodroot or *puccoon*." He continued to talk about plants, but his mind was lingering on what she had said about future walks.

Nothing could make him happier. She had quickly stolen his heart.

"As you know, it is from this bluff that I have watched you when you have been on your horse," he said, intentionally changing the conversation to something more personal.

"I know," Chandra said, smiling timidly at him. "I felt your eyes on me. Do you not recall? I gazed up at you. Even then I felt something magical between us."

"I, too, felt it, and that is why I hurried for home," Midnight Falcon admitted. "I was stunned. Were you, as well?"

"No, I wasn't stunned, I was entranced," Chandra said, finding it easy now to be truthful. "What do you think of my horse? Her name is White Iris because she is the color of the white irises my mother grows back in Liverpool."

"She is magnificent. And the name is something that someone as gentle and perfect as you would choose for an animal."

He picked up a pebble and tossed it over the edge of the bluff, toward the river below. "My people have had the opportunity to own horses, but we are not interested," he said. "We travel by foot or by canoe when we travel by river to places far from our village."

"Tell me more about your people," Chandra said. "While living in England, I often wondered about the Indians of America. I tried to find books to learn the customs of various tribes, but I only found a few. In those there was no mention of the Powhatan people. What I know about your tribe is what I have learned since my arrival here."

"The name Powhatan was the name of the village of chief Wahunsonakok. The first English to come here could not pronounce the chief's name, so they called him—and all our tribe—Powhatan," Midnight Falcon said. "I am sure you have heard about Pocahontas. Chief Powhatan was her father. He reigned as head chief until he died. Since then, there have been many local chiefs, for none carried the same sort of power over all Powhatan people as he did."

"And you are now a chief," Chandra said, again feeling awed by him.

"Yes, after my chieftain father's death, I was named chief," Midnight Falcon said, a haunted look in his eyes.

"Midnight Falcon, should your people find out that you have befriended me, a white woman, and that my niece is friends with your sister, would they disapprove?"

Chandra was troubled that he didn't respond to her question right away, but instead grew quiet as he gazed out over the lovely James River. She wished that she was a mind reader, for she would love to know what he was thinking at this very moment.

Her question had caused his silence. Now she wished that she hadn't asked it.

Midnight Falcon knew he should be troubled

by the bond that was growing between him and Chandra, and by the one between the two young girls. If he were not his people's leader, this wouldn't be an issue.

But he was, and he had always considered his people's feelings before his own.

This time, his feelings must come first, he decided. He had been alone in his bed for too long now. He would be a better leader if his heart was filled with joy and love.

Yes, he must make his people understand.

"Should your people find out that you have befriended me, an Indian, would they approve?" he asked her instead of answering her question.

Chandra could not find it in her heart to tell him about her brother.

He was getting worse at lording over her. She was glad that she had stood her ground with him of late, and that he had somewhat backed off, for she never wanted to be put in the position of reminding her brother that it was she who owned everything he depended upon to live. She knew that behind her brother's cross words was a vulnerable man whose mind could snap at any time.

She hoped that her friendship with Midnight Falcon wouldn't jeopardize Jan-Michael's standing in the community, since it was he who had more to lose should people look down on her for her behavior. He wanted to start a business, and he had a young daughter to raise. She hoped that her actions didn't threaten a secure future for Shannon in the white community of Jamestown.

Determined to change the subject, Chandra told Midnight Falcon more about White Iris. "Even though you do not wish to own a horse, would you like to learn how to ride mine?" Chandra asked. "Would you like to ride White Iris today?"

Midnight Falcon looked quickly at Chandra. "You wish to have me ride on the hoofed animal with you?" he said, fascinated by the idea.

And it was a way to be alone with Chandra for a while longer, before his prolonged silences frightened her off.

"Would you like that?" Chandra asked.

Her pulse raced at the very thought of having him that close, his body next to hers, as they shared the saddle.

Of course, she knew that she was tempting fate by riding out in the open with him. It would give her brother a better chance of seeing them together.

She would have to explain and hope he understood.

"But if we do ride together, we must ride where my brother won't see us," she said before Midnight Falcon had answered her. "He has bad feelings toward Indians. His wife was found murdered after an Indian ambush when we were stranded waiting for our ship to be repaired. He cannot separate one tribe from another. He sees all red men as responsible for the acts of one."

"He is wrong to feel that way, because it was not our tribe that did that to his wife," Midnight Falcon said, offended. "But I am used to prejudice and understand your need of secrecy. That will not keep me from riding with you, if you still wish to go."

Chandra leaped to her feet. "I shall go now and get my horse," she said, her voice filled with joy. "If you wait at the foot of the bluff, I shall return soon with White Iris."

"I will wait with an eager heart," Midnight Falcon said, moving to his feet.

"You will?"

They gazed into one another's eyes for a moment, and then Midnight Falcon grabbed Chandra into his arms and gave her a deep, hot kiss.

Chandra felt her insides melt. She was lost, heart and soul, to him.

But what if she was with child?

No, she wouldn't think about anything now but the moment . . . of finally having found a man who made her heart sing.

Midnight Falcon tried to hide how passionately shaken he was by the kiss and the sensual way she responded to it. He stepped away from Chandra and reached a hand to her lips. Slowly he ran a finger across them, feeling the heat of her flesh against his.

He then pulled her back into his arms and kissed her again, fiercely aware of how she strained her body hungrily against his.

Afraid of losing control, Midnight Falcon broke free of her again.

His breathing was labored. His heartbeats were erratic.

"I will wait for your return," he said.

Chandra nodded. She was almost too weak with passion to walk away, yet she knew that she must, or she would give herself wholly to this man, who was still only a stranger to her.

"Yes, I'll go now," she said. She almost stumbled over her own feet as she backed slowly away from him. "I . . . I won't be long."

Forcing one foot after the other, she turned and ran down the steep slope.

Still overwhelmed by the passionate kiss and the heat of his body against hers, Chandra reached the stable where White Iris waited.

Just as Chandra told the stable boy to ready White Iris for riding, Jan-Michael appeared, his eyes accusing, as though he knew everything.

Their eyes locked in silent battle.

Chandra prayed that her brother would not push too hard this time, for she could take only so much more of his bitter mood.

And nothing, especially her brother, would keep her away from Midnight Falcon, ever.

He was a part of her now.

Midnight Falcon was her destiny!

9

Escape me?
Never—
Beloved!
While I am I, and you are you.
—ROBERT BROWNING

Jan-Michael took a step closer to Chandra. His gaze stayed on her face. "Why are your cheeks flushed?" he asked. "Where is Shannon? You left together to dig for mussels. Why didn't she return with you? Scottie returned home long ago alone."

Chandra felt trapped under her brother's scrutiny, as though his eyes could look deep into her soul and see that a man had caused her cheeks to flush.

She was afraid that if she spoke, her voice would give away her excitement. Only moments ago, the most handsome man in the world had held her and kissed her. Moments ago she had become alive as never before.

She had been dazzled by a man for the first time in her life.

No other man's arms had made her dizzy with desire.

No man had ever given her such a passionate, heartfelt kiss.

She still felt the warmth of his lips on hers and the pleasure of his kisses.

She was no longer the same person she had been the last time her brother saw her.

The kiss, the embrace, had changed her forever.

She forced a smile and found the courage to finally speak. When she did, she was relieved that her voice sounded no different.

"Shannon is still digging for mussels," she said, feeling guilty at the lie. She had never made life easier for herself by telling lies.

But this was different.

Her entire future could be threatened by saying the wrong thing now to her brother, who still looked accusingly at her.

She knew that her future had been altered by the Powhatan Indian chief, and she found it hard not to reveal how thrilled she was.

But her brother was a man who despised even the mention of Indians. How would he react to learn that his sister was captivated by one—was in love with one?

"She is, is she?" Jan-Michael said, turning to look in the direction of the river. "Why aren't you with her? Don't you think it's dangerous for her to be out alone so often?"

"Jan-Michael, you know as well as I that Shannon learned back in England how to fend for herself, and it is no different here, except that she doesn't have drunken, foul-mouthed ruffians to

watch out for as she did on the streets of Liverpool."

Even Chandra had learned early on how to defend herself against such riffraff. It had been necessary in order to survive.

"There weren't any Indians in Liverpool to
worry about as there are here in America," Jan-
Michael said. He placed his fists on his hips. "Go
and get Shannon. Tell her time's up today for her
explorin'. I can find somethin' for her to do." He
nodded toward the door. "I've got things to do or
I'd go and fetch her myself."

"Let the girl enjoy this new freedom, this new
land," Chandra said. She sighed heavily. Her hand
was eager to grab her horse's reins from Tommie,
who stood aside holding them for her.

White Iris sensed that freedom from the stable
was near and whinnied and dug at the straw-
covered floor with a hoof.

Chandra quickly grabbed the reins. "Let *me*
enjoy *mine*," she said, stubbornly lifting her chin.
"As for Shannon, she is a bit disappointed that
she's not found a purple pearl. I am, also, not for
myself, but for my niece."

Chandra felt uncomfortable having to talk about
something that had not even come about today.

Purple pearls, indeed.

The reason for Shannon taking Chandra away
from their home this morning was something far
more exciting.

And if her brother wasn't so pigheaded about

things, so opinionated, then lies would not be necessary.

Chandra didn't like keeping things from him, because deep down he was a kind and caring man and had Shannon and Chandra's best interests at heart.

Chandra would love to share her heart with him as she had when she was a little girl. She had idolized her big brother.

As they grew up, they had grown apart. Her brother had made friends that Chandra felt uncomfortable around, friends who later had joined up with him to be his crew on his fishing boat. He had worked hard to save for that boat, ever since he had been old enough to earn a coin or two by any means he could find.

But she knew that if Jan-Michael discovered his daughter's friendship with an Indian girl, and her involvement with an Indian chief, he would go into a fitful rage and forbid them both from ever seeing them again. He might go as far as to lock his daughter up to keep her from being with Little Snow Feather.

He might even insist on going back to England, no matter that returning to their homeland would mean many weeks at sea again.

No.

She doubted that he was ready for that.

He had barely made it to America with his sanity, so real had his fear of water become.

She had begun to doubt that he would ever change.

And as for returning to England, she didn't want to even consider it, but the baby would be the deciding factor.

Jan-Michael grabbed Chandra by her shoulders and gently shook her to bring her from her deep thoughts. "Where on earth has your mind drifted to?" His eyes slowly raked over her. "And why are you behavin' so peculiar this mornin'?"

"I was just trying to figure out why you have changed so much these past years," Chandra said.

She shrugged his hands from her shoulders. "I understand some of it," she said. "But for the most part, I don't know you anymore. You rarely smile these days. And I miss your laugh so. We used to have such fun together."

"Don't try analyzin' me." Jan-Michael stepped away from her and slid his hands in his rear breeches pocket. "Just go on. Take your ride. And while you're out, tell Shannon to not stay much longer. I do worry about her."

Chandra sighed with relief. She swung herself into her saddle. "I do love you so much, big brother," she said, seeing how that made his eyes waver.

She sank her heels into the flanks of her horse and rode free of the stable, stiffening when Jan-Michael shouted at her.

"You should have at least taken time to change

into proper ridin' attire! A silk dress is not for horseback ridin'!"

"I know, but I'm too eager to ride to care," she shouted over her shoulder at him, then rode off.

She galloped across the wide, green pasture of her estate. As her dress fluttered up past her knees, and her long hair flew in the wind behind her, her heart raced with the thought of Midnight Falcon waiting for her.

Surely this was a dream, she thought to herself, again recalling his powerful arms and the press of his lips against hers.

She made a sharp turn with her horse and rode along the James, farther and farther away from her home and Jan-Michael.

If she *was* only dreaming, she never wanted to wake up. It was a wonderful, sensual dream, and in it Midnight Falcon had fallen in love with her.

But her own feelings were too deeply felt, too real, for her to be dreaming. She was in love.

"I'm in love with a Powhatan chief!" she whispered into the wind, giggling at the wonder of it.

It was not a dream. It was a miracle.

10

The Devil hath not, in all his quiver's
 choice,
An arrow for the heart like a sweet voice.
—Lord Byron

Purple clover blanketed a wide stretch of land,
the blossoms beckoning to Shannon and Little
Snow Feather as they ran hand in hand, carefree
and radiant.

"It's so pretty!" Shannon said, her auburn hair
bouncing on her shoulders. She and Little Snow
Feather began skipping through the flowers. "It's
as though I am back in England running through
a field of heather! Oh, but those times were too
few! And to get to the heather fields, Chandra and
I had to walk so far. Sometimes, that took a lot of
the fun out of it."

Breathless, her eyes shining, Shannon stopped
and faced Little Snow Feather, who stopped alongside her. "One day, as my aunt and I were ready
to head back for home, there was a horseman there
blocking our way on the most beautiful white
horse you have ever seen! He was a kind man,
older. He offered to give both me and Chandra a
ride back to the city." She giggled. "Of course, we

had been told not to trust all that easily. But who could refuse a ride on a horse like that?"

"And so you did?" Little Snow Feather asked, her eyes wide.

"Yes, even though it was hard for three of us to sit on the one horse," Shannon said, giggling again. She spun around, her arms outstretched before her. "But we managed. I sat in front of the gentleman and Chandra sat behind him, clinging to him for life as we went back to town. Oh, what fun! I will never forget it!"

"Did you ever see the man again?" Little Snow Feather asked.

Shannon stopped spinning, and the girls sat down amidst the clover.

"Yes, many times," Shannon said. She began picking long-stemmed clover blossoms. "Although we never told my mother or father, or Grandmother Neal, Chandra and I met the gentleman often, and he was the one who taught us both how to ride."

Shannon sighed. "Chandra even began wishing that this man was her father," she said. "You see, Chandra never did get to know her real father. He left when Chandra was a baby and never returned. Grandmother Neal raised two children all alone, and helped take care of me, too, when I came along."

"Perhaps this man *was* Chandra's father," Little Snow Feather said, captivated by the story.

"Perhaps that's why he came and offered you rides, to spend time with you."

"If so, Chandra said it would be even more cruel than having left his family to fend for themselves," Shannon said. "But possibly you are right, for the man never shared his full name with us. He told us to call him Thomas. Then one day he stopped meeting us. Chandra and I never saw him again. But at least he taught us how to ride horses."

"The white horse," Little Snow Feather said, following Shannon's lead by plucking clover blossoms, and laying them, one by one, on her lap, "did you not see it again, either?"

"No, and oh, how we missed riding her!"

"The horse your aunt rides is white," Little Snow Feather said. "It is so beautiful."

"Yes. She chose a white horse for herself when we reached America and had money enough to afford such things," Shannon said, now tying one clover stem to another.

"Why didn't you pick a white horse, too?" Little Snow Feather asked, watching curiously as Shannon continued to tie clover stems together. "Yours is brown instead of white and it is much smaller than your aunt's."

"Mine is a pony because it fits my size better," Shannon said, nodding. "I chose my pony because his large, dark eyes seemed to call me to him when I first saw him."

"What have you named him?"

Shannon giggled. "I named him Thomas," she said, her eyes twinkling.

"The name of the man who taught you to ride?"

"Yes," Shannon said. "I wonder what Thomas would say if he knew."

"He would be pleased to be remembered, don't you think?"

"Yes, I think he would," Shannon said, slowly nodding.

"I have been watching you tie clover together," Little Snow Feather said, raising an eyebrow. "What for?"

"I am making you a crown of clover," Shannon said, tying the final link in the circle of flowers. Her eyes shone as she placed the flowers on Little Snow Feather's head. "You are a princess for your people and now you have a crown."

Little Snow Feather reached up and gently touched the flowers on her head, then smiled widely. She began tying the clover stems that she had plucked into a circle. "I shall crown you, as well," she said. "You shall be a queen."

"Oh, what fun," Shannon squealed. "I shall make you a bracelet to match your crown." She eagerly tied more flowers together.

"Pocahontas came to me last night," Little Snow Feather blurted out, looking almost timidly up at Shannon. "I asked her if she might allow you to at least see her."

"Oh, truly? You asked Pocahontas if I could see

her? What did she say?" Shannon's words came out in a rush, her voice breathless with excitement.

"I am sorry, Shannon, but she said no." Little Snow Feather sighed. "She told me that it was best this way. Pocahontas comes only to watch out for me, nothing else. I am her namesake, and, like she was, I am my people's princess."

Shannon could not hide her disappointment from Little Snow Feather, but she did try hard to understand. She still wanted to believe that her friend was not telling her a tall tale by saying that she had seen and talked with Pocahontas's ghost-spirit.

Shannon so badly wanted it to be true.

"Pocahontas was very special in her time," Little Snow Feather said, as though she felt Shannon's doubts inside her heart. "That is why she has the power to return in spirit. When the white man arrived on the James River, Pocahontas was curious and worried. The Powhatan princess helped our people and the English become friends, and she saw to it that corn, venison, and other foods were brought to the colonists, who were not used to this land. That's when she met the white man, John Rolfe, and married him."

"That couldn't have made your people happy," Shannon said, forgetting the clover as she became caught up in the story. "Wouldn't they have rather she stayed away from the white people?"

"Pocahontas knew that once the white people came, nothing could stop them, so she felt it was important to work with them instead of turning away from them," Little Snow Feather explained. "And by marrying a white man, the man she truly loved, she brought peace between her people and the whites. She was smart, knowing that no one would win in the end by fighting!"

"I heard that she even became a Christian," Shannon said. "Is that true?"

"Yes, and in a strange way it brought our two peoples even closer," Little Snow Feather said, placing her finished crown on Shannon's head. "But my people never forgot our own god."

"And who is your god?" Shannon asked, smiling as she adjusted the crown on her head.

"There are more than one. But Okeus, the Devil God, is the main one," Little Snow Feather said, pleased that Shannon liked her crown of flowers.

"A devil god? Why would you call it that?"

"Because children used to be sacrificed to Okeus," Little Snow Feather said matter-of-factly.

"Truly?" Shannon gasped, paling at the thought. "Were white children ever sacrificed?"

"No," Little Snow Feather said. "The children were always Powhatan." She reached over and took one of Shannon's hands. "Come. I will take you to our people's temple to see the four-foot idol of the Devil God."

Shannon grabbed her hand back from Little Snow Feather. "No, I don't think so," she said, visibly frightened. "And what if you got caught taking me, a white girl, into your people's temple?"

"It would surprise no one," Little Snow Feather said, her eyes twinkling. "You see, I am my people's princess, the chief's sister. I can do things others dare not even think about, much less do."

"That surely does not go as far as being so friendly with a white girl, or you would not have kept our friendship a secret."

Little Snow Feather shrugged. "My people have to find out some time, why not now?" she said. She leaped to her feet and held her hands out for Shannon. "Come with me. You are my friend. Do not be afraid."

Shannon thought for a moment, then moved to her feet and took one of Little Snow Feather's hands. "If you think it's all right," she said, still somewhat reluctant.

"Yes, yes," Little Snow Feather said eagerly.

"Then let's go," Shannon said. Her heart began to race at the thought of doing something so risky, yet too exciting to refuse.

With their crowns of flowers, they left the field of clover behind and rushed into the dark shadows of the forest, heading for the Powhatan village.

Shannon hoped that Pocahontas really did watch out for Little Snow Feather, since they might need help if it didn't go well.

Her father's angry face came to her mind's eye. Shannon blinked her eyes, and then he was gone.

Smiling, she ran onward with her friend.

11

Ah, love, let us be true
To one another! for the world, which
    seems
To lie before us like a land of dreams,
So various, so beautiful, so new,
Hath really neither joy, nor love, nor light.
—MATTHEW ARNOLD

Chandra stood back and watched Midnight Falcon riding White Iris.

The sight made her forget everything—the black clothes she had recently stopped wearing, her brother's troubled moods, and even her concern about being caught with Midnight Falcon.

She marveled over the fact that he seemed born to ride horses. Chandra watched him gallop toward her after having ridden some distance across the brilliant green and grassy meadow.

She had only ridden with Midnight Falcon once on the horse, instructing him how to hold the reins and control them, and how to balance himself. Once was all it took for him to catch on to how it was done.

By the shine in his eyes and the smile on his lips, she could tell that he loved riding her horse as much as she loved watching him.

This would be a sight that would remain in her heart and mind for the rest of her days, how Midnight Falcon's hair fluttered down his back in the breeze, how the muscles of his legs and arms flexed, and how he held his magnificent shoulders so square and proud.

As he approached her now, smiling widely, everything within Chandra thrilled. She was lost in her love for him.

She returned his smile, looking into his eyes as he drew a tight rein beside her.

He bent low to one side on White Iris, reached out for Chandra, and swept her from the ground. Her breath was stolen away. He placed her on his lap, facing him.

Her heart throbbed as he drew her closer. He ran his hand through her hair, bringing her lips closer and closer to his.

And then all she could see was sparkles of sunshine behind her closed lids, as she was overwhelmed by the pure, sweet wonder of his kiss.

She entwined her arms around his neck and strained against his powerful chest.

The cry of a red-tailed hawk circling overhead momentarily startled them, and they drew their lips instantly apart. But they gazed into each other's eyes, and both of them could see the passion that remained.

"Come to my village with me and see how I live," Midnight Falcon said, breaking the magical trance between them. "Come with me now. I want you to learn more about my life now, not later."

"You want me to go with you?" Chandra asked, stunned by his suggestion. Although his kiss and his embrace proved that he cared about her, was he really ready to announce to his people that he wanted a white woman in his life?

Was she? Although she knew that she loved this man with all of her heart and never wanted to let him go, there were still too many things in her own life that were not settled.

But Chandra could not deny how much she wanted what Midnight Falcon seemed ready to offer her—a life of love and wonder.

His invitation touched her heart deeply. In truth, they had only known each other for a very short time.

Instant love.

From the moment she had first seen him on the bluff, without even exchanging one word, this special bond had begun.

"You do not answer my question," Midnight Falcon said. "Does that mean that you are not ready to take this next step? It was in your kiss how deeply you feel for me. It is in your eyes even now as you gaze into mine."

He placed a hand on her cheek. "How can you be unsure about anything between us? Don't you wish for the same thing as I?"

"What is that?" Chandra asked carefully. "What *do* you wish for? Are you asking me to . . ."

He slid his hand gently over her mouth, stopping her questions. "You know what is in my heart. You felt it when I kissed you."

He slowly slid his hand away. "If you are hesitant to go with me because of your brother, I understand," he said. "But if it is because you are concerned about how my people will feel, it is nothing for you to fear. Whatever I do, my people know that I do it with much thought beforehand. When they see you with me, they will know that I have made peace with it, and so then should they. I am their chief. They want for me what I want for myself, for as my goal is to serve them, theirs is to see that I am happy."

"Still, I don't know if I should," Chandra said, swallowing hard. "I am worried about my brother. But I am also worried about your people. Although you say they will accept your decision, will they truly? Or will they, deep down, resent me? My skin is white."

"Whether your skin is white, red, or the color of the sun, my people would soon learn about my feelings for you, anyhow," Midnight Falcon said.

He stopped to brush a soft kiss across her lips.

He gazed into her eyes and smiled. "There is no need to delay the inevitable, is there?" he said, reaching a hand to brush a fallen lock from her brow. "Let us go. Put your concerns behind you. Let us enjoy our time together, the love we have found so quickly in a world that is too often filled with mistrust and hate."

The strength and conviction of his feelings filled Chandra with a soft warmth. "Yes, let us go," she said. "Let us go now."

She giggled as he turned her around so that

she now faced away from him. She could feel his hard-muscled chest against her back when he drew her close to him before snapping the reins and starting off toward his village.

"Your people will get more than one surprise today," she said, giving Midnight Falcon a mischievous glance over her shoulder. "Can you imagine their surprise when they see you on White Iris, actually in control of her reins? They will be even more in awe of you than before."

"Riding came quickly to me only because it was you teaching me," Midnight Falcon said. He chuckled. "And, yes, my people's eyes will be full of wonder when they see me arrive on your steed."

"They might not even pay attention when they see that I am on the horse with you," Chandra said, her smile waning. She watched ahead of her for the first signs of his village in the distance. "Oh, Midnight Falcon, what if they truly hate me?"

"Never," he said.

She didn't tell him that she was more afraid of her brother's reaction when he found out, which, in time, he would. Being among a whole village of Indians sounded scary, but Midnight Falcon would be with her, and he was their chief. That was reason enough for her to feel safe.

But Jan-Michael? What *could* she expect from him now that she had placed her mourning behind her and had fallen in love with another man so quickly?

And not just any man, she reminded herself— a man whose skin was the same color as that of the men who took the life of his precious wife.

They rode along the James River, the thundering of the horse causing various forest animals to scamper for cover. Chandra got a glimpse of two red foxes as they dove behind a thick stand of brush. She smiled as several brightly winged parakeets flew past her to hide in the hardwood trees.

She was filled with such joy that it made her feel as though she had taken wing and was flying amidst the fluffy clouds in the blue heavens.

But she wasn't flying. She wasn't in the clouds. She was on White Iris, and Midnight Falcon was holding her close as he led them farther and farther away from her home, and closer to his.

"I feel as though I am an extension of your magnificent horse!" Midnight Falcon said, brimming with excitement. "Today I have discovered that a horse is a wonderful way to travel!"

"Yes, it is," Chandra said, reminded again of his natural skill.

"Ahead is my village," Midnight Falcon said, pointing.

Chandra's heart lurched in apprehension. She swallowed hard when she saw the village of longhouses nestled near the James. Smoke was spiraling from the rounded roofs. Children's laughter filled the air.

Dogs howled, sounding like wild wolves.

Sensing her sudden uneasiness, Midnight Falcon drew a tight rein and stopped the horse. He placed his hands at Chandra's waist and turned her to face him. He was struck by an unpleasant thought, that she might see the homes of the Powhatan as something lowly and undesirable compared to hers.

If so, he would give her reins back to her, dismount, and ask her to leave. Had he been wrong to believe that there could ever be anything between them, that their cultures would not clash too often?

"Is seeing my village and how we live the cause of your uneasiness?" Midnight Falcon asked. "Are our homes so undesirable to you?"

Chandra realized where he was going with his questions. Their homes *were* different, even more different than she had imagined. She had expected either wigwams or tepees. Instead there were longhouses.

But such things didn't matter. She had been misjudged back in Liverpool because she was poor, and she knew better than most that it was one's heart that measured one's worth.

"Entering your village is so very exciting," she said. "I am in *awe*. That is why you sense a difference about me."

She swallowed hard. "But I can't help but still be afraid that I won't be accepted."

Relieved, he felt a little foolish at having

thought she would judge him in that way. He gazed at her with love in his eyes, his smile warming her through and through.

"I will be with you," he said. "Is not that enough?"

Chandra smiled weakly and nodded.

And then he kissed her, but this time it was not a kiss of hungry passion. It was sweet and delicious, causing all of Chandra's fears and apprehensions to melt away.

"Now let us go," Midnight Falcon whispered against her lips. "All will be well. You will see."

Chandra sighed contentedly as he turned her again to face forward.

She was glad, though, when he took one of her hands and held it as he once again urged the horse toward his village.

12

There be none of Beauty's daughters,
With a magic like thee;
And like music on the waters
Is thy sweet voice to me.
—LORD BYRON

Little Snow Feather led Shannon around behind the village, staying far enough in the shadows of the forest so that no one could see them. She knew that she had a right to take a friend to the temple to teach her the ways of the Powhatan, since doing so might help her people in the future. Shannon could, in turn, teach *her* people about Powhatan culture and make whites realize that Indians were not savages. But Little Snow Feather knew that it was best to avoid being detected just yet. One of the villagers might get upset and try to persuade Little Snow Feather's brother to stop her alliance with Shannon. She wanted nothing to get in the way of her friendship.

Still, her brother would not step in and forbid anything of the kind, not now.

Little Snow Feather would never forget that moment when she saw her brother and Chandra hug, knowing then that both his life and her own would be better because of it.

She knew that the future would bring many more whites to the area. Like Pocahontas, she felt that alliances between her people and the whites would only benefit everyone.

Little Snow Feather stopped when she saw the back of the temple, which sat at the very far end of the village. She squeezed Shannon's hand.

"There is my people's temple," Little Snow Feather whispered, nodding toward it.

Shannon looked stunned as she stared at the largest longhouse in the village.

Little Snow Feather tilted her head and squinted at Shannon. "Why do you look so strange?"

Not wanting to embarrass Little Snow Feather, Shannon tried to hide her surprise over the shabby appearance of the temple. Shannon had imagined a grand, tall building covered in gold.

"It is only that I am a little afraid to go inside," Shannon whispered back. She was not lying, for she did feel nervous about what they were going to do.

It seemed unholy somehow for Little Snow Feather to be taking a stranger, a white stranger, into her people's place of worship.

Yet Shannon kept telling herself that Little Snow Feather surely knew what she was doing. And wasn't she their princess? Shouldn't she know what was right and wrong? And what *could* it hurt? Shannon was just a little girl, and she wanted to see inside.

And Shannon was ready to risk as much as Little Snow Feather. She was risking the wrath of her

father should he ever discover any of her es-
capades, especially those today!

"I have thought it through and I feel there is
nothing wrong in taking you inside my people's
temple," Little Snow Feather whispered. "I want
you to see something very special. Please come."

Shannon took a deep breath, then nodded. "All
right," she said. "But let's not stay long. If my
father caught me . . ."

"He will not catch you in a place where he himself would not go," Little Snow Feather said. She
tightened her fingers around Shannon's. "Let's go
now. I am so excited over sharing this with you."

The excitement felt contagious, and Shannon
listened eagerly.

"We must hurry along the side of the longhouse
to the front and get inside as quickly as possible,"
Little Snow Feather said. "No one should be there
now, but I don't want anyone to see us go in."

Again Shannon nodded.

They quietly went around the side and darted
through a door at the east end, but not so quickly
that Shannon didn't catch a glimpse of two fig-
ures that stood at the door on each side, carved
to resemble dragons.

Breathlessly, Shannon followed Little Snow
Feather farther into the temple. She looked
around, surprised by how dreary and unimpres-
sive it was.

Again, she had expected something grand, but
it was nothing much to look at. The birchbark

walls were bare. The floor was covered with mats, and along the walls there were benches that also had mats on them as cushions. Torches were positioned along one wall.

In the center of the floor was a large open space surrounded by rocks, where a fire burned slowly, its smoke spiraling upward through an aperture at the peak of the roof.

As Shannon's eyes grew more used to the dim lighting in the room, she saw something that completely puzzled her. A velveteen sofa, looking so out of place among the other simple things, sat alone against the far wall.

It was faded and the velvet was worn. One leg supporting it was gone, leaving the sofa to lean precariously. It looked quite old. It wasn't how the sofa looked but the fact that a piece of furniture used by white people was there, in the Powhatan temple, of all places.

Shannon stared at Little Snow Feather with wonder.

"Come. I shall show you," Little Snow Feather said, taking Shannon's hand and leading her toward the sofa.

As they came closer, Shannon saw something else. A crown of rare jewels sat on the sofa.

"Long ago, in the time of Chief Powhatan and Pocahontas, a treaty between my people and the king of England included Chief Powhatan receiving this sofa and crown in exchange for a small parcel of land near where Jamestown now stands."

"Truly?" Shannon gasped.

"Chief Powhatan met the king face-to-face on the king's boat with its large white wings," Little Snow Feather said. "The king sat on this sofa and wore this crown on the boat. Chief Powhatan could not help but want them for himself."

"And the king gave them to him?" Shannon asked, fascinated by the tale.

"Yes," Little Snow Feather said. "It was a part of the treaty signed between them. After the sofa was taken from the king's ship and placed here in the temple, only Chief Powhatan and Pocahontas sat on it. Only he wore the crown. They are kept in the temple now to honor Chief Powhatan's memory and how smart he was to take from the king what he knew was so important to him."

"That's so interesting," Shannon said.

Little Snow Feather led her away from the couch to where another fire burned, but this one was in a much smaller opening in the floor.

From where she was standing, Shannon could not make out an object that lay on a table just past the fire space.

She shuddered, suddenly feeling that she was in the presence of spirits.

Little Snow Feather tugged on her hand as she tried to encourage her to walk toward the smaller fire and the small table.

"I don't know," Shannon whispered, grimacing.

"Why are you afraid?" Little Snow Feather

asked, an obvious hurt in her voice. "You should trust me."

"I sense we are not alone," Shannon said, looking around her and moving closer to Little Snow Feather. "Do you also not feel it?"

"I always feel that way when I am in my people's holy place," Little Snow Feather said matter-of-factly. She shrugged. "But that is good. You should enjoy the presence of your loved ones who visit you while you visit the temple." She looked heavenward and smiled. "I feel my mother and father's presence. I also feel Pocahontas's."

"Are they smiling or frowning over you bringing me here?" Shannon asked, more and more convinced that her friend did have the power to feel and see such things.

She was beginning to see why many people were afraid of Indians. They seemed closer to nature and heaven than whites ever could be.

"I am loved by them all, so they trust who I bring here," Little Snow Feather said. "Please come now and see what I have been wanting to show you."

Shannon knelt beside Little Snow Feather in front of the small fire.

With true interest, she listened to her friend, more intrigued the more she listened.

"As I have told you, the most powerful of the Powhatan gods is Okeus," Little Snow Feather said. She gestured toward the idol that lay on the table in the light of the fire. "The idol is in the holiest area of the temple, and the priests keep a fire burning to keep the god happy. Look at it. See how beautiful it is?"

Shannon *was* in awe of the idol, especially since she had never seen an idol of any kind before. That her friend was showing her something so holy made this moment even more special.

The idol was made of wooden crosspieces padded with moss. The body was painted black. The face was white. It was decorated with strands of pearls.

"The priests of my people teach that Okeus causes all the evil in the world and can make people sick, or destroy their corn, or make wives hate their husbands," Little Snow Feather said. "We must always remember the power of Okeus and be good in his presence."

Little Snow Feather smiled at Shannon. "Less powerful than Okeus is Ahone, the Powhatan god of goodness," she explained. "Ahone is friends with the sun. In his name, the Powhatan bathe in a stream at morning or at sunrise. Then we place dried tobacco in a circle around one who is praying. That person raises his arms to the sun, and then slowly lowers them to the earth."

"And how often is this done?" Shannon asked, eyes wide.

"Whenever anyone feels the need to feel close to Ahone. Special times call for special prayers."

"Earlier, when you were talking about Okeus, you said something about sacrificing children,"

Shannon said, staring at the idol. "Is that done now?"

"There is a time when it is necessary—" Little Snow Feather stopped when she heard footsteps behind her. Startled, she rose quickly to her feet. She heard Shannon move just as quickly to her feet and felt her standing very close to her side.

". . . Limping Fox!" Little Snow Feather stammered as she stared at her people's head priest.

Shannon's heart thundered inside her chest. The most peculiarly dressed man she had ever seen, or perhaps would ever see, stood before them. The elderly man, whose wrinkled face was painted with streaks of red and white, wore a headdress of dyed deer hair gathered into a topknot and crowned with feathers, from which dangled a dozen or more snakeskins. A knee-length shift of quilted rabbit skins was the only covering on his body, which was painted black. In his ears he wore various ornaments, dangling claws of fowls inset with copper.

If that weren't enough, something else that Shannon saw made her weak with fear. She stared at the live green garter snakes woven along with strands of fresh-water pearls through his floor-length gray hair. The snakes flicked their tongues out and hissed as their beady green eyes glared at her. In disbelief she gulped for air.

Little Snow Feather realized that because of the deep respect he had for her as their people's princess, Limping Fox was not openly scolding her for having brought a white girl into the temple. But the anger in his eyes said it all.

"Limping Fox, this is my new friend," Little Snow Feather said, ignoring how he stared at her as though Shannon wasn't there. "She wishes to know the ways of our people. I feel it is important for her to know. She is teaching me things I did not know about her people. And we are bringing happiness to one another's hearts."

Limping Fox still did not look at Shannon. He stepped closer to Little Snow Feather and placed a hand on her shoulder. "I understand your need to learn things that you hope will, in turn, help your people, but be careful of who you befriend," he said. His voice was deep and authoritative. "What good will such a friendship bring your people?"

Almost as quickly and quietly as he had come into the temple, he turned and left again.

Suddenly too afraid to stay, Shannon ran from the temple and fled into the darkness of the forest.

Not seeing a gnarled thick root that had grown up from the ground beneath an old oak tree, Shannon stumbled. Sprawled on the ground, she started to cry.

Finally catching up with Shannon, Little Snow Feather fell to her knees beside her and slid her arms around her waist. She hugged her tightly. "Let no one, not even my people's head priest, frighten you away from our friendship."

Shannon clung to her, her sobs drowning out the forest sounds around them.

"He spoke about me but did not look at me once," Shannon sobbed. "It was like I wasn't there."

"I know that he must have studied you well when he first arrived, before we knew that he was there," Little Snow Feather said. "As I talked to you, he watched and listened. He saw your true interest. He even saw your sweetness, or he would not have been as kind to us."

"Do you feel sorry about taking me there?" Shannon asked. She leaned away from Little Snow Feather and wiped her eyes with the back of her hands.

"No, I do not think I was wrong," Little Snow Feather said. "Nor does Limping Fox, not really. We have talked often about things, about our people's past and future. He has seen it in the stars, how many of them there are overhead, telling him how the whites will, also, become many across our land. It is something that no one can stop. Being friendly with whites is the only way we, as a people, can learn to live with them."

"Even so, I don't want to go back there ever again," Shannon said, shuddering.

"Do you mean my village? Or just the temple?"

"I'm not sure."

"Please do not let one visit keep you from coming back." Little Snow Feather's eyes searched Shannon's. "Please?"

"I won't," Shannon said, smiling. "But I don't think I want to go back for a while."

"I will know when the time is right," Little Snow Feather said. She smiled broadly, glad that they would be able to share more things.

Shannon rose to her feet and brushed her skirt free of leaves and twigs.

"Let us do something fun," Little Snow Feather urged.

"Like what?" Shannon asked, twining her fingers through her long hair and drawing it back from her face so that it hung long and loose down her back.

"Let us wade barefoot in a stream where there are many tadpoles to kiss our feet and ankles," Little Snow Feather said excitedly.

Not sure if she should linger any longer with Little Snow Feather, Shannon smiled weakly, but when Little Snow Feather took her hand and they began to run away from the village, she forgot her fears. She ran through the forest with her friend, laughing.

"It will be such fun!" Little Snow Feather cried.

Coming out of the forest, they raced through the clover field where they had made their crowns.

"Yes, such fun!" Shannon echoed, feeling like a young girl again who for the moment forgot that she had ever had a worry or a fear.

13

Never love unless you can
Bear with all the faults of man.
—Thomas Campion

Chandra looped the reins around a small tree limb on the riverbank to secure her horse. She thought this would be wiser than riding with Midnight Falcon to the Powhatan village for all to see, as they had originally planned. A movement to her left caught her attention out of the corner of her eye.

For a moment, she thought that it was Shannon running with Little Snow Feather through the forest.

But at second glance, she saw a deer leap into hiding behind a bush, and realized that must have been what she had seen. Her imagination was playing tricks on her, since she had just been thinking of her niece, wondering where she had gone with Little Snow Feather. The longer Shannon stayed with the Powhatan princess, the more chance she might be seen by her father.

But perhaps that might be best, Chandra thought as she stepped away from her horse and began walking with Midnight Falcon up the incline toward his village. It made her feel guilty to deceive her brother.

In time he must be told, and Chandra would tell him, for both herself and Shannon, when she felt the time was right.

That time was not now, not when her brother's mood was so dark that he might come into the Powhatan village with a firearm and do something reckless.

She pushed thoughts of her brother aside. Only a few moments from now, she would be the center of attention among Midnight Falcon's people, so she focused on being with the man she loved.

As they walked away from the James River, she became aware of how the Powhatan settlement, which overlooked the water, was located on higher ground. The bark houses, with their arched roofs, were long and narrow, and were scattered randomly throughout the village.

Some houses had sides covered with mats woven of reeds, while others were covered with large patches of bark that looked as though they could be rolled up and removed in warm weather. This must be to permit air to circulate through the dwellings.

The roofs were thatched with marsh grass or bark.

Having first thought, from a distance, that smoke came from chimneys, now she could see that they weren't chimneys at all, but smoke holes left in the centers of the roofs.

Interspersed among the houses and square gardens behind them were groves of trees, which provided shade from the sun and shelter from the wind and rain. There were great stands of pine, cypress, and walnut. She also recognized mulberry trees, from which the Powhatan undoubtedly obtained juicy fruit.

She could see that pumpkin, maize, and beans grew in the gardens, as well as tobacco that grew at the far end of each field.

They were not far enough into the village to draw his people's attention yet. Chandra tried to familiarize herself with everything.

"I noticed that each house has its own garden," she said, breaking the awkward silence that had fallen between them.

She supposed that Midnight Falcon's silence was caused by apprehensions he did not want to share with her. Although it was his decision to bring her to his people, she imagined that he would be somewhat uncomfortable at first.

She understood.

It would be the same, even worse, should she enter the town of Jamestown with Midnight Falcon at her side. It was taboo between the two cultures, something that both she and Midnight Falcon had chosen to ignore.

"Yes, each family cares for their own food supply," Midnight Falcon said, glad to have something to talk about. He was watching out for the first person who would see him with the white woman.

Although nothing would be said to him since no one ever openly questioned his right to do anything, he knew that many would silently wonder.

He had thought it over very carefully, and knew that it could be no other way.

Now that he knew that Chandra loved him, he would pave the way for their eventual marriage, and their children.

"Do the women care for the gardens?" Chandra asked, her pulse racing as the hill flattened out into the outskirts of the village, where the first longhouse sat.

As they walked past it, she could hear people chattering from inside. She heard easy laughter, and then more talk.

Farther ahead, she saw others coming and going from their lodges.

She could hear children squealing as they played, but she couldn't see them.

And again she could hear the howling of the Powhatan dogs.

"Yes, the women plant and care for the crops that we eat, but it is the men who cultivate the tobacco," Midnight Falcon said. He gazed down at Chandra and saw that she was closely observing everything and everyone.

He could tell that she was tense, and he understood. It was up to him to lighten her mood and make her feel comfortable so that she would not be afraid to come here again.

"Once planted, the corn emerges first, and by the time it has a good stalk, beans come up and twine around it," he said, nodding toward a garden that was close by. "Four kinds of corn are planted. Two ripen in early autumn, which are called flint corn and she-corn, and two ripen early in summer so that two crops can be raised each year. There are two kinds of beans. The smaller ones are called *assentamens*."

"Now that we are closer I can see many types of melons, too," Chandra said, just as she noticed people stepping to their doors to stare at her and Midnight Falcon.

Midnight Falcon also saw his people. He smiled and nodded to each villager, yet kept talking to Chandra to help get her past the growing fear that he saw in her eyes. "There is squash, including gourds, muskmelons, and *maracocks*, or passion flowers, which are planted between the corn and bean clumps and allowed to run along the ground," he said. He was relieved that his long-house was near, for he could tell that Chandra was even more tense than earlier. "Any corn not ripened by the end of the harvest season is gathered and roasted in hot ashes, then kept for winter, when it is boiled with beans for a special dish we call *pausarowmena*."

"Your homes are different than I would have thought them to be," Chandra said, smiling awkwardly as a girl stepped closer to get a better look at her. "I thought Indians lived in tepees or wigwams."

Midnight Falcon nodded hello to Evening Star, a young maiden his sister's age. She kept pace with them, her eyes, filled with curiosity, never leaving Chandra.

"Our houses are called *yi-hakan*, longhouses," he said. He swept an arm around Chandra's waist, ushering her toward his lodge door. "To you, who lives in a wealthy white man's lodge, this must seem drab, but it is how the woman who will be my wife will live."

He stopped just before entering his home and turned her to face him. He had to be sure. "Is this house distasteful to you?" he asked quietly, so no one else would hear. "I had to bring you and show you to give you a chance to back away from me and my way of life should you want to, before my heart is lost more deeply to you."

She had not had the chance to see the inside of his home, but she did not even care how much it differed from where she lived now. Chandra forgot everyone around her and smiled up at Midnight Falcon. Were he to see how she had lived before she married Sir Lawrence O'Banyon, he would realize that anywhere else would be paradise in comparison.

"How can you think that where I live would make such a difference?" Chandra said. She was glad that everyone seemed to be losing interest in them. One by one they were returning to their chores, and now she and Midnight Falcon were alone at his door.

"I saw what white man's wealth bought to make you comfortable," Midnight Falcon said. "There is no way I can shower you with such gifts and fancy clothes. What I will offer you is made from Mother Earth, and by the hands of my people."

The children Chandra had heard laughing before had run up behind Midnight Falcon and were staring at her questioningly.

"Can we go inside and talk there?" she asked.

Midnight Falcon saw how uncomfortable Chandra looked and followed her gaze. When he saw the children, he smiled and hurried her inside his lodge.

Midnight Falcon rushed into the lodge away from her, and the room was so dark she could not tell where he had disappeared to. She became frightened.

"Where are you?" Chandra called. "Why did you leave me?"

"My fire," Midnight Falcon said from somewhere in the darkness. "There is hardly a trace of fire left burning in the firepit. There are only embers, and they are dying. I must tend to it quickly."

He immediately began rekindling the household fire by chafing a dry pointed stick against a hole in a little square piece of wood. The heat that was generated caught some moss and leaves on fire.

Satisfied, yet making sure the fire caught hold strongly enough, he waited and watched as each spark of fire spread. Then he began adding wood to the kindled flames.

The longer Chandra stood there, the more her eyes adjusted to the darkness. At first the smoke hole overhead was the only source of light. But then she saw the glimmer of ashes and could make out the silhouette of Midnight Falcon kneeling beside the firepit.

Soon she saw a fire burning brightly in the firepit, which was surrounded by a circle of rocks on a dirt floor. As she waited there for him to come back to her, she looked slowly around her.

She saw that there was one large central room flanked by several smaller rooms, with a small corridor leading to them. There was little furniture. There were mats made of buckskin, some plain, some embroidered, and some decorated with white pearls and beads.

Along one far wall she saw a long bench, under which were buckskin bags, probably filled with Midnight Falcon's personal belongings.

Hanging from pegs on the walls were his bow and quiver of arrows, and pelts taken from various animals, all looking rich, expensive, and thick.

She presumed all cooking utensils and other such things were in the other rooms.

She strained her neck to look down the small

corridor. She wondered what his bedroom was like and on what sort of bed he slept. She wondered which room was his, and which was Little Snow Feather's.

She noticed how clean his dwelling was, and how it smelled pleasantly of pine needles and perhaps something similar to sage.

"Come now and sit with me beside the fire," he said, gently taking her by an elbow and guiding her onto soft mats.

"You seemed in a hurry to tend your lodge fire," Chandra said. She thought he looked relaxed now, watching the flames hugging the logs.

"I was startled when I saw that my fire was almost out," Midnight Falcon said. "It is my people's belief that we must keep fires going in our homes at all times. If the fire goes out completely at any time, it is taken for an evil sign."

More and more Chandra was discovering just how superstitious the Powhatan were.

"Our people believe in signs and things that you might find hard to understand," he said, turning to gaze into her eyes. "I told you before that we believe in reincarnation."

"Until I met you, I never thought much about reincarnation," Chandra said. "Please tell me about it."

"At death our people's spirits climb to the top of a tall tree supporting a bridge that leads to the sky," he said. "There they live until, after dying a second time, they are reborn from the womb of an earth woman, to experience a second life on earth. It is a privilege for a family when a spirit is brought among them for a second life."

"That is so interesting," Chandra said, truly in awe of everything that she learned from him.

"I hope to teach you everything about my people." Midnight Falcon reached for her hands and held them. "I plan to share everything with the woman I wish to marry."

"Marry?" Chandra gasped, her heart skipping a beat. "You are speaking of me? You want me to be your wife?"

"When you feel that an appropriate time of mourning your husband is past, yes, I want you to come live with me as my wife," Midnight Falcon said. He wrapped his arms around her waist and brought her closer to him. "But that can only happen if you can accept everything about my people. Some have said our culture is one of dark superstitions and devil worship, a culture of easy cruelty and primitive social accomplishments. How do you see us so far?"

"Devil worship?" Chandra tried to absorb his words. "Cruelty? Who said this about your people?"

"First there were black-robed men who came and tried to change our religion, and then there were the English," Midnight Falcon said. "There have been many on the English side who choose to believe such evil things about my people."

"How could they?" Chandra said, wanting to

believe there was no truth in it. Why would anyone think the Powhatan worshipped the devil, unless they were referring somehow to their belief
in reincarnation.

"Many white people will say, do, and believe
anything, if it can successfully discredit us," Midnight Falcon said, his voice low. "Devil worship-
ping tales began about my people when whites
realized that we do not share the same belief in
creation as the black-robed priests preach from
their black book they call the Bible."

"I'm sorry for the ignorance of those white people who purposely stir up trouble for the
Powhatan in order to gain more land for themselves." She moved into his arms and gently
hugged him. "Greed is the cause. Ignorance and
greed are the enemies of the white community,
not the red man and his beliefs."

Midnight Falcon framed her face between his
hands and gazed at her with deep emotion. "I
want you to be my wife," he said, his eyes searching hers. "When the time is right for you, it will
be for me. Will you marry me?"

He wanted to tell her that should she become
his wife, she would gain the title of queen. But
he had to wait until they were man and wife; then,
and only then, would he tell her. He was not sure
if being his people's queen, his queen, might over-
whelm or frighten her. He would not take that
chance.

"It is like a dream that you are even asking me

to be your wife," Chandra said, her head reeling over the very idea of living forever with this man. "Are you certain? We . . . we have not known each other for very long. What if you are wrong about me? What if you begin seeing my flaws after it is too late?"

He chuckled. "You? Flaws? If there are any, they are very well hidden."

He brushed a soft kiss across her lips, then smiled at her. "My woman, I know that we have only just met, but that should not matter. Too often time is our enemy, especially if we wait too long for what we know is right for us," he said. "Ours is a special love, born of the stars, moon, and sky. Let us not wait too long to share it as man and wife."

Midnight Falcon crushed her lips with his and Chandra moaned with pleasure. She clung to him for a few moments before she had to pull herself free or else never leave his dwelling again.

"I must go," she said, breathing hard. "My brother might come looking for me. I'm not ready yet to face him. I hope that it won't be long before he works out the demons inside his head. Then I shall be free to do as I wish. But until then, please be patient. He has a lot to get over, and I do not want to make things worse."

"I will wait until you say the time is right," Midnight Falcon said. "But my heart will ache until I can hold you again."

"I will try to make sure that it will not be for

long," Chandra said. "I will ache when we are apart as well."

"Meet me tomorrow," he said as he rose to his feet before her. He slowly walked her toward his door. "I want to take you fishing. It will be a way to learn more about me, and my customs."

"Oh, I would love to do that." She placed a hand on his face. "But I must warn you, I have never fished before. My brother is the fisherman of the family."

She lowered her eyes and swallowed hard. Although she had been trying to encourage her brother to get on his new boat and start his fishing business again, she, too, had become afraid of water.

She did not blame herself for the boating accident, as her brother did, but she had attended the burials of all of the men who had died. She had seen the grieving widows and children. And she had begun dreading ever going out on water again.

The long voyage from England had been an ordeal for her to begin with, but then she had watched her husband's body lowered into the ocean. It was hard to erase from her mind the sight of the water swallowing her husband's body like some hungry sea monster.

She knew that drowning could be the same.

She never talked about these feelings with her brother or anyone because she was too busy trying to encourage *him* not to be afraid.

Now she knew that she must be tested. She would not deny herself the pleasure of going fishing with Midnight Falcon tomorrow.

"I'm afraid of water," she said.

Midnight Falcon tried to hide the surprise in his voice. "I vow to keep you safe while we fish from my canoe," he promised. He did not think this woman would be afraid of anything after seeing her ride so bravely on horseback.

"Canoe?" She found that thought even more terrifying than she had expected. Canoes seemed so dangerous, so easily tipped over.

"I have mastered my canoe as you have mastered your horse," he said, encouraging her. "You, too, will master the canoe. I will teach you everything about it."

"While I am with you, I'm sure nothing will frighten me," Chandra said. "But I really must leave now. And if I keep busy, won't tomorrow seem to come so much more quickly?"

"Yes, but in my heart it is here already," he said, pulling her close, answering her outcry of passion with a fiery kiss.

Then he stepped away from her and walked her to the door.

As he opened it, she noticed something that she had not seen in the dark of the room earlier. She jumped back with alarm and stifled a scream.

"Do not be afraid," Midnight Falcon said as she stared at an object hanging on the wall beside the door.

"What is it?" Chandra asked, daring to take a step toward it.

"That is my family's coat of arms. Every prominent Powhatan family has their own coat of arms, some particular bird or beast that belongs to that family," he explained. "The cardinal is our family's crest, which is tattooed on our bodies. This fox, which has been skinned and stuffed, is my family's coat of arms."

Chandra could not help but recall the two beautiful red foxes she had seen at play many times. She shivered at the thought of anyone catching and killing them.

"It is just one of the many customs of my people you will be introduced to," Midnight Falcon said, recognizing her uneasiness. "Will you be able to adjust to such customs?"

Chandra took a deep breath and turned to look at Midnight Falcon. "For you, I will do anything," she said. She flung herself into his arms and hugged him tightly. "I do love you so."

He slowly closed the door so that he was able to kiss her again without being seen, but after a moment he broke free, sensing that their passions were becoming too heated. He opened the door and walked with her to the outer fringes of the forest.

"Until tomorrow," she said, and smiled.

She ran from the village, mounted her horse, and rode in a hard gallop beside the river toward home.

She had never been as happy, or filled with such bliss, as now. She felt as though she was floating amidst the clouds, for she had finally found a man she adored.

She would not spoil the moment by thinking about him being an Indian, or his strange customs, or that he was forbidden to her.

She couldn't wait much longer to share everything, especially lovemaking, with Midnight Falcon.

She knew that she could never love anyone but him, and nothing or no one would keep them apart.

An image of her brother flashed before her. She would have to tell him soon.

14

Love at the lips was touch
As sweet as I could bear;
And once that seemed too much;
I lived on air.
—ROBERT FROST

Chandra thought that the tension in the parlor was so high that something would soon snap. Jan-Michael often glanced at her from where he sat before the fire playing chess with Shannon.

He hadn't even mentioned the empty birdcage since she had set the lovely parakeet free.

Chandra tried to ignore his scowl as she turned the page of her poetry book and began reading aloud a poem by Sir Thomas Browne: "Sure there is music even in the beauty, and the silent note which cupid strikes, far sweeter than the sound of an instrument. . . ."

Reading poetry gave her peace, as she had discovered shortly after meeting Sir Lawrence O'Banyon. His first gift to her had been this very book of poetry.

When she had read the personal inscription on the inside cover, where he declared his love to her, she had realized that if she wanted it to, her life could change forever.

It was then that she had begun to feel as though she was being pulled in two directions. She had always been a person of much pride no matter how she lived, and she was afraid that if she accepted a life of luxury, it would take away her pride in who she truly was.

Yet she had wanted to explore this vastly different life, even though it had never been her desire to wear velvet and silk clothes, or sparkling jewels.

Not wanting to be accused of being a vain, money-hungry person, she had almost decided against marrying Lawrence—until her brother's accident.

Seeing her brother falling deeper and deeper into despair, so deep that he had talked of wanting to take his own life, had made the true difference in Chandra's decision.

She placed a velvet ribbon between the pages of her book so she would know where to begin tomorrow. Closing the book, she looked at Jan-Michael again.

His gaze was no longer on her, but on his game of chess instead. Shannon had just checkmated him and she smiled broadly at Chandra. Only moments ago, Shannon had looked worried, as though she was waiting for the room to explode in words. She knew that her father sensed there was something secret between her and his sister, yet pridefully did not pursue what it might be.

It thrilled her that Midnight Falcon had actually talked of marriage, although they were so new to one another. She was afraid that once he had time to think about what he had done, he might change his mind.

She knew for certain that she would never change her mind about wanting to live the rest of her life with the wonderful Powhatan chief.

Her heart filled with joy, and she smiled to herself as she thought of tomorrow's planned fishing expedition.

She gazed at the clock on the fireplace mantel and watched the pendulum sweep back and forth, filling the room with its steady, rhythmic sound.

Yet Chandra felt time was passing too slowly. If she could she would will the hands of the clock to the hour tomorrow when she would already be with Midnight Falcon in his canoe, watching his muscled arms as he brought fish out of the water.

"Chandra, I went into Jamestown today and posted notices about hirin' men to start my fishin' business in America," Jan-Michael blurted out, eliciting gasps and stares of surprise from both his sister and his daughter.

His eyes wavered as he gazed at Chandra. "I know that I must find the courage to set sail again," he said. "What I keep thinkin', though, is how mastering my own boat is much different than ridin' the seas under someone else's command. Should my boat capsize again, it is I who again will be responsible for the loss of lives."

Chandra remained quiet so that he could say everything that he needed to say. She even waited

as he paused to reach for his pipe and bag of tobacco.

After filling the bowl of his pipe, lighting it,
and taking several puffs, he stared at the chess-
board for a moment, then looked at Chandra
again.

"I have never told you how I have such terrible dreams, where the faces of my lost crew haunt
me," he said, his voice breaking. "Lord, if I lose
anyone else like that, I will be livin' in hell for
eternity."

Not realizing it had been that bad for her
brother, Chandra now understood so much about
his attitude these past weeks and months. She laid
her book aside and hurried to Jan-Michael.

She bent low and hugged him.

And when his arm wrapped around her and
she felt the desperation in his grip, she, too, became afraid for him. She knew now just how close
he was to the edge.

"Things will be all right," she murmured. She
eased from his arms and took his hands and urged
him up from his chair. "Come and walk with me
in the moonlight? It's been so long since we did
that. Big brother, I do love you so."

Shannon realized that her game of chess was
over and she would have to accept that her father
had ignored her last move.

She plopped down on the sofa where Scottie
was napping and drew him onto her lap.

Filled with peace over her father finally getting

involved in his fishing business again, she watched them leave through the open double doors that led out to the veranda.

Shannon stretched out on the sofa beside Scottie and napped, as well, as the fire's orange flames flickered around the logs.

Outside, Chandra and Jan-Michael walked beneath the moonlight, and Chandra allowed her brother to lead the way. As the moon sprayed its silver light down onto the boat in the river, Chandra prayed that her brother was going to finally board it.

"I'm so glad that you are finally looking for a crew," she said. She felt disappointed when he stopped and stared at the boat, still seeming not to have any plans to board. "What caused you to change your mind about hiring a crew?"

He placed his hand on her shoulder and turned her to face him. "I have watched you, little sister, and how you have gotten past your mourning so well," he said. "I knew that I must do the same." He swallowed hard. "But I was mourning more than a wife. I was mourning my crew, and perhaps even a part of me that died with them."

"But accidents happen, you *know* that," Chandra said softly. "It is a risk one takes when going out to sea, especially when one has to go as often as you did to succeed in your business."

"Had I been that successful, I would've made a better life for Mother and you, and especially for Shannon and my beloved wife."

"Jan-Michael, you knew from the beginning that fishing for a living scarcely makes one rich," Chandra said, sighing. "But you put food on our table and clothes on our backs. Don't you know how grateful we were for that, especially since Father abandoned us and cared nothing about how we would survive?"

She placed a hand on his cheek. "Never see yourself as any less than a knight in shining armor, which is what you became for us in the absence of our father."

"Knight in shinin' armor?" Jan-Michael said, laughing. "Chandra, you read too many books."

"They became my escape," she said, smiling up at him. "They made life tolerable. Now I have . . ."

She caught herself just before saying something that might change her brother's mood back to somber.

She felt the color drain from her face when he gazed intensely at her. He frowned, as though he could look clean into her heart and see Midnight Falcon's face there.

"What were you about to say?" Jan-Michael asked. "It was somethin' about what you now have?"

"Freedom," Chandra blurted out. It seemed enough to satisfy her brother.

"Ay, freedom," he said, turning from her to again gaze at his boat. "I, too, crave it. I hope I do have the courage to feel free again, especially of my demons."

Now she dreaded, even more, the moment she would tell him about the man she loved.

And what would he do when he discovered that his very own daughter was keeping something so secret from him?

She had to find a way to make him understand for both herself and Shannon.

Jan-Michael turned toward Chandra. "I noticed that you no longer have the parakeet," he said.

"Yes, I set it free," she said. "You see, it, too, deserves the freedom it was born with. . . ."

Jan-Michael nodded, then again turned toward his boat, Chandra watching him.

15

The eyes, those silent tongues of Love.
—MIGUEL DE CERVANTES

The moon shone down the smoke hole onto the flames of a fire in the council house firepit. Many eyes were on Midnight Falcon as he sat with his warriors in a half circle.

"As you all know, word has been received that Chief Black Rock and his Pocoughtaonacks tribe are moving south out of Canada in hopes of conquering more land for their people," Midnight Falcon said. He looked each warrior in the eye before continuing. "I believe his true reason is to attack our village again. We must prepare ourselves for their arrival."

Midnight Falcon opened the door and peered out. He looked imposing in his council clothes, the skin of a wolf over his shoulder, with one arm left bare. "Our people have suffered enough at the hands of the cannibals," he said. "I still ache inside my heart for the family I lost."

He spun around and glared from warrior to warrior. "Choose among you the warrior who has the most stamina, so that he can leave soon to scout the land and report whether Black Rock and his men are on their way here," he said, his voice filled with a measured anger. "Chief Black Rock must be stopped this time. He must die!"

The council had already been long and much had been discussed. With the main points now decided upon, Midnight Falcon hungered for the privacy of his lodge. "I will go now, my warriors," he said. "Prepare for what might lie ahead of us. Choose carefully the man who will scout for us. As you know, Chief Black Rock has ways of eluding even the most clever eye."

"He will not be returning to Canada if he is foolish enough to leave and dare the Powhatan into another fight," Feathered Hawk said, rising to his feet. He went to Midnight Falcon and placed his hands on his shoulders. "If it pleases you, as well as everyone else, I would like to volunteer to be our scout. I will go, even now, to search for signs of Chief Black Rock and his warriors. Do I have your permission to do this? Do I have your blessing?"

Touched deeply by the faithfulness of his best friend since childhood, Midnight Falcon worked hard to keep his emotions in check.

He reached up and placed a hand on one of Feathered Hawk's. "No vote in council is needed for this decision," he said. "Go. Do your duty to your chief and your people. Your devotion will be rewarded upon your return."

"No physical reward is needed," Feathered

Hawk said, proudly squaring his shoulders. "The true reward lies in being Powhatan!"

A low rumble of approval swept through the warriors, and soon they were all on their feet thanking Feathered Hawk.

Midnight Falcon caught Feathered Hawk's eye and received a friendly nod and smile in return for his own. Seeing that he was no longer needed, with everyone involved with Feathered Hawk, he left the council house and hurried to the quiet peace of his own lodge.

After stirring the coals in his lodge fire and adding more wood, Midnight Falcon sat down before the dancing flames. He could not help but think back to when Chandra had been there with him.

In fact, she had been with him ever since, in his heart, his mood, and his every action.

He was surprised by his intense feelings for her. While he had been in council, his mind had strayed far too often to the white woman with the hair of sunshine, aching for tomorrow.

He knew that the only way he might stop getting distracted was to marry her soon and have her there with him all of the time.

"My wife," he whispered to himself. "I have asked her to be my wife."

Marrying her was what he deeply desired, yet he could not shake the feeling that this was happening too quickly.

Was it too quickly for him to be certain that his

feelings were genuine? Might he simply be intrigued by her loveliness?

Or might he just be lonely in his blankets at night?

And there were the obstacles in the way of their being together as man and wife. She had a family, who perhaps she should be making more important in her life than a Powhatan chief.

Something else had begun to bother him, something he tried to fight with all of his strength—that she might be infatuated with him because of his title. Since he had become chief, had that not drawn many women to him, as bees are drawn to honey?

How could he truly know that Chandra loved him, and for the right reasons?

He had waited too long already to take a wife. But should it be her? She was white. She lived a life of luxury. Her customs differed so much from his.

"Tomorrow," he whispered, nodding.

Yes, tomorrow he would get the chance to study Chandra more intensely, to look inside his heart and decide his true feelings. He hoped that she would be searching for the same answers about him.

While fishing they would be alone—alone with their feelings.

A part of him was almost afraid to know the true answer, but a part of him found it hard to wait. Whatever he discovered tomorrow, it would give him the true direction for the rest of his life.

He was unable to forget how it had felt when they had kissed and embraced. To live without her surely would be to feel like a man sentenced to death!

16

Live now, believe me, wait not till tomorrow;
Gather the roses of life today!
                                    —PIERRE DE RONSARD

It just didn't seem real to Chandra that she was actually in a canoe with Midnight Falcon, away from her family and the only world that she had ever known.

For so long she had placed herself second to everyone else in her life, putting the needs of her family before her own.

Back in England she had always sought ways to make things easier for her mother. It did not seem possible that there could be so many miles dividing them now. She did sorely miss her.

But Midnight Falcon was giving Chandra a life that she felt she could now call her own, and she could not help but dream of a future with him.

For the moment, she had even placed the concern of being pregnant from her mind. She was going to enjoy this private time with Midnight Falcon to the fullest. That way, should they never be able to be together again, she would have her sweet memories to nourish her. A part of her would be lonely forever without him.

"Are you all right?" Midnight Falcon asked. He

paused from his paddling to look over his shoulder at Chandra, where she sat in the canoe behind him. "Are you afraid?"

"No, I am anything but afraid," Chandra said, feeling foolish for having mentioned her fear of the water. While she was with him, she felt safe and cared for. She knew that he would never allow anything to happen to her. The love he felt for her was in his eyes, and in the smile that now tugged gently at his lips.

"That is good," Midnight Falcon said, nodding. "Soon you will see how I fish, and then I will instruct you how to do it yourself."

She nodded eagerly. She clung to the sides of the canoe as Midnight Falcon resumed rowing beneath trees along the James River far from her home, and his.

Along the shore, she saw many honey locusts casting their lacy shadows in the water. She admired the stately ginkgoes and the thick trunks of lime trees.

Chandra's eyes shifted upward as an eagle dove from the clear sky and settled somewhere amidst the black and green of spruces and pines.

A noise to her far left caught her attention. She smiled when she saw a moose wading chest-deep in the rushes. A loon, resting on a low branch, had fixed its red eyes on her.

As they traveled, she silently marveled over Midnight Falcon's canoe. It was much larger and sturdier than she would have imagined it to be. It was made of cypress.

He had explained to her how he had constructed it. He had cut down a cypress tree and hollowed out the trunk by gradually charring patches and scraping them away with stones and shells. The Powhatan dugouts were long, round-bottomed, thick-walled crafts that could be up to fifty feet long and carry forty men.

But most were smaller. His was a personal canoe with enough space for four people and room at the bottom for his catch of fish.

Sometimes he guided the canoe with a paddle, but sometimes, when he reached a shallow spot in the river, he would stand and propel the vessel through the water with a long, rounded-off pole.

Besides the paddle and pole, the canoe held his fishing gear and mats, which he had said could be used for a temporary shelter if a sudden squall drove them ashore. He had told her that such mats were also used for covering houses and doors, covering sleepers within the house, wrapping corpses for burial, and for drying food.

Baskets made of the same material as the mats were used for sieving, gathering corn, berries and nuts, and storing food.

He had explained to her that some baskets and mats were decorated with designs made from the bloodroot plant.

Her mind slowly drifted back to that morning

and how she had escaped from her home as early as possible, as soon as breakfast was finished and her brother had excused himself to his study.

She knew that once he was there, he would probably spend hours with his books as he waited for responses to his advertisements in town. He loved to read almost as much as Chandra.

Chandra enjoyed this time away from home and was so glad she had come. Now that the mist had burned off the mirrorlike river, the air was so still that she could hear deer in the brush along the shore.

"We are almost there," Midnight Falcon said over his shoulder. "Do you recall what I told you about the different ways that can be used to fish from the James?"

"Yes," Chandra said, picturing how Midnight Falcon looked when he described everything to her before they set out in his canoe.

He had told her that fish-angling was done with rods, lines, bait, and hooks. The rods were small, just little sticks, with a cleft at the end where the line was fastened. The fishhooks that the Powhatan used were made from pieces of bone ground into a hook shape, or from splinters of bone.

They tied big, fat worms onto the hooks as bait.

The most amazing way that he told her that fish, especially sturgeon, could be caught was to lasso lines around their tails. Fish were sometimes even shot with long arrows or caught in nets made from deer sinew. One way he had described made her shiver. The Powhatan sometimes poisoned fish, which they called "stunning." Juice from a certain herb was cast on the water, causing the fish to rise to the surface where they could then be caught by hand.

Her thoughts were interrupted when she felt the canoe suddenly stopping.

She looked around to see where Midnight Falcon had finally decided to do his fishing.

They were mid-river, the banks far from them on each side.

"Today we are fishing for shad," Midnight Falcon said, grabbing a fishing rod.

She shuddered as he removed a worm from a buckskin bag and wound it onto the bone fishhook at the end of his long line.

Chandra had never gone fishing with her brother, so today was truly a new experience for her.

As she watched Midnight Falcon bring one big fish after another into the boat, securing each of them in a buckskin bag at the bottom of the canoe, she could not help but feel excited.

But that excitement changed to apprehension when Midnight Falcon handed the rod to her, the worm wriggling on the fishhook.

"It is your turn now," he said, still holding the rod out for her even after he saw her hesitation. "One learns best when one joins in the doing."

"But I have never fished before," Chandra said,

hardly able to take her eyes off the poor worm that was still trying to get free of the hook.

"After today you will not be able to say that," Midnight Falcon said, placing the rod in her hand. "Now stand up beside me."

Swallowing hard, her knees weak, Chandra pleaded with him with her eyes.

But when he didn't budge, or show any signs of changing his mind, Chandra saw no choice but to do as he told her.

And she knew that he would not tell her to do this unless he truly believed that she would enjoy fishing as much as he. He just didn't seem to understand that she hated killing any living thing.

"Besides fish and food from your gardens, what else do your people like to eat?" Chandra asked, in an attempt to delay the inevitable.

Realizing what she was doing, Midnight Falcon's eyes twinkled. "The hunting of land animals is as important to the Powhatan as fishing from their canoes," he said. "It is done by way of trapping, stalking, and surrounding."

She seemed pleased to have momentarily sidetracked him. He would play along to appease her, but for only another moment or two.

"Hunting for smaller game is preferred by many," he said. "Beaver, in particular. Their meat, and especially their tails, are a great delicacy to the Powhatan."

"Their tails?" Chandra was repulsed by the thought of eating the tail from any animal, but especially from a beaver. To her beavers were fascinating creatures, with their flat tails that thump-thumped in water, sometimes sounding like a drum.

"Beaver traps are smeared with a pulverized form of hunting root to attract the animals," Midnight Falcon said, noticing how Chandra seemed to dislike even the thought of someone eating the tails of beavers.

That, as well as many other things that the Powhatan considered delicacies, might displease her. It would be a part of what she would have to grow accustomed to when she became his wife.

And he knew that she could.

She was a determined woman, a woman of much will power, which might be required to transform her life into something so different from what she had always known.

She was learning to be Powhatan!

"Now is the time to fish, not hunt," he said, watching her reaction. He hoped that she was past her uneasiness over what she needed to do today as one of her first lessons to be a Powhatan wife.

"Well, all right," Chandra said, sighing heavily. Her knees shook when she rose to stand beside Midnight Falcon.

Everything seemed to change into something magical when he wrapped a muscled arm around her waist and covered her hand with his.

That he was so near, his breath hot on her cheek,

was enough to make her forget any discomfort that fishing had momentarily caused her.

She laughed along with him as he guided her into casting one time, and then another, until the line was finally straight out from the boat and resting in the water.

"Now wait for the fish to bite," Midnight Falcon said, his arm still around her waist. "Watch. And be aware of the weight changing on your pole. That will mean that a fish has—"

When the bait and hook were suddenly yanked down beneath the surface of the water, Chandra squealed and clung more tightly to the pole, both hands now on it, holding it steady.

"I did not tell you that sometimes shad can be a yard long!" Midnight Falcon shouted as he realized that the fish on the end of this line had to be quite big. It was yanking fiercely, bending the pole almost in half!

"Sometimes, such a large fish can pull a man overboard," he said, although he did not believe that this fish could be that large, since the ones he had just caught were of a normal size.

Chandra gave Midnight Falcon a frenzied look. "A yard long?" she cried. "How on earth can I possibly pull such a thing from the water?"

She became frantic when Midnight Falcon stepped away from her and only watched.

"What are you doing?" she shouted, fighting even harder to keep the pole in her hands.

"You will be much prouder if you pull the fish

out by yourself," he said, still believing she would have no trouble with it.

He thought that she must haul this first fish in alone to realize the victory.

After she felt the wonder of success, she would never be apprehensive about it again.

She would be eager to join him in his fishing canoe!

Chandra gave Midnight Falcon a look of utter disbelief that he was going to make her bring in the monster fish by herself. Then she concentrated on doing it, to prove that she could.

When the fish gave a much harder yank on the line, Chandra screamed and found herself being pulled overboard into the river.

Frantic as she went beneath the surface, she released her hold on the pole.

She couldn't swim!

Always having been afraid of water, she had never learned how to swim.

She panicked when she swallowed a great gulp of water into her lungs, and then another.

She struggled to get back to the surface, but as the water kept her from taking air into her lungs, she believed that she was experiencing her last moments of life.

As she thrashed beneath the surface, in her mind's eye she saw Midnight Falcon's face. She felt his hands on her cheeks, caressing her. She tasted his lips on hers.

Suddenly she *did* feel strong arms surrounding

her and felt herself being lifted toward the surface.

When she was finally above the surface, she clung to Midnight Falcon as she coughed up water and gagged.

He held her in his arms and carried her toward shore. She gazed into his eyes and saw how sorry he felt.

She could not find it in her heart to be angry at him over encouraging her to do something that had almost caused her to drown, for she was too embarrassed over her failure to catch the fish, and even more embarrassed over her inability to swim.

At that moment she realized that instead of Midnight Falcon having to swim to get her to shore, he was walking.

She was even more embarrassed now that she knew the river had not been all that deep.

Had she gathered her wits, she could have stood up and saved herself!

As they reached shore, Midnight Falcon gently laid her on the ground. He knelt over her and lovingly swept her hair back from her eyes.

"I should have never allowed that to happen," he said, his eyes filled with apology. "I promised to care for you. I should have never forced you to pull the fish in by yourself."

"Please don't blame yourself for my inadequacies," Chandra said, hating herself for making him feel so guilty. "Any other woman could . . ."

He placed a hand over her mouth. "You are not

just any woman," he said. "You are *mine*. And I promise never to put you in such a position again. How could I have ever let you do something that was not safe? Do you forgive me, Chandra?"

"There is nothing to forgive," she said, reaching out for him, glad when he allowed her to wrap her arms around his neck and draw him next to her. "Please just hold me."

And he did. He held her in his arms, and then his lips moved to hers so gently, so sweetly, she felt as though she was being swept high above herself, into the heavens.

Her moments in the water weren't forgotten, but instead she felt blessed for them, for they had brought her to this moment with the man she loved.

"I need you," she whispered against his lips. "My body, my heart, aches for you."

"I want you so much," he whispered back.

He rose and stood over her. "Wait here for me until I beach my canoe, and then I have a place to take you."

Her eyes filled with joy and she nodded.

She sat up and hugged herself, watching as he dove into the river and swam out to his canoe, and then soon had it secured on shore.

Throwing a soft pelt across his arm, he went to Chandra and swept her into his arms. He carried her across a stretch of land that led away from the river.

Chandra laid her cheek against his chest, sighing, as they passed under towering oaks and elms, where birds sang and flew, and where wild roses filled the air with their sweet scent.

She gradually became aware of a roaring sound. Chandra leaned away from Midnight Falcon to look ahead and saw something that took her breath away.

He was carrying her toward a vast, beautiful waterfall.

"You have not seen the Fall of the James before?" he asked.

"No, and I think I shall never see anything as beautiful again," Chandra murmured. She marveled over how he stepped up to one side of the falls and began edging behind it, on a ledge only large enough for him to walk across.

The waterfall splashed into a pool far below them, causing the water to bubble up and hiss like some monster sea serpent. Even though she could look down and see just how high they were, she was not afraid.

She again laid her head against Midnight Falcon's chest, and soon he had her in a cave behind the falls, with a fire burning and the pelt spread beside the fire.

Without further words, they undressed one another in the seclusion of the cave.

After leading her down onto the pelt, he blanketed her with his body, warm against hers. He plunged deeply into her with his throbbing heat.

As their bodies moved together, Midnight Falcon needed no more convincing about the truth of their feelings for one another. He knew that what they shared was genuine, and wonderful.

Chandra had never imagined that making love could be so beautiful. Lawrence had never inspired such feelings in her during lovemaking, since all he needed was to satisfy himself.

Today, in the arms of the man she loved, with his hard body against hers and his hands awakening her every sensual place, she was filled with a hot, pulsing desire.

Midnight Falcon's mouth seared her flesh as he kissed one breast, and then the other, his fingers stroking her throbbing sex. He dazzled her senses.

He covered her mouth with his and molded her closer to the contours of his lean body, his steady rhythmic strokes filling her deeply. She shuddered with desire and clung to him, thrilled by the wonderful new sensations.

As he cupped her breasts with his hands, he felt himself burning inside like a flame. His mouth seared hers with an intensity so strong it left him breathless and trembling.

Their wild passion grew and one kiss blended into another as their bodies rocked and swayed together. Their moans echoed through the dark spaces of the cave.

His arms anchored her against him as they both quaked and shook, their climax soon complete.

Feeling stunned by the rapture that she had

been introduced to, Chandra lay quietly beside Midnight Falcon.

He sensed her quietness. He gazed at her as she turned and stared into the rolling flames of the fire. Gently placing his hands on her shoulders, he turned her toward him.

He smiled, but the smile faded when she did not quickly smile back at him. Instead, she looked at him as though she was troubled by something.

"What is it?" he asked, his hands slowly moving away from her. "What am I seeing in your eyes? Are you filled with regret over what we just shared?"

Seeing how troubled he was, Chandra sat up quickly and wrapped her arms around his neck. She brushed a kiss across his lips, then smiled at him.

"I have never experienced anything as beautiful," she said. "I . . . I guess I was still somewhat stunned. That is why you saw something in my eyes you could not read."

She had told him what was in her heart, except for one thing—the child.

At this moment, when things seemed to be so right in her life, when she loved and was loved, there was still the fact that she might be with child!

Oh, how could she tell Midnight Falcon now?

Would he not think her deceitful for having allowed the lovemaking while all along possibly carrying another man's child?

"It seemed different than that," Midnight Falcon said. He reached his hands to her hair and gently pushed it back from her face. "Is there something you need to tell me? Or is that look of worry only about how you are going to tell your brother that you are going to be my wife?"

Her brother!

She had managed to forget about Jan-Michael, and the reminder now came to her like a sword inside her heart.

She was no longer sure what to say or do, but she did not want such thoughts to matter at this moment.

It was such a precious time and she wanted to savor the many beautiful awakenings inside her body, heart, and soul.

Everything else would come later, when she was no longer with Midnight Falcon.

"There is something else that I have not mentioned," she said, moving to her knees before him. "I am so hungry! Do you think you might go and get one of those fish that you caught? Wouldn't it taste delicious cooked over this fire?"

His eyes twinkling, Midnight Falcon hurried into his breechclout and moccasins. He gave her a tender smile, then left the cave.

Still fighting off her concerns, Chandra dressed in her nearly dry clothes and waited for Midnight Falcon's return.

As she watched the fire, she jumped with alarm. In it she thought she saw her brother's likeness, looking accusingly at her and angrily shaking a finger.

Her heart thumping, she looked quickly away. When Midnight Falcon came back with a string of the fish that he had caught, she leaped to her feet and ran to him.

She soon forgot everything but their shared laughter, and the delicious baked fish. It seemed like a moment that only happened in fairy tales, she thought to herself as she watched Midnight Falcon eagerly eating the fish.

"One day I shall catch up with the shad that got away today," he said, chuckling.

"Yes, the fish that got away." Chandra laughed.

She was filled with such happiness, yet the longer she was in the cave, the more she became aware of the passing of time and knew that she must leave soon. She did not want her brother to have to search for her. He would know about her love affair soon enough, for she *was* going to tell him.

And soon she would seek the expert advice of a doctor. She had no choice.

As the days passed, one by one, and her monthly flow didn't arrive, she became more and more certain that a child was growing inside her.

17

Cupido,
Upon his shuldres wynges hadde he two;
And blynd he was, as it is often seene;
A bowe he bar and arwes brighte and
   kene.
                              —GEOFFREY CHAUCER

"I love the water," Shannon said as she and Little Snow Feather sat dangling their bare feet in the river. Scottie was close by, napping, his shiny black nose twitching when a bee buzzed around it.

Shannon glanced over at her dear new friend. "My father used to, but when we lived in England his boat capsized in rough waters, killing many of the men who worked for him catching fish. Since then he's seemed afraid of water. I don't know how he even made it from England to America on a ship. During one of the storms, he was as pale as a ghost. I thought he would faint."

"Do you think he will ever board the boat you showed me, the one with white wings?" Little Snow Feather asked as a soft breeze fluttered her hair down her back. "I have watched him from a distance, how he sits on the riverbank staring at it. I studied his eyes. He looks like he wants to go."

"Yes, but he doesn't know how," Shannon said, sighing. She plucked a clover blossom and twirled its stem around and around between her forefinger and thumb. "I hope today will be different. It would be so wonderful to look out across the James and see my father sailing by, happy again. His sadness was worse, though, when Indians . . . carried my mother away."

Shannon's eyes wavered. She slowly tossed the flower into the water. "And then Father found Mama's body," she said, shuddering. "It was so . . . so horrible."

Shannon looked at Little Snow Feather. "That's why he won't want us to be friends," she said, her voice breaking. "You are an Indian. When he sees any Indian, he sees how Mama died. I don't share his feelings about all Indians, or . . . or we wouldn't have ever become such special friends."

"I am so glad that you know there is no cause for your father's ill feelings toward me or my people," Little Snow Feather said. She quickly reached over and hugged Shannon. "My people are good. So good and decent. They would never have hurt your mother."

"I know," Shannon said, returning the hug.

Then Little Snow Feather leaned away from Shannon and a frown creased her brow. "But I do know that some people with skin coloring matching mine can be bad," she said. "Very, very bad." She sighed heavily as she looked into Shannon's eyes. "There are the Pocoughtaonacks. They are a cannibal tribe, evil, through and through."

"Cannibal?" Shannon gasped, paling. "You mean they eat . . ."

"I have never personally seen it, but that is what is said about them. They are the tribe who came and killed so many of my people . . ."

Little Snow Feather did not want to think about what had happened that day when Chief Black Rock and his warriors came into her village, ambushing her people in their sleep. She did not want to mention the possibility that Black Rock was on his way to her village again, even now, as she and Shannon spoke.

"Let us swim," Little Snow Feather said, jumping to her feet. She reached a hand out for Shannon. "It is much better to swim than talk of things that hurt our hearts."

Shannon watched, too surprised to rise to her feet or say anything back to Little Snow Feather, as her friend took off her buckskin skirt and blouse and was now removing her moccasins.

"You are going to swim nude?" Shannon asked, finally getting to her feet.

"I swim without my clothes all of the time," Little Snow Feather said, placing her moccasins right next to her clothes. "Swimming without clothes makes me feel so free!"

She gestured with a hand toward the river. "Come with me, Shannon," she encouraged. "Take off your clothes and let us swim free in the river."

"But what if someone should—" Shannon started to say, but Little Snow Feather interrupted.

"We are at a very secluded place," Little Snow Feather said. She motioned with her hand toward the tall cane stalks that grew on the riverbanks like a great wall. "Should a canoe or ship come by in the middle of the river, the people aboard could not see past the cane stalks."

Shannon turned and looked behind her, where the forest stretched out without even a path cutting through it. It did seem private enough.

She turned and smiled at Little Snow Feather. "It does sound like fun," she said, giggling. "Yes, I'll do it. But not for long. My father has been noticing how long I've been gone lately, and I am sure he's getting suspicious. If he wasn't so sad these days, I imagine I would have never gotten past the front door to go out exploring with you."

She hurried out of her clothes, then ran into the water, squealing.

The sun was bright overhead.

The breeze was warm.

Birds were the only other creatures that could be seen, and their song could be heard coming from the thickness of the forest.

Shannon and Little Snow Feather had waded to their knees in the water when Shannon saw something on Little Snow Feather's right, outer thigh. "A tattoo?" she gasped, drawing Little Snow Feather's eyes to her. "You have a tattoo, and it looks like it is in the shape of a cardinal!"

Little Snow Feather's eyes gleamed and she smiled almost mischievously at her.

"Little Snow Feather, I have seen tattoos before, but they were always on men, never women," Shannon said. "Especially not on girls our age."

"All of the Powhatan, men and women, boys and girls, have tattoos somewhere on their bodies," Little Snow Feather said, allowing Shannon a better look. "Each family has the same design. It is their personal family crest."

"Then Midnight Falcon has one, too, in the shape of a bird?" Shannon asked, still studying the tattoo.

"Yes, my brother has the same cardinal tattoo." Little Snow Feather slowly ran her fingers over the image and giggled. "But his is not on his thigh."

"Where is it?" Shannon asked, intrigued by this custom.

Little Snow Feather giggled again, then moved close to whisper in Shannon's ear. "On the left cheek of his bottom," she said, watching Shannon blush.

Little Snow Feather reached down and let water run through her fingers. "Tattooing is called 'pouncing,'" she said matter-of-factly.

Pouncing, Shannon repeated, trying to absorb everything that Little Snow Feather said to her about the Powhatan way of life. It made her feel important that Little Snow Feather felt comfortable enough to bring Shannon into her world.

After her friend finished explaining, Shannon reached over and gingerly touched the cardinal tattoo, then slowly eased her hand away. "Can I have one?" she asked. "Can I have a tattoo just like yours? It could be done in a place where my father would never see it." She giggled. "It would be fun to have a secret like that between us, wouldn't it?"

"There is only one way that you can have such a tattoo," Little Snow Feather said, taking Shannon's hands. "It can only be done if you became a part of the tribe. It could happen if your aunt marries into the tribe, which would make you a part of it, as well. We must work harder. We must find more ways to bring your aunt and my brother together. If they marry, then we can have an open friendship." She yanked on Shannon's hands. "Come, let us swim!"

They ran further into the water, then dove in and began swimming. They stopped, laughed, and talked of things, then dove again and swam again, their laughter filling the air with happiness.

Suddenly Scottie began barking frantically as a shadow fell over the water, alarming Shannon and Little Snow Feather into turning with a start.

Shannon's heart sank when she saw her father standing on the bank of the river, his arms crossed, his face beet red with anger.

"Papa!" she gasped. He had found her. Not only with an Indian, but nude in the water!

Her heart pounded as the minutes passed and she waited for his outburst.

Shannon heard the whinny of a horse and knew

that it came from her father's steed, which he must have tethered somewhere in the dark shadows of the forest away from where they could see it.

The laughter must have led her father to the river while he had been horseback riding.

The forest did not extend very far. It ended abruptly next to a large meadow where her father must have chosen to ride today.

She was relieved to see that he had finally broken free of the house and had managed to go horseback riding, which must mean that he was recovering.

But how ironic that he had chosen this route! That he would find his daughter doing not only one thing that would anger him, but two!

"Out of the water," Jan-Michael growled, his chest heaving in anger. He looked from Shannon to Little Snow Feather, and then again at Shannon as she slowly came from the water, her nudity like some dark sin.

"How dare you do this to me," Jan-Michael said, his voice filled with loathing. He tried not to look at his daughter as she pulled on her dress. He glared at Little Snow Feather, who still huddled low in the water, her heart thudding, her arms across her chest, her eyes wide and fearful.

"You in the water, you who are the naked daughter of the Devil, stay away from my daughter!" Jan-Michael shouted as he waved a finger at the frightened Indian child.

Then he turned and grabbed Shannon by her

shoulders and pulled her close so that his eyes almost branded her with accusation. "I don't know how this friendship has come about, and perhaps it's best that I don't know, but I am telling you now that I forbid you to play with that little savage ever again."

Shannon's knees shook as she stared with wide, frightened eyes up at her father. She even feared for Scottie as he growled and snapped at her father's boots in an effort to protect her.

Jan-Michael ignored the dog. He stared at his daughter, his eyes narrowing even more angrily the longer he stood there, knowing the extent of her misbehavior today.

"Do you hear me, Shannon, do you hear what I said?" he roared.

Shannon knew that she couldn't ever agree not to see Little Snow Feather again, but she also knew that she had no choice but to pretend to now, so she nodded.

"I understand," she said, hating being forced to lie to her father, for she did love and respect him so much.

But she felt that he was wrong to feel this way about a people who had never done him any harm.

It had been a different band of Indians, perhaps even the cannibal tribe that Little Snow Feather had talked about, who killed her mother!

Then, embarrassed and humiliated over her father's rudeness toward Little Snow Feather, and so badly wanting to give her friend the privacy she needed to flee from the water and hurry back to her home, Shannon began to cry. She ran off in the direction of the horse's whinnying, Scottie beside her.

To herself she vowed not to ever let her father stop her friendship with Little Snow Feather. If he was not such a prejudiced man, he would see that he was wrong to view the Powhatan people, especially sweet Little Snow Feather, as savages.

She hoped that in time he might come to understand this.

Glad to finally reach Thunder, her father's black stallion, Shannon mounted quickly. She stiffened when her father jumped into the saddle. His large arm anchored her against him as he wove his steed in and around the trees in the forest, then rode free across the meadow in a hard gallop. Scottie followed, panting.

When Shannon turned her head and strained her neck to try to get a glimpse of Little Snow Feather, her father slapped her.

"You had better listen to what I have to say," he grumbled, as Shannon rubbed her stinging cheek and gazed up at him with deep hurt in her eyes. This was the first time he had ever laid a hand on her.

"I forbid, absolutely forbid, you to ever be with that heathen again," Jan-Michael said. "Do you hear me? Do you hear that word 'forbid' and understand its true meanin'?"

Sobbing, Shannon forced herself to nod, but deep inside she was even more resolved not to let her father rule her in this decision.

"That's more like it," Jan-Michael said. He placed a hand gently on her cheek, which held the imprint of his flesh. "I love you so, Shannon girl. That is why I am so protective of you." He swallowed hard. "I should not have hit you. For that I am sorry."

Hearing his apology melted some of Shannon's anger. She knew he hadn't meant to hurt her. She turned in the saddle and he gave her a big hug.

"I love you, Papa," she whispered. She clung to him, her cheek resting against his chest as they rode on toward their home.

She had so much to work out inside her heart and mind. She never wanted to do anything that disappointed her father, but she knew that as far as this one thing was concerned, she would not obey him . . . ever!

18

Twice or thrice had I loved thee,
Before I knew thy face or name.
—JOHN DONNE

As Chandra walked away from White Iris's stall in the stable, she stopped and stared at her brother's horse. It was breathing hard, and she saw the sweat on its mane.

She smiled at Tommie, the black, twelve-year-old stable boy who came in with a brush and towel to care for the horses.

She was torn over how to feel about the fact that her brother had finally gone horseback riding after only having gone a few times since their arrival in America.

She was glad that he had left the house, which proved that he was fighting to get past his dark moods.

Yet seeing the horse in such a shape, exhausted and almost foaming at the mouth, made Chandra realize that her brother's outing had not been a usual one. He respected animals and never rode his horse hard. Although he was moody and mean recently, this was out of character.

"Ma'am, ah'll see to Thunder," Tommie said in a slow drawl. "He's needin' seein' to pretty bad."

"Thank you," Chandra said, stepping back so that Tommie could get into Thunder's stall. She watched Tommie pick up a bucket of water and offer the thirsty horse a drink. She asked him to tell her about her brother's ride and not to spare the truth.

"If I can say so, ma'am, he shouldn't ride his horse so hard, especially when he has Shannon with him. My pappy, before he died in the river, always said if you're goin' to have an animal, you must treat it right."

The mention of Shannon being with Jan-Michael made Chandra's heart skip a beat.

She stared at Tommie for a moment, then lifted the skirt of her dress and ran from the stable toward the house.

Her eyes scanned the windows on the second floor of the back of the mansion until she found her niece's room.

The drapes were drawn, which meant that Shannon was there, and Chandra guessed she was upset and possibly in bed to have closed the drapes at this time of afternoon.

"Where did Jan-Michael find Shannon?" Chandra whispered to herself. "Oh, Lord, please not with Little Snow Feather."

She stopped with a jolt and looked quickly down at her dress. It was a mass of wrinkles after its soaking in the river. She knew that if her brother saw her dress, he would ask questions about her day's activities that she would not want to answer anymore than Shannon surely had.

The back stairs, she thought to herself, again running toward the house, praying that Jan-Michael wasn't watching her from a window.

Guilt flooded her as she ran up the back steps and into the house, closing the door behind her as quietly as possible.

She hated betraying her brother time and again by keeping so many things from him. She hurried on, past the closed kitchen door where food cooking on the stove smelled tantalizingly wonderful.

It was time to find a way to come clean and hope that her brother would reach into his heart and accept his sister's new love, and his daughter's new playmate, regardless of the color of their skin.

But Chandra knew that this was not going to come easily for her brother, and it was going to take some deep deliberation on her part to figure out how to break the news before things got out of hand.

She flew past the maid's quarters, then up the back staircase, breathless when she finally reached the second-floor landing.

On hearing Shannon's deep sobs and seeing that her niece's bedroom door was closed, Chandra wanted to rush to her side and comfort her. She knew that Shannon would need her, would want to open up to her and tell her what had happened.

But Chandra could not do this immediately. First she had to change her dress.

Her mind swirling with thoughts of Midnight Falcon and the memories of making love with him, Chandra was scarcely aware of the time it took to change into something freshly ironed, put on new sandals, and brush her hair until it was glistening. The river water seemed to have given it an added luster.

Finally presentable, Chandra left her room and went to Shannon's, stopping just outside the door. She knew that her brother would soon realize that she was home and be full of questions for her about where she had been for so long on White Iris.

No longer hearing Shannon's sobs, Chandra thought that she might have cried herself to sleep. She hesitated knocking on the door.

Then she heard the sobs again, but thankfully this time they did not sound so painful.

She raised a fist and gently tapped on the door.

There was a long moment before the door creaked slowly open. When Shannon saw that it was Chandra, she jerked the door all of the way open and rushed into her aunt's waiting arms.

Chandra held Shannon close as the girl wept openly, clinging to her.

"Papa found us together," Shannon said between sobs, trying hard to be quiet so that her voice would not carry to her father. She wasn't ready for another confrontation with him. Although they seemed to have made their peace with one another on their way home, the minute they were inside the house, he had ordered her to her room and begun his ranting and raving all over again.

"No!" Chandra exclaimed. She stroked her fingers through Shannon's hair. "How? Where? Oh, no, how did he treat Little Snow Feather? Did he shout at her? Did he hurt her?"

Swallowing another deep sob, Shannon regained control of her emotions. She stepped away from Chandra and circled her fingers around the doorknob. "Come inside my room," she whispered.

Chandra went with her, but just as she closed the door, Jan-Michael opened it again in a burst of fury. He stood there, his fists on his hips, his eyes glaring from his sister to his daughter.

He had just gone to his room when he had heard voices in the corridor. He had headed for Shannon's room, pausing only long enough to look down at the stable, his heart filled with shame over how hard he had ridden his stallion.

That, as well as other things, proved that he must get hold of himself and take some control of his life. His sanity depended on it.

But the way he had found his daughter with the wanton savage was almost too much for him to accept.

"Have you told your aunt where I found you today?" Jan-Michael practically shouted. Those moments on his horse when he had thought he had found some peace inside his heart were again forgotten.

Now, seeing in his mind's eye all over again the shameful way he had found his child, and with whom, he could not help but feel rage.

"Shannon, have you told Chandra who you were with? Have you told her the shameful way I found you? Have you?" Jan-Michael asked.

Ducking her head to avoid her father's threatening glare, Shannon slowly shook her head back and forth. "No, I haven't had the chance to tell her anything yet," she said, her voice scarcely audible. "She . . . she only just arrived."

"Then I'll tell her myself." Jan-Michael unfolded his fists and slipped his hands into his front breeches pockets. His eyes narrowed as he kept his gaze on Shannon, yet spoke to Chandra. "This daughter of mine, who I've taught right from wrong since the moment she could understand the difference, shamed her family today. I not only caught her with a savage, but she was swimmin' nude in the James with the red-skinned girl!"

A hush fell across the room as Chandra gaped at her niece, stunned over what she had done.

Scottie lay at the foot of the bed, his head resting on his paws. He looked from one to the other, his tail wagging.

Of course, Chandra had already accepted Little Snow Feather into their lives, but for Shannon to be so careless as to go swimming with her, naked, was such a shock that Chandra could not find the words to respond.

She knew that she had to be careful, for she did not want to allow Jan-Michael to believe that she was his ally in condemning Shannon for being with an Indian.

She did think Shannon had been wrong to be this reckless, but she knew that she herself was guilty of behavior her brother would condemn.

She was so mixed up about things, her head was spinning.

"Your silence proves that you feel the same as I do about what Shannon did today," Jan-Michael said, less angry now. "Talk with her, Chandra. Give her a mother's advice about her actions."

He sauntered to a window, drew back the drapes, and gazed out toward the river. "This new world we have come to is a place of heathens," he said. "We should've never come." He turned slowly back to Chandra. "Perhaps we should leave and return to England?"

Stunned by his suggestion, wanting anything but to return to England, Chandra swallowed hard and could not answer him.

"That's all right," Jan-Michael said, clasping his hands together behind him and rocking slowly on his heels. "If we do, it won't be anytime soon. I've devils still to fight inside my brain before settin' out on a boat for Liverpool."

Relieved, she knew that she had a little more time to work out how to tell him that she was never going back to England, that she had found a reason to stay. Chandra went to her brother and flung herself into his arms.

"Please do not be so quick to make decisions that would alter all of our futures," she said, glad when he wrapped his arms around her.

She stood there with him for a moment longer, then stepped away and gazed into his eyes. "And do not be so quick to condemn your daughter, or sister, for things we might do."

"You know the right and wrong of things," Jan-Michael said. He nodded toward Shannon. "She does, too, but I think she needs a bit of reminding, don't you?"

"I'll talk with her," Chandra said, nodding.

Her brother's gaze held hers for a second, and in his eyes she saw a look of lonesomeness and pain.

But she also saw much respect and love there, and it was at this moment that Chandra felt she might have gotten her brother back, at least a little.

"I'll return to my own room now," Jan-Michael said, interrupting her thoughts. He glanced over at Shannon before leaving the room, closing the door behind him.

Chandra took Shannon's hand and led her over to the bed where they sat down, side by side.

Sobbing anew, Shannon flew into Chandra's arms and clung to her. "I know it was wrong to swim naked with Little Snow Feather," she cried. "But it was such fun."

"I will not scold you for what you did, for your father has said enough to convince you not to swim again in the nude," Chandra said. She looked her in the eye. "My worst fear is that your father now knows of your friendship with Little Snow Feather."

"Papa forbade me ever to see her again," Shannon sobbed. She reached up and wiped tears from her cheeks with the palms of her hands.

"I'm sure he did," Chandra said, realizing now just how hard it was going to be to tell her brother about Midnight Falcon.

But she had to. She loved Midnight Falcon, and she would not give him up for anyone, not even her brother whom she adored.

"Chandra, I don't agree with him. It's my life and I want to be friends with her."

Chandra honestly was at a loss for words.

"I know how hard it is for you," Shannon said. She reached out and took Chandra's hands. "You love an Indian, don't you? And so do I, in a much different way, as sisters love sisters. It would break my heart if I couldn't see Little Snow Feather. We are best friends and I shan't allow Papa to keep us apart."

Chandra smiled. She slid a hand free and smoothed a lock of hair back from Shannon's face. "You are still such a child," she murmured. "But you have the heart of an adult."

"Then you understand?" Shannon asked. "Whether or not anyone would believe it, my friendship with the Powhatan princess might some day help all of us. She is teaching me so much. I am also teaching her things of our people."

"I will never forbid you such a friendship," Chandra said. "I hate to go against your father's wishes, and I do not want to encourage you to do the same, but let me say that I do understand, and I, personally, will not stand in the way."

She brushed a kiss across her niece's brow. "Let us pray that in the end your father will come to his senses. But never do anything so foolish again. You *have* been taught right from wrong, and what you did was wrong."

Shannon nodded, then again wrapped her arms around Chandra. "Thank you for being you," she said. "Thank you for understanding my feelings as I know my mother would have understood."

"I'm always here for you, little darling," Chandra said, touched deeply by Shannon's trust. She could not help but think about her responsibility to Shannon and feel ashamed that marrying Midnight Falcon might mean failing her niece. And what about her unborn child?

19

Pains of love be sweeter far
Than all other pleasures are.
—John Dryden

Trying to soothe her brother's woes, Chandra had stayed home for two days since the confrontation with Shannon, although she was afraid of what Midnight Falcon might be thinking—that she might have decided against meeting him again.

Chandra was sitting in the library before a fire in the fireplace, with Scottie snoozing at her feet. She was attempting to concentrate on a novel, while all along she kept seeing Midnight Falcon in her mind's eye and remembering their last moments together.

She knew that he had other things besides her on his mind, so perhaps he was not yet that concerned over her absence. He had told her that he had sent his scout to see if Chief Black Rock was headed toward the Powhatan community.

Suddenly Chandra's arms itched, and the intensity of it interrupted her thoughts.

After laying her book aside on the table next to her chair, she shoved the long sleeve of her dress halfway to her elbow.

The sight of blisters breaking out on her skin caused the color to drain from her face.

She recalled an epidemic of smallpox a few years ago in England.

Her mother had kept her and Shannon inside, protecting them from the deathly ravages of the disease. They thought that as long as Jan-Michael was away on the water fishing, he was safe enough.

They all had happily survived the disease, which some had begun calling "the plague."

But to have contracted it now? Chandra's pulse raced at the thought of how quickly one's life could be snuffed away by the disease.

The voyage over from England! Perhaps someone on the ship unknowingly had been ill with smallpox!

She studied the blisters more closely. She had never actually seen smallpox, but she knew that its onset was marked by an itchy rash on one's flesh.

"What are you lookin' at on your arm?" Jan-Michael asked as he entered the library, coming to sit down before the fire with Chandra. He moved over to her and leaned low to stare at her arm.

He quickly stepped away from her, in his eyes the fear of what she had felt inside her heart.

"Is it . . . smallpox?" she asked, her voice breaking. "Oh, Jan-Michael, what if I contracted smallpox on the ship from England?"

"I'll go into Jamestown and get a doctor," Jan-Michael shouted over his shoulder as he left the library.

He stuck his head back inside. "Stay away from Shannon," he said, his eyes wavering. "Go to your room. Isolate yourself there. Lock the door. No matter what, do not allow Shannon in the room with you until we see what you have. Lord, pray that it's not smallpox."

Tears filling her eyes, Chandra nodded. Shaking, she rose from the chair.

Many things played through her mind—her concern for her brother and niece, and for the child that she might be carrying. She wasn't sure how a baby might be affected, even if she survived such a debilitating disease.

"And Midnight Falcon?" she whispered as she walked from the library in a haze. "Did I expose him? Will his people be plagued with smallpox?"

She didn't want to even think about such possibilities, but she knew how the disease had wiped out a sizable English population as it spread.

Surely it would likewise devastate the Powhatan.

Her mind numb with worry, her whole body now seemingly on fire with itching, she went to her bedroom and locked her door behind her.

Shannon was in her own room, having thought of little else these past two days besides how to be with Little Snow Feather again without upsetting her father. Even after telling him that Little

Snow Feather was a princess, special in many ways, he still had forbidden her to see her.

Chandra went to her window to watch for her brother's return. She prayed that the doctor wouldn't be afraid to expose himself to the disease, or else she was doomed to die!

"Let it not be smallpox," she whispered, unable to stop scratching her arms.

She lifted the skirt of her dress and groaned when she saw that the blisters had begun to appear on her legs.

She scratched one so hard that it burst open, and an almost translucent liquid flowed from it.

It was then that she willed herself to stop scratching, afraid she might spread the plague to every inch of her body with her fingers!

Feeling somewhat sick to her stomach, Chandra stretched out on her bed.

Slowly her eyes closed and she welcomed sleep, a reprieve from the horrible itching.

"Chandra?"

A voice woke her up with a start, and when she heard the voice again from behind the closed door, she was awake enough to know that it was Shannon.

"Chandra, why do you have the door locked?" Shannon asked, trying the doorknob. "What's wrong? And where did Papa go in such a state? I would have come earlier to ask you about it, but I was afraid that you two had had words again. I . . . I didn't want to get in the way."

Chandra leaned up on an elbow. "Shannon, your father has gone for the doctor in Jamestown," she said.

"Doctor?" Shannon asked, her voice filled with fear. "Why? What's wrong?"

"It's nothing for you to worry about," Chandra said. "But I can't let you in my room, not until the doctor has diagnosed my illness."

Too curious to leave it alone, Shannon kept prodding Chandra until she finally blurted out her worst fear.

"Smallpox?" Shannon gasped. "Oh, no, it can't be!"

"Don't worry, not yet," Chandra said, trying to sound brave. "I probably have something quite different."

She heard Jan-Michael's horse and looked quickly toward the window.

She listened intently for the arrival of another horse, but heard none. That had to mean that the doctor was too afraid of the disease to come to their home.

She didn't even get out of bed as she waited for Jan-Michael to come and give her the disappointing news.

When she heard his footsteps on the staircase, and Shannon's frightened voice questioning him about the doctor, Chandra finally left the bed and unlocked the door.

Jan-Michael convinced Shannon that she

shouldn't enter the bedroom, then came inside the room himself.

"He didn't want to come," Chandra said, moving away from her brother.

"No, it's not that," Jan-Michael said, drawing Chandra into his arms.

"Jan-Michael, please," she said, pushing away from him. "Why put yourself in any more danger? Please keep your distance."

"Chandra, if it is my fate to get what you have, I will," Jan-Michael said, taking her hand anyway. "The doctor was away somewhere deliverin' a baby. No one knows when he will return to town. And there are no other doctors in the area. We'll just have to wait."

He reached a hand to her cheek, wincing when he saw the fresh blisters there.

Shannon had heard enough through the closed door. Frightened for her aunt, and determined not to just stand around and wait for her to die, she refused to think about her father's wrath when he discovered her gone and fled down the stairs.

Knowing that the commotion of getting her pony would draw too much attention, she ran on past the stable and raced toward the Powhatan village to see if there was anyone there who could help Chandra.

She raised her eyes heavenward. "Oh, please, Lord, if ever you hear my prayers, hear mine today," she whispered. "Please let me do something that will help my aunt. Oh, please don't let her die!"

She truly didn't think that she could stand losing another loved one.

She would rather die herself!

20

Give all to love;
Obey thy heart;
Friends, kindred, days,
Estate, good fame,
Plans, credit and the Muse,
Nothing refuse.
—RALPH WALDO EMERSON

Breathless, her heart pounding, Shannon ignored the stares of the Powhatan people as she ran through their village toward the longhouse that Little Snow Feather shared with the Powhatan chief.

All that she could think about was Chandra.

Tears came to her eyes and a desperation she had never felt before forced her small feet to go faster, her soles pounding hard against the ground.

As she wiped the tears from her face, she said a silent prayer that Midnight Falcon would know what to do. Yet she knew not to ask him to bring their shaman to Chandra, for at first sight Shannon's father would surely kill him.

Shannon would ask Midnight Falcon if his people had any sort of medication for smallpox, since no white doctors had ever found anything effective against the dreaded disease.

Shannon stopped, with weak knees and anxious heart, in front of the longhouse that Little Snow Feather had pointed out to her. She said another prayer before knocking on the door, hoping that Midnight Falcon was there, for she did not have the courage to ask anyone else in the village for help.

Her hand shook as she curled her fingers into a fist and knocked on the door, her eyes wide as she waited for it to open.

And when it did, and Midnight Falcon was suddenly there, a look of utter amazement on his face, she could not help herself.

Sobbing, she flung herself into his arms as though she had known him forever. Her trust in him was that deep.

The fear in Shannon's eyes and the desperation in her hug told Midnight Falcon only one thing—something was wrong with Chandra.

He felt cold inside, for he had wondered these past two days why she had not met him on the bluff, the place they had chosen for their rendezvous. He had assumed that it had something to do with her brother, that perhaps he had discovered her feelings for him.

Or perhaps it had something to do with her brother's discovery of his daughter with Little Snow Feather in the river. Little Snow Feather had confided everything to Midnight Falcon. She had come home in tears, frantic with worry over never seeing Shannon ever again.

He had thought that Jan-Michael had taken his anger out on his sister, perhaps even ordering both Chandra and Shannon to stay away from redskins.

But he did not think that Chandra would allow her brother to dictate anything to her, for she had proved to him that she was independent and strong-minded. Surely no brother could change her mind about the man she loved.

Midnight Falcon had decided to wait it out. He knew that Chandra would come to him soon, one way or the other.

Now with Shannon before him, he felt a prickle of fear. What if Chandra had disobeyed her brother and he had caught her? Would he have harmed her?

He gently gripped Shannon's shoulders and moved her away from him so that he could look into her eyes.

Past her tears he saw a painful fear.

He was almost afraid to ask her why she was there, but he had to know. If Jan-Michael *had* harmed Chandra in any way, he would answer to Midnight Falcon.

No, he would not just answer to him. The white man would die!

"Tell me why you are here," he said, trying to keep the anger out of his voice.

"It's Chandra," Shannon sobbed, her eyes wavering as she saw a strange sort of angry light deepen in Midnight Falcon's eyes. "She is ill."

She was afraid to say the word "smallpox." After arriving at the village and seeing the innocence of the Powhatan people, she realized that even the mere mention of the word might send a frantic fear into all of their hearts. She would have to be careful how she asked for assistance from Midnight Falcon.

But by holding back, she knew that he would have to go to Chandra, which would put him in danger—of being shot by her father, and also of contracting the smallpox himself.

She had no choice. Midnight Falcon might be the only one who could help Chandra. She had heard that Indians had cures for almost everything. Even knowing that her father would resist Indian help, Shannon had to risk it in order to try to help her aunt.

"She is ill?" Midnight Falcon said, slowly lowering his hands from her shoulders.

He could not help but still blame her brother.

His fingers tightened into fists at his sides.

"What is wrong with her?"

"I don't know," Shannon answered, scarcely able to breathe. "And there are no doctors to care for her. The one Jamestown doctor is away, helping a woman give birth." She desperately grabbed Midnight Falcon by an arm. "Please, Midnight Falcon. Please help her."

In his eyes she saw a mixture of different emotions.

"I will go to her," Midnight Falcon said, stepping away to fasten a sheathed knife to the waist of his breechclout.

Watching him, Shannon felt guilt splash through her. She hoped it might be something besides smallpox, something that was not as lethal. She could not help but think that she might be sending him to his death.

She prayed over and over again that her father would be civil toward Midnight Falcon at such a time as this, especially when Midnight Falcon had cared enough to risk death to go to his woman's side.

She was going to have to confront her father herself, and she knew just how angry he was going to be at her for having gone to the village and for having brought a Powhatan warrior home with her.

But she couldn't worry about that.

She was too concerned about Chandra to allow anything to get in the way of helping her.

"I will go to your house to see what I can do for your aunt, but I urge you to stay here with Little Snow Feather until I return, for I know the rage your father is going to be in once I show myself at your door," Midnight Falcon said, gesturing toward his sister, who stood in the shadows.

He wanted to take his shaman with him but refused to place the man in harm's way by bringing him to a white man's house.

For Chandra, though, Midnight Falcon was ready to defy this white man, even risk being killed by him. She was everything to him.

Her name was whispered inside his soul with his each and every heartbeat!

He could never love anyone as much, ever again. And he knew that she loved him in return.

They were destined to meet. They were soul-mates!

"I don't know," Shannon said, swallowing hard. "I'd better not . . ."

"You must," Midnight Falcon said in the flat, authoritative tone that he often used as a chief. "You, even more than I, know the depth of your father's wrath."

"Little Snow Feather told you about us getting caught as we swam in the river?" Shannon asked, a flush of embarrassment rushing to her cheeks. She knew that if her friend told him about the episode, she would not have left out the most embarrassing part—that they were caught nude.

Midnight Falcon nodded and glanced at Little Snow Feather over his shoulder. She stood behind him now, in her eyes a look of mischief that he knew well, for she was not ashamed of what had happened.

It was a natural thing for the children of his village to swim without clothes in the river. It was just another way to enjoy their freedom of life, and he explained this to Shannon.

Then he dropped his hands to his sides as his face took on a look of fierce determination. "I will go now," he said.

He turned to Little Snow Feather, gave her a quick hug and a look that Shannon did not understand, and left the lodge in a hurry.

Sobbing again, Shannon fell into Little Snow Feather's arms. "I'm so afraid," she cried. "I'm afraid for my aunt, and also for your brother. My Papa, he . . ."

Little Snow Feather placed her hand gently over Shannon's lips. She did not want to even think about what might happen when her brother faced the hard-hearted white man.

At this moment, she was very afraid for her chief!

21

Thou art to me a delicious torment.
—RALPH WALDO EMERSON

As he approached the imposing stone mansion, Midnight Falcon did not hesitate. He ran up the front steps, pulled open the door, and rushed inside, stopping with a start when he found himself face-to-face with Jan-Michael.

Midnight Falcon realized that Jan-Michael must have seen him coming. The white man leveled a long-barreled firearm at Midnight Falcon's belly, his eyes filled with a dark rage.

In an instant, Midnight Falcon grabbed the firearm away from Jan-Michael and aimed the barrel at his adversary.

Chandra had watched her brother turn away from her bedroom window, as if he might have seen something, and rush from her room, his heavy footsteps sounding like claps of thunder as he raced down the stairs.

Although she felt weak, Chandra had managed to climb out of bed and leave her room. Just as she reached the head of the stairs, she saw Midnight Falcon take the firearm from Jan-Michael.

She felt as though she might faint when Midnight Falcon aimed the gun at her brother.

"No!" she screamed, hanging onto the banister for dear life as her knees threatened to buckle beneath her.

At this moment, she even forgot the terrible itching and how it had made her feel so ill. All that she could think about was Midnight Falcon being there, pointing the gun at her brother.

"Please don't kill him!" she cried. She hoped that Midnight Falcon would look up at her and reassure her that he wouldn't hurt her brother.

She understood when he didn't, though, for he surely knew that her brother would quickly gain the advantage if he looked away.

"This is no time for a fight," she cried. "I'm ill. Please leave. I don't want you to catch . . . smallpox."

The word "smallpox" filled Midnight Falcon with dread. He had heard of tribes that had been annihilated by the disease.

Until now, it had not reached Powhatan land.

That his woman had such a life-threatening disease made him feel ill himself, inside his very soul.

But he had to keep his wits about him. He had to deal with her brother first; then he would do what he could for her.

He would not flee her house like a scared rabbit, not when her life might lie in the balance.

At this moment, he was a man in love, not a chief who was thinking of himself, or his people.

He could not, he would not, walk away from the commitment he had made to this woman, a commitment that he had made for their lifetime.

"I will not shoot your brother if he agrees to allow me to come to you," Midnight Falcon said, hating each moment that kept him from his woman's side.

"You are speakin' to my sister as though you know her, and she seems to know you." Jan-Michael's gaze slowly moved up to Chandra. "Chandra, tell me why," he said. "How does he know you?"

As he waited for her answer, he realized that something didn't make sense. How could this Indian know that Chandra was ill? Only one other person besides the servants in the house knew.

Shannon!

Jan-Michael looked down the long corridor behind Chandra and shouted his daughter's name. When Shannon didn't make an appearance, he knew not to shout for her again. She wasn't there.

It had to have been Shannon who brought the news of Chandra's illness to this savage.

His heart sank as understanding dawned on him. Not only had his daughter befriended the Indians, but his sister must have as well. And Shannon had gone to this warrior because Chandra must be important to him.

He turned back to Midnight Falcon. "Get out of my house," he growled.

Chandra realized that Midnight Falcon was not

going to leave, no matter how much Jan-Michael berated or threatened him. She was deeply touched that he cared so much for her that he would chance getting the terrible disease himself. Thinking that he had already been exposed just by being in the house, Chandra grabbed hold of the banister with both hands and shakily worked her way down the stairs. Her eyes never left the firearm still aimed at her brother.

When she reached Midnight Falcon's side, she gave her brother a pleading look. "Please, Jan-Michael," she begged. "Tell Midnight Falcon you won't do anything you'll regret if he agrees to give me the gun."

There was a long pause as Jan-Michael ran his fingers through his hair, then nodded. After Midnight Falcon lowered the gun, he stomped away, disappearing through the door to the study.

Chandra smiled softly up at Midnight Falcon and reached a hand out for the gun. "I know that he won't do anything now to harm you," she said.

She felt a deep relief when Midnight Falcon handed her the firearm.

"You do not have smallpox," he said, reaching a hand toward her face. "I recognize immediately what is wrong with you. You must have come in contact with a poison ivy plant in the forest. It is only contagious to those who touch your blisters, and, even then, it is not something serious. The blisters will go away soon, especially after I treat them with medicines from the forest."

"Poison ivy?" Chandra said, raising an eyebrow. She was unaware of such a plant, yet she was thrilled that he didn't think she had smallpox. The relief in his eyes when he first saw her up close convinced her that he was right.

"Yes, poison ivy," he said. "When we are in the forest together again, I shall point the plant out to you so that you can avoid it in the future. You can then, in turn, point it out to your sister." He looked past her to the closed door of the study and frowned. "Even your brother. He should also know to avoid the plant."

When Chandra unconsciously reached to scratch one of the blisters, Midnight Falcon grabbed her hand and stopped her. "Do not scratch," he said. "That will scar the flesh."

"It will?" Chandra asked, wincing. Then she sighed heavily. "Thank the Lord I don't have smallpox. I was so afraid. I had just found such happiness. It was not fair that I would not live long to enjoy it."

Midnight Falcon took her hands. "I, too, was afraid that our time together would be cut short."

He again looked past her at the study door, then gazed down into Chandra's eyes.

"You will be all right once you are medicated properly," he said. "I will leave now, for the longer I stay, the more your brother will resent me. But first let me tell you about the healing plant you should look for in the forest."

"Which plant is that?" she asked.

"The spotted touch-me-not plant," he said. "You should boil the plant, then spread the warm liquid over your blisters."

"I would never find the plant," Chandra said, sighing. "I have no idea how to. I don't know what it looks like."

"Are you strong enough to go with me to find it?" he asked, even though he knew that Jan-Michael would fly into a rage if he continued his relationship with Chandra and Shannon. He wanted to be sure she could find the plant on her own, in case he was not nearby to help her if this happened again.

Jan-Michael would have to get used to the idea, since Midnight Falcon was not going to let this woman go.

If it came to blows between himself and the white man, so be it!

"It's so strange," Chandra said, "but I suddenly feel better." The sick feeling at the pit of her stomach was gone, and she no longer felt weak in the knees.

She must have worked herself into such a state over believing she had a deadly illness that she literally had made herself sick over it.

She smiled broadly. "Yes, I do feel well enough to go with you to look for the plant," she said. "And the sooner the better. I really hope it can help stop the itching."

She looked over her shoulder at the closed door of the study. She knew that her brother would be livid if she went with Midnight Falcon, yet she also knew that he had to accept the idea of them being together. Soon it would be forever!

"Let's go," she said, lifting her chin defiantly. "Please show me the spotted touch-me-not plant."

"After we find the plant, I would like you to go to my lodge with me so that I can prepare it for your use," Midnight Falcon said as they walked outside and down the steps. "Shannon is waiting at my village for my return. Come. Let her see for herself that you are not as ill as first thought."

"Yes, that's best," Chandra said. "I am anxious for Shannon to know that I'm all right. How better than for her to see me?"

As Chandra took the last step, she felt somewhat light-headed.

Midnight Falcon saw her teeter and wrapped an arm around her waist. Holding her close to his side, he walked away from the house.

Chandra looked nervously over her shoulder at the study window. She shivered at the sight of her brother holding aside the sheer curtain, staring angrily down at her.

She turned away from him.

She didn't even want to think about what his next move might be!

22

If the heart of a man is depress'd with cares.
The mist is dispelled when a woman appears.
—JOHN GAY

Waiting outside the longhouse with Little Snow Feather, Shannon was getting restless. Midnight Falcon had not returned yet with word of Chandra's health, or of whether he was even allowed to enter the house to see her.

She had accepted food to help pass the time, and had enjoyed the shellfish boiled in a bisque thickened with cornmeal.

She had tried to be patient, but finding it hard to sit beside the lodge fire, Shannon had finally told Little Snow Feather that she must go outside and watch for Midnight Falcon.

The longer Shannon stood there, the more afraid she became that something terrible might have happened when Midnight Falcon arrived at her home. She knew that her father would not take his arrival well, or the fact that his very own daughter disobeyed him and became involved with Indians again.

She dreaded returning home.

Squeals of laughter and giggling drew her eyes to a garden area behind the longhouses. Most families had their own gardens, but this garden seemed to be a communal one.

She saw Powhatan children climbing in and out of small, covered scaffolds that were scattered here and there in the garden.

"Little Snow Feather, what is the purpose of those things, and why are children climbing into them?" Shannon asked, watching with wonder.

"The children serve as scarecrows," Little Snow Feather said, waving to one of her friends who was perched close by. "Look around. Do you see any pesky birds among our crops?" She laughed softly. "Hear the crows in the trees beyond the garden? They are squawking angrily because they are too afraid to come to the garden and eat the fresh sprouts of corn and squash."

Little Snow Feather grabbed one of Shannon's hands. "Come, I see a scaffold that is not being used," she said, yanking on Shannon's hand. "We shall climb onto it together. We will keep the crows away ourselves."

So glad to have something to take her mind off of Midnight Falcon's return, Shannon ran with Little Snow Feather between the furrows on the ground, where various plants sprouted, green and delicate.

Shannon could not help but giggle as Little Snow Feather helped her up onto the scaffold, then climbed up and positioned herself beside her.

"Should I wave my arms to be sure the crows see me?" Shannon asked. She watched one large crow flying overhead, its beady dark eyes seemingly on her. She shivered when she saw the sharpness of its beak and hoped sitting on the scaffold was enough to keep the bird away. She didn't want to think of what that sharp beak could do to her!

"Just sitting here is enough," Little Snow Feather said, also watching the bird circling slowly overhead. She waved her arms anyway and shouted at the bird, relieved when it flew away.

"There are other ways to frighten the crows from our crops," Little Snow Feather said, now resting her hands on her lap. "Do you see? There are strings of bark tied from pole to pole around three sides of the field."

Little Snow Feather pointed elsewhere. "We also hang gourds on top of poles where small birds nest, and the gourds spin around in the air and scare off the large birds."

"Do you help with the planting?" Shannon asked, genuinely curious.

"Yes. We plant by digging holes between the tree stumps with a crooked piece of wood. We drop in corn kernels and space beans about four feet away. The corn plants emerge first and by the time they have a good stalk, beans come up and twine around them. Squash and *maracocks*, or passion-flower plants, are planted between the corn and beans and allowed to run along the ground."

"And when is all of this eaten?"

"Autumn is the time of the largest harvest,

when my people have their main feasts and sacrifices," Little Snow Feather said. She heard her friend gasp.

"Sacrifices?"

The girls heard the sound of a horse's hooves thudding like thunder against the ground.

Shannon looked around and saw no horse, yet the sound of hooves was getting closer.

"Who would be coming to the village so quickly?" Shannon asked. She and Little Snow Feather exchanged questioning looks. "It wouldn't be Midnight Falcon, would it?"

"My brother does not own a horse, nor does he know the skills to ride one," Little Snow Feather said, scanning the land for the rider.

Just then the horse and rider rounded a wide bend of land, where trees and meadow came together a short distance from the outskirts of the village.

"Papa!" Shannon cried, so stunned by his appearance that she felt frozen to the scaffold. She watched him growing closer and closer on Thunder.

Her heart sank when she saw that he had spotted her, his eyes dark with rage, his heels sinking into the horse's flanks to urge the animal into an even harder gallop.

He rode through the crops, smashing them along the way, steering around one scaffold and then another. Children climbed down from them to flee, their screams filled with fright.

Shannon felt faint when her father halted beside her scaffold and dismounted, his angry, accusing eyes locked with hers.

Jan-Michael grabbed Shannon from the scaffold and carried her screaming and kicking toward his horse.

Midnight Falcon and Chandra arrived at the village in time to see what was happening in the garden.

Chandra was stunned to see her brother there, knowing that he must have left the house right after she and Midnight Falcon.

He must have heard Midnight Falcon tell her that Shannon was with the Powhatan, and had planned to arrive at the village before Chandra and Midnight Falcon returned from the forest so that he could get Shannon while they were not there to interfere. She was grateful that her brother had not known exactly where the village was located, or else he would have arrived much sooner and would have already taken Shannon away.

As it was, Chandra felt as though they were just in time. She hoped they could save Shannon from whatever fate awaited her at the hands of her angry father.

Chandra broke away from Midnight Falcon and ran up to her brother. "Jan-Michael, put Shannon down," she said, trying not to reveal just how angry she was over his prejudice against Indians. "Put Shannon down this minute."

"Stay out of the way, Chandra," Jan-Michael

said, holding Shannon against him as she wriggled to get free.

"You don't want to do this," Chandra said, meeting her brother's glare. "Release her. Go on home. We will be there soon."

"I'm taking her home with me now." Jan-Michael turned to stare accusingly at Midnight Falcon. "And no one had better try and stop me."

Chandra felt afraid for her niece and knew that she had to do everything within her power to keep Jan-Michael from taking her home to punish her. She wished that they hadn't taken the time to stop and pick the plants for her wounds so that they could have arrived at the village before him. Chandra gave Midnight Falcon a pleading look.

Reading her feelings, Midnight Falcon saw the danger himself. Jan-Michael might do something terrible if he were allowed to take Shannon home without Chandra there to intervene.

He slid a comforting arm around Chandra's waist and drew her closer to him, then met the challenge in Jan-Michael's stare with his own.

"*Tassantasses*, it is best that you put your daughter down now," Midnight Falcon said in warning, his tone suggesting that he had the upper hand.

"You do not address me by my name? You dare to insult me?"

"It was not meant as an insult," Midnight Falcon said. "I called you English in my language."

Jan-Michael doubted that Midnight Falcon was telling the truth when several of his warriors began to surround this place of confrontation, their eyes steady on him. Some had spears, others had knives or arrows notched onto large bows.

Jan-Michael knew when he was outnumbered.

And although he hated all redskins with a vengeance, he knew that he had no choice but to back down this time.

His one consolation was that he knew these Indians were not going to harm his daughter, even though he resented the fact that they were dictating to him how he should treat her.

He slowly set Shannon to the ground.

As he looked from warrior to warrior, he backed up closer and closer to his steed.

Chandra hated to see her brother feel so trapped, even though he had been about to mistreat Shannon. She wanted to go to him and try to see if she could soften his mood.

But his expression told her that now was not the time to attempt to reason with her brother.

She wondered if she ever could.

He was being humiliated in front of an entire village of Indians.

She worried that he might not be able to forgive her.

After Jan-Michael mounted his stallion, he dared to edge closer to Midnight Falcon. "You interfered with me today," he said. "That was not a wise thing to do."

"Yes, *Tassantasses*, I can see how you might think that," Midnight Falcon replied. "But you were wrong in how you were treating your child. Shannon is safe among my people. No harm could ever come to her while with them."

"She is my daughter and it is my right, only mine, to decide what is best or what is not best for her," Jan-Michael said. He stole a glance at Shannon, who was clinging to her aunt.

Jan-Michael lifted Thunder's reins. "Chandra, I'll be expectin' you home soon with my daughter," he said. He turned his horse and rode past the garden, then disappeared around the bend, leaving silence behind him.

Chandra was hurt that her brother had not even asked how she was feeling. It wasn't all that long ago when she thought she had smallpox!

His lack of concern made her concern for him deepen. Although they were very different, sometimes so much so that she wondered how they could be brother and sister, she still loved him and knew how rough this past year had been for him.

"I'm so confused," Shannon sobbed. "Papa was never so mean to me. And I didn't mean to make him so mad." She swallowed hard. "But I had to come for Midnight Falcon. I thought he could help you."

Remembering why she was there, Shannon stared at her aunt. "Why aren't you at home?" She winced when she saw the newest blisters on Chandra's face. "You shouldn't be here."

"I am going to be fine. I don't have what we

thought I had. It cannot spread to others unless a person touches the blisters on my skin," Chandra explained.

"What is it?" Shannon asked. She was glad when Little Snow Feather came and squeezed her hand.

"It is called poison ivy," Midnight Falcon said, smiling at Shannon. "It is from coming in contact with the poison ivy plant. Your aunt, or my sister, can point this plant out to you so that you can avoid it yourself."

Midnight Falcon gazed at Chandra. "I know that you feel the need to get home and talk things out with your brother, but I urge you to come into my lodge and stay long enough for me to apply the medicine, as we planned. The sooner your skin is medicated, the sooner you will heal."

"Yes, I'll stay long enough for you to make the medicine for me, but I will apply it myself. I would not wish these itchy things on anyone, and would not want you to get it from touching me."

Midnight Falcon nodded. "Stay outside with Little Snow Feather," he told Shannon. "This will not take long."

Shannon ran off with Little Snow Feather into the field to try to help undo the damage from her father's horse.

Once inside, Midnight Falcon busied himself with preparing the medicine. He dropped the leaves in a small container of water that he had already set in the hot coals of the lodge fire. Chandra sat on a mat, watching him.

"When you return home you must talk at length with your brother about everything," he said, his voice filled with feeling. "You do know what I am referring to, do you not? Us. You and I, and our future together. You need to find a way to make your brother understand how things are to be. Once he realizes that he cannot control your destiny, and that your destiny includes a man with red skin, he will also realize that his daughter has her own destiny and choices. He must accept this."

"I doubt that now is the time to talk with him about anything," Chandra said. "But I doubt, also, that there will ever be a perfect time when he would listen with an open heart."

"I understand that he is a man of many moods, most of them dark, but he must either get past those moods, so that everyone can live in some sort of harmony, or lose both you and Shannon forever. Are you not her mother and don't you have a say in her upbringing?" As he talked, Midnight Falcon continued to prepare the spotted touch-me-not plant for use against Chandra's poison ivy.

"I hope so, but I would never take her away from her father altogether," Chandra said, her voice breaking. "No, I must find a way that will not tear my family apart. I must make my brother see reason and get past his hatred of Indians. I must make him understand that there are bad Indians, just as there are bad white men, but that not all Indians are bad."

"You are a wise woman, a caring woman, who is loyal to her kin, and that is admirable," Midnight Falcon said. "I trust you can work this out, for I would not want to think that anyone can keep us apart now that we are committed to one another."

"I assure you that no one will keep me from my future happiness with you," Chandra said, trying not to think of the child that might be growing inside her.

She smiled weakly at Midnight Falcon as he took the container of medicine from the fire and set it beside her.

Testing it for warmth, she was relieved that the liquid wasn't too hot to spread across her flesh. She drew her dress over her head so that she could get to all of her blisters, but she did not feel any uneasiness over being nude in Midnight Falcon's presence. It was not the first time he had seen her without her clothes, and she hoped it would not be the last.

As she applied the medicine, she thought of what lay ahead of her.

First she would deal with her brother's wrath, and as soon as things were calm between them again and they had come to some sort of understanding, she would have to go into Jamestown and see a doctor to confirm that she was with child.

When finished, Chandra dressed and went outside to get Shannon.

After saying their good-byes, they left the village. As they reached home, Jan-Michael came out on the steps and glared at them.

"Both of you listen to me," he said, placing his fists on his hips. "Never put me in such a position again as you did at the Powhatan village today." He shifted to look at Shannon. "Daughter, I am tired, so I won't punish you for what you did, but let that be the last time you are with the savages. Do you hear me?"

Shannon burst into tears and ran up the steps past him and into the house.

Jan-Michael glared at Chandra. "I have no control over what you do, because you are an adult and you have always had a mind and strong will of your own," he said. "If you want to waste your life on a savage, so be it. But never come cryin' to me how wrong you were to do it."

Then his expression softened. "Were you able to find somethin' to help the rash?" he asked, his voice breaking.

Stunned at how quickly his mood could change, yet relieved that he was finally showing some concern over her health, Chandra nodded. "I applied an herbal medicine, but it is too soon to know whether or not it will be effective. I must admit, though, I don't itch as badly."

She started to say something else, but suddenly she felt so nauseated that she thought she might vomit. She grabbed her stomach with one hand and covered her mouth with her other as she ran past Jan-Michael and into the house.

"Chandra, what's wrong?" Jan-Michael shouted, following her. He watched her hurry up the stairs. "Damn it, it's probably whatever the Injun concocted for your sores! You should've never gone there, Chandra. You should've never paid any attention to their hocus-pocus."

Not even hearing her brother, she ran to her room. She knew what might be causing the nausea and decided to go into Jamestown tomorrow to see the doctor.

Chandra sank a cloth into a basin of water, then wrung it out and laid it across her forehead. She climbed into bed and lay down on her back.

She willed the sickness away, but nothing could erase the fear of telling Midnight Falcon the truth.

How would he be able to accept the fact that she had made love with him while she might be pregnant with another man's baby? Would he think that she was trying to trick him into marrying her, to secure his love in order to have a father for her child?

Surely Midnight Falcon would not think that she would try to trap him. Given the way things were between her people and his, he would think that if she wanted to trap a man, it would be someone of her own skin color.

Why was she even thinking of the word "trap"?

she argued to herself. She had been married when she had conceived, if she had conceived.

"Tomorrow," she whispered.

Yes, tomorrow she would know for sure.

Even if Midnight Falcon accepted her in this delicate condition, her brother might be more adamant against allowing a man whose skin was a different color to be a father to her baby.

"Please, please let everyone understand," she prayed.

23

The supreme happiness of life is
the conviction that we are loved.
—VICTOR HUGO

Telling her brother that she felt much better, Chandra used the excuse that she wanted to buy a new book of poetry to go to Jamestown. Jan-Michael had not sensed it was a ploy. Chandra sat in the doctor's office, awaiting his return after he had left her to get dressed again.

She felt anxious, the doctor having given her no clue whatsoever about her condition. During the examination, he had seemed more interested in how she had medicated her blisters, which had dried up almost magically overnight.

Chandra thought about Jan-Michael.

She was glad that he had not mentioned anything about the prior day's exploits as they had sat at breakfast. But she could tell by Shannon's silence as she sat eating her oatmeal that she had been reprimanded by her father. For the moment, it seemed that she would obey his order not to go among the Powhatan again.

As soon as breakfast was over, Shannon excused herself and returned to her room, where she had remained as Chandra boarded her buggy for the trek to Jamestown.

When Shannon had not asked to go with her, Chandra knew that the child was holding a lot inside. Chandra had to find a way to convince Jan-Michael that it was wrong to keep Shannon and the sweet Indian princess apart, but first she had to settle things in her own life.

"Where is that doctor?" Chandra wondered aloud as she looked around the gloomy interior of the doctor's office. A strong medicinal aroma filled the room.

There were many bottles lining shelves along the walls, and the table on which she had been examined sat off to one side.

She shuddered at the indignity of having had to spread her legs to a total stranger as he probed her.

He hummed a strange sort of tune, the smell of cigar smoke strong on his dark suit. She hated to think of this man delivering her child if she was pregnant. He was short, squat, bald, and wore thick-lensed, gold-rimmed glasses. His hands were rough and cold.

"Well, young lady, I think we have your answer," Doc Cline said as he walked back into the small room. He readjusted his eyeglasses on his round nose, then squinted through his lenses at her as he sat down at his desk opposite her chair.

Chandra's heart skipped a beat. She leaned forward, nervously picking at invisible dirt on her dress.

"Tell me," she said, her heart now pounding. "Am I . . . with child?"

"Yep, seems you are," Doc Cline said, pressing his fingertips together before him. "I'd say six or seven weeks along. But don't fret about showing anytime soon. I predict you will not gain all that much weight and you will carry the child well."

Chandra felt numb at the news, even though the doctor had only confirmed what she had suspected to be true.

Things would have been so much easier if it were not so.

But now that she knew there *was* a child, she had no choice but to tell the man she loved and pray that he would still want her. However he reacted would make or take away her future happiness.

"You are a widow," Doc Cline said, his voice solemn. "You don't have a husband to help you raise the child. But you have a brother. He will take over the same responsibilities that a father would, won't he?"

Chandra nodded, unable to tell the doctor about the strain between herself and her brother.

She pushed herself up from the chair, trembling.

When her knees almost buckled beneath her, the doctor hurried from his chair and placed a steadying arm around her waist.

"Do you need someone to accompany you to your home?" he asked. "Are your emotions too strong to be alone? Knowing that you are with child must make you miss your husband."

"I'll be all right," was all that Chandra answered.

She eased away from him, smiled clumsily, and left the room. She walked out to her horse and buggy as though in a daze.

Once on the seat, her reins in hand, Chandra knew there was only one place to go.

To Midnight Falcon.

She could not wait any longer to get his reaction.

As she guided her horse and buggy down the dirt street amidst the hustle and bustle of other buggies, wagons, and men on horseback, Chandra tried to be happy about her pregnancy.

A child! She was actually carrying a child!

How she loved children. When she was a child, she often had thought about how it would feel to be a mother.

But she had dreamed of having a child with a man she would die for.

She had met that man, but he was not her child's father.

Soon she would know whether or not she would marry Midnight Falcon.

If he rejected her, how could she ever be happy again?

She tried to focus her thoughts on the beauty

of the day. The sky was bright and blue. The sun was warm on her face. A breeze lifted her long hair from her shoulders.

Birds flew from tree to tree, the parakeets the most lovely of them all.

The river lapped at its banks while a pair of woodchucks romped along the muddy shore.

She caught her first sight of the village. Everything about it seemed so peaceful until she heard the sound of drums.

Never before had she heard drums in Midnight Falcon's village.

Was it a good sign—or bad?

With each rhythmic beat of the drums, she thought she could feel her throbbing heart.

When she finally rode into the village, she saw much more activity than usual between the men. They seemed excited about something. Some even had their faces and bodies painted, the designs on a few of them grotesque.

She saw Midnight Falcon as he stepped from his longhouse, his eyes filled with fire, his stance angry.

When he saw her approaching, he stopped and stared before running to meet her.

She drew a tight rein and got out of the buggy. "What's happened?" she asked, looking around.

She gasped when she saw weapons being piled in front of the large council house.

Warriors began to dance and yelp around the

large open fire, swinging tomahawks in their hands.

"Our scout returned with news that Chief Black Rock of the Pocoughtaonacks is not far away," Midnight Falcon said, gently placing his hands on her shoulders. "It is not a good time for you to be here. Return home. When the warring is over, I shall come for you."

His gaze swept slowly over her. He noticed her lovely gathered dress, the pink of her cheeks, and how her hair was drawn back from her face and tied with a velvet bow.

He looked into her eyes and saw something new there, a desperation.

Then he looked past her and studied the horse and buggy.

"Why have you not come on foot, or on White Iris?" he asked. "Is there trouble? Has your brother caused it?"

"No, Jan-Michael has said no more about my relationship with you," Chandra said. She wanted to tell him that Jan-Michael had even, in a strange way, given his blessing, a blessing made of mockery and vengeance. "I . . . I came today . . ."

She paused, because she knew now was not the time to tell Midnight Falcon about the baby, not when he had warring on his mind. The thought of him going to fight his bitterest enemy made her quiver with fear.

"You came today because . . . ?" Midnight Falcon prodded.

"I sensed that I should," Chandra said, then flung herself into his arms. "Must you go to war? Must you? I would die if you were taken from me."

He held her tightly. "This must be done," he said, then framed her face between his hands. "It seems the Pocoughtaonacks tribe has misjudged us, forgetting that we will be out for blood if they show their faces to us again. Or they remember and smugly think they can be victorious again. They aim to expand their fur-hunting territories by taking our land away from us and by eliminating as many Powhatan people as they can in the process."

"I'm afraid for you," Chandra cried, tears filling her eyes as she stepped away from him. "Perhaps they have come to speak peace with you. Do you truly think they have war in mind?"

Midnight Falcon laughed sarcastically. "They have more than war on their minds," he said. "As I told you before, this tribe is known to torture captives to death, then eat parts of their bodies. My warriors and I must stop them before they get closer to my village."

Chandra grew pale at the thought of cannibals being anywhere near. "I am now even more afraid for you," she said, shuddering.

"I see and understand your fear. Just remember this, that if I do not stop those warriors, and they succeed at killing off my people, they will then proceed into the white community to feed their appetites. I will, I must stop them, at all cost."

"At all cost?" Chandra said. "Even your life?"

He ran a finger over her face, changing the subject. "The blisters are all but gone," he said, smiling. "My medicine worked well."

"Yes, very well."

"And Powhatan medicine will bring me home to you," Midnight Falcon said. He pulled her into his arms and held her close.

"Go home and stay safely there and be sure that Shannon stays with you," Midnight Falcon said, releasing her. "When I return, if I return, I will come to you."

"If . . . ?" Chandra stared at him, her eyes wide.

When he said nothing, she flung herself into his arms and clung to him with all of her might.

She still hadn't told him that she was with child. Now she might never get the chance.

He gave her a long, deep kiss, then carried her to her buggy and placed her on the seat.

"Remember not to wander from your home until you know things are back to normal."

"I shall wait anxiously for your return," Chandra said.

Then, with a sob she could not hold back, she snapped her reins and rode off, her heart aching.

Behind her Midnight Falcon and his warriors began in earnest to prepare for war. Chandra felt cold on hearing them chanting war songs, low-pitched and menacing.

Midnight Falcon seemed so different from the man she had grown to know, yet she realized she was seeing another side of his culture. She must accept it or lose everything, for without accepting his customs, all of them, she couldn't have him. He would not want her halfway.

24

A hope beyond the shadow of a dream.
—JOHN KEATS

Although Chandra had not wanted to leave Midnight Falcon, concerned that the Pocoughtaonacks tribe might attack, she had reluctantly returned home.

Dispiritedly, she walked down the hall toward the front staircase, then stopped with a start in front of the library.

She was surprised to hear her brother talking behind the closed door. She had come in the house by the back way, which did not give her a view of the front hitching rail where horses might be tied.

But she knew, by the varied voices, that there had to be several men with her brother.

One of them mentioned how glad he was to be hired to work for Jan-Michael on his fishing boat. Chandra's heart leaped with happiness. Her brother was finally moving forward with his life. It wasn't just idle talk. He was doing it.

He had actually hired men!

This could be the turning point in her family's lives, Chandra thought, and she felt hope for the first time since their arrival in America that perhaps things might turn out all right for everyone.

Her joy was short-lived. One of the men in the library absently mentioned the cannibal tribe that was on its way to wreak havoc on the Powhatan.

He said that Chief Midnight Falcon and his warriors were going to meet the Pocoughtaonacks in battle.

Jan-Michael showed an intense interest in the news, asking the man how he knew about the two enemy tribes. The man said that he had an Indian friend who kept him informed about anything that might eventually affect the Virginia settlers.

Another man chimed in that nothing would please him more than to see all redskins leave the area. The only good redskin was a dead one, he said.

Chandra shivered at the callousness of that remark. Her hope that her family would come together faded into an almost unbearable dread.

She stifled a gasp when she heard her brother suggest a plan that no longer had anything to do with fishing.

Her pulse racing, Chandra stepped closer and listened to Jan-Michael as he told the men that he saw the Indian war as a golden opportunity to rid himself of the Powhatan chief, then explained why—how his very own sister and daughter had become involved with the savages.

Chandra felt increasingly sick the longer she listened to the men and how they quickly sided with Jan-Michael. Tears spilled from her eyes on hearing one of the men say that he would like nothing more than to take away the Powhatan's strength and hope by killing their chief.

Another man said that he'd personally like to exterminate the Powhatan the same way he had enjoyed helping exterminate the pesky wolves in the area. The only difference was that he would not want any savage's hide to hang in his cabin.

When the room was filled with much laughter, and Chandra became certain that these men would work together against the Powhatan, she turned to run to her room. She must think and make plans of her own to warn the Powhatan that they had more than the Pocoughtaonacks to fear. But her brother's voice came to her again, measured and determined, stopping her cold in her tracks. She listened to how he made plans with the men to ambush Midnight Falcon and his warriors just before the Powhatan reached the cannibal tribe. They would kill Midnight Falcon and his men, but it would look as though they were killed by the Pocoughtaonacks.

Jan-Michael laughed as they worked out the details of the plan. They would kill many Pocoughtaonacks and chase the rest back to Canada so they could not reveal the true fate of the Powhatan warriors. With Midnight Falcon out of the way, at least Chandra would have no more reason to visit the Powhatan. And if she didn't, surely his daughter would lose interest in them, as well.

Another man laughed and said that the Powhatan might be so afraid for their lives, since their chief and warriors were killed so easily, that they might flee to parts unknown. That would ensure that Jan-Michael's sister and daughter had no way to involve themselves with them again.

Chandra was appalled by what her brother and the men were so coldheartedly planning. She wanted to rush into the room and tell them that their plans wouldn't work, for she would not allow it. She wanted to shame her brother into changing his mind!

But from recent experience, she knew that he would ignore anything that she said. He was in one of the darkest moods that she had ever seen him in, and she knew that nothing she said would penetrate the wall he had built around his heart.

That left Chandra only one choice. She had to find Midnight Falcon, yet he must be far from his village by now.

She shouldn't ask his people to send warriors after him, because that might make the village too vulnerable and leave it unprotected. Once her brother and those men were engaged in mischief, who was to say they wouldn't go to the Powhatan village and start trouble there?

Chandra hurried to her room and changed into her riding attire, only to realize her mistake. She couldn't reach them by horse. She remembered that Midnight Falcon and his warriors had planned to take a water route to surprise Chief

Black Rock. That meant that she would have to travel the same way to catch up with them.

She had never taken charge of any type of boat, let alone a canoe.

And she hated water!

Determinedly fighting back her fears, Chandra changed again into more comfortable clothes and went to Shannon's room to tell her where she was going.

Shannon was gone.

"Little Snow Feather," Chandra whispered, figuring that when she found Shannon, she would find her with the lovely Powhatan princess. It was obvious that Shannon would never give up that special friendship, especially not for a father blinded by prejudice.

Knowing this was not the time to worry about anything except Midnight Falcon's welfare, Chandra set aside her concerns about Shannon and crept down the long corridor to the back stairs.

She recalled having seen several canoes not far upriver, where they were kept by a family who enjoyed canoeing on clear days.

She had wondered how they had managed to have canoes, whether they had stolen or traded, or the family had made them themselves.

Now none of that mattered to her. Getting up the nerve to steal one of the canoes and board it was all that was important—that, and keeping Jan-Michael from catching her.

For the moment, he was too involved in making plans to be thinking about her or Shannon. As far as he knew, both were in their rooms. He must have heard her return in the horse and buggy and probably thought that she was off somewhere reading.

Praying that neither Jan-Michael nor any of his cohorts were looking out the window, Chandra broke into a run across the front lawn.

She breathed a deep sigh of relief when she got over the slight incline of land next to the river, reaching a blind spot from the house. She had only one more thing to do—steal the canoe—and then she would be free and clear.

All she could think about was Midnight Falcon and how much she loved him. She must do everything within her power to save him, even at the expense of her very own brother. She knew that after Midnight Falcon learned of her brother's plans, he would have to stand up against him and the other white men.

In the end she might lose one of them.

Or both.

That thought filled her with dread, yet she had to warn the man she loved from a mindless ambush. Perhaps the Lord above would find a way to save both men in the process.

Running along the embankment, she searched until she found the beached canoes.

As she ran toward them, she realized they were made exactly like Midnight Falcon's. She figured that the owners had traded for the canoes, not stolen them, or else the Powhatan would have seen the whites in them and demanded them back.

She hoped that no one stopped her once she was in one of the canoes. She prayed that she would have the courage to ride the river's currents, and that she would have the skill to keep the vessel upright.

Her knees shaking, her heart throbbing, she studied the cabin nestled in the trees a short distance from the river. She could hear voices but she couldn't see anyone. She needed to get far enough upriver before anyone realized the canoe was missing.

And she needed to be brave. The idea of paddling out to the middle of the river, where it was the deepest, made her feel heartsick with fear.

But she had no alternative.

This was the only avenue of travel that would get her where she wanted to go in time. She couldn't paddle close to land because along the shore there were obstacles such as drifting logs and beaver dams.

She would have to stay mid-river.

After struggling with the canoe, which was much heavier than she had realized, and getting it in the water, Chandra climbed aboard and lifted the paddle.

Remembering how Midnight Falcon had done it, she began drawing the paddle through the water.

Memories of spilling overboard while fishing came to her, making her feel cold.

But she put it from her mind and concentrated on the chore at hand. She searched ahead of her for signs of Midnight Falcon in his own canoe.

She understood the danger that she was putting herself in, as well as her unborn child. She had no idea how far she would have to travel to find Midnight Falcon, if she ever could find him.

But at least it gave her a small ray of hope that if she couldn't find Midnight Falcon, her brother couldn't either.

And she had a head start on Jan-Michael and his crew of madmen!

All that she could do was give it her best.

When she reached a point where she knew that she was not very far from the Powhatan village, she was tempted to stop and ask for help.

But again she reminded herself that the warriors who had stayed there must remain to protect the rest of the tribe in case Chief Black Rock eluded Midnight Falcon and came to attack.

She kept telling herself over and over again that she could succeed, for if she didn't, she might lose everything.

Suddenly she heard voices shouting her name.

She saw Shannon and Little Snow Feather waving at her, beckoning for her to come to shore.

She was torn. If she stopped, it would delay her mission. But what if the girls had something important to tell her, perhaps something about Midnight Falcon?

Needing to know, Chandra turned the canoe toward shore. Once there, she discovered that all the girls had wanted was to know what she was doing in a canoe, and where she was going.

Shannon knew of Chandra's dislike for the water and had never seen her traveling that way alone.

"Let us go with you," Shannon begged after Chandra outlined her plan to the girls.

"Three paddling a canoe will get you where you are going much faster," Little Snow Feather said, looking anxious.

Chandra saw the logic in Little Snow Feather's words, and knew that she would feel much better if she wasn't by herself.

And she realized that the Indian girl knew the lay of the land and every bend in the river, since she had been born and raised in the area.

Her only fear was that the girls might become harmed in some way, and Chandra would never forgive herself if that happened.

"*Please*, Chandra?" Shannon asked.

The most important thing to think about was Midnight Falcon and his welfare. If Chandra didn't find him before her brother and his men did, the man she loved might die!

"Yes, come on," Chandra said, already reaching down for two more paddles.

The girls splashed into the water and climbed into the canoe behind Chandra.

With each of them manning a paddle, they pushed off and headed upriver, traveling much faster than she had alone.

Chandra leaned her head sideways and tried to listen as Little Snow Feather whispered something to Shannon, just barely loud enough for Chandra to hear.

She thought that Little Snow Feather was telling Shannon that Pocahontas was with them in the canoe, and that she would keep them safe.

Chandra looked from side to side, then all around her, and strangely enough she did feel a presence. She smelled something sweet. Might Pocahontas wear flowers in her hair?

Chandra shook her head to clear her thoughts, figuring that she had misunderstood what the Powhatan child had said. She glanced over her shoulder at the two young girls who gave her innocent looks.

Chandra smiled and turned back around.

She must have been imagining things. Pocahontas had been dead for a long time, and there wasn't such a thing as ghosts!

But spirits? She wondered, her eyes widening as she thought of how Indians believed in such things, especially the Powhatan. Was it possible?

Again she turned to face Little Snow Feather.

When Little Snow Feather slowly nodded and smiled so sweetly, yet mischievously, Chandra felt that the child understood what was on her mind. Maybe Pocahontas's ghost-spirit *had* just visited them!

Swallowing hard, Chandra faced the front of the canoe and made herself concentrate on the task at hand.

Midnight Falcon.

Only Midnight Falcon!

It was all up to her to save him from her scheming brother!

25

Beyond a mortal man impassion'd far
At those voluptuous accents, he arose,
Ethereal, flush'd, and like a throbbing star,
Seen mid the sapphire heaven's deep
repose.

—JOHN KEATS

The muscles in Chandra's arms ached from the incessant paddling. Just when she wasn't sure if she could go any farther, she got her first sight of Midnight Falcon. Three warriors were in his canoe with him, followed by five other canoes filled with Powhatan warriors.

They had all painted themselves for war, crossing their foreheads, cheeks, and the right sides of their heads with clay mixed with pulverized bloodroot.

She could see that they were well equipped with full shooting gear—bows made of witch hazel, bowstrings made from deer gut, arrows fletched with turkey feathers with deadly arrowheads, some fashioned from stone, others from wild turkey spurs.

It was all too real, how she might lose Midnight Falcon before they had a life together as man and wife. The thought made her heart ache, yet she knew that what he was doing was a part of his culture that she must accept. But this was the worst so far of those things that came with loving him.

Midnight Falcon's canoe was at the lead, the others skimming along the water in single file, moving steadily but unhurriedly forward.

"There they are!" Chandra pointed out the canoes to the girls, who did not seem to have noticed them yet. She felt a mixture of relief that she had reached Midnight Falcon before anyone else, and fear of what might lie ahead. Chandra doubted that her arrival would stop any fighting, for it had taken her a long time to reach Midnight Falcon.

Her brother and his men probably were not far behind her in their more substantial boats. She was certain by what she had overheard that her brother had put his fear of water behind him. She wished that it had happened earlier so that he would have been too wrapped up in his daily fishing to be aware of what was happening between the two tribes. He would have centered all of his energies on how many fish he would catch, not on how many Indians he might kill.

As it was, the enemy tribe would not be that far away now, ready to clash with Midnight Falcon and his warriors.

Chandra knew that she might have brought herself and the girls into the middle of the fighting, but she had to chance everything to save Midnight Falcon. Everything!

"Paddle harder!" Chandra cried, wincing in

pain with each draw of the paddle through the water. "Hurry! We might be running out of time!"

She could hear the girls moan, but they, too, pushed harder and harder with the paddles.

As they drew closer to the Powhatan canoes, Little Snow Feather shouted at Midnight Falcon in her Powhatan language.

He turned with a start when he recognized his sister's voice.

He went cold inside when he saw who was there with Little Snow Feather.

What did this mean? he wondered.

He instructed the warriors in his canoe to make a wide turn in the river and they hurried to meet the approach of Chandra's canoe.

He guided his canoe next to hers and stopped.

"I had to come," Chandra blurted out. She knew by the look on his face that Midnight Falcon was puzzled, and also knew that by the time she told him everything her brother or the enemy tribe might have caught up with them.

Stunned, Midnight Falcon listened intently to Chandra's hurried explanation of her brother's plan.

And even before he had the chance to reply, his attention was diverted elsewhere. He spotted Jan-Michael and his cohorts moving toward them in several boats, and then he became aware of a splashing sound coming from another direction. He turned to see Chief Black Rock and his warriors closing in from the opposite side.

He was trapped between two evils.

To him, one was no less his enemy than the other. Realizing that he now had his woman, her niece, and his sister to protect, Midnight Falcon suddenly came to his senses.

He shouted commands at his men then stole a glance at Chandra.

His heart ached knowing that she was now in dire danger, yet he was touched by her caring enough to risk everything to warn him.

He had not misjudged her as a woman of courage. She had looked past her fear of the water, and of possibly being caught in the middle of a battle, to do what she could to save him.

"Chandra, hurry to shore," he insisted. "Take the girls and hide. Do not come out until I say the time is right."

He reached a hand to her cheek. "And thank you, my woman," he said softly.

Swallowing hard, her eyes filled with tears, she nodded.

As Midnight Falcon and his warriors turned the canoe around to join the rest of the Powhatan, Chandra and the girls rowed as hard as they could toward shore.

When they reached land, they leaped from the canoe and ran into the dark cover of the forest. They hid behind some trees and reluctantly prepared to watch the battle.

Chandra peered out at her brother, a man she scarcely knew anymore. As each day passed, he was becoming more of a stranger, a stranger who was now in trouble. He had brought this on himself, yet he clearly had not thought it would be so dangerous.

She could see how wild his eyes were and how he seemed frozen, no longer paddling as he watched the cannibals approach. He looked with fear at Midnight Falcon and his warriors, who were taking control of the situation. The Powhatan were now out of the water, their canoes tipped onto their sides to use for cover as they prepared to fight off two deadly enemies.

Chandra felt faint when she realized that her brother and the other white men would soon be attacked by the cannibals.

She gasped at the sight of Midnight Falcon with two arrows in his bow hand and two between his teeth!

Midnight Falcon set the notch of an arrow on his bowstring, his fingers cold, his muscles straining. His men filled their bows, aimed, and sent volleys of arrows at the cannibals, inadvertently protecting the white men. Jan-Michael and the others rowed frantically toward shore, all seemingly forgetting their plan to harm the Powhatan.

Once safe on land, Jan-Michael and his frightened men hid behind trees and began firing at the cannibals, who didn't have a chance now.

Soon the remaining Pocoughtaonacks began fleeing in retreat.

Knowing that Chief Black Rock was among

those still alive, Midnight Falcon went after him alone.

Chandra watched in fear as he dove into the river, a knife secured between his teeth.

When he didn't surface immediately so that she could tell where he was going, or if he was even still alive, she died a slow death inside as she waited.

Suddenly she caught sight of him again just as he surfaced to push over a canoe, throwing an Indian into the water.

"It is Chief Black Rock," Little Snow Feather cried, seeing what her brother was up to. "The Pocoughtaonacks chief managed to live through the attack! The coward he is, he left his men to fend for themselves while he tried to escape alone in his canoe. My brother! Oh, if he does not stop him this time . . ."

"Chief Black Rock?" Chandra paled as she watched the two men grapple in the water.

When both men went under, Chandra held her breath as she waited for Midnight Falcon to surface again.

An icy fear spiked through her. She watched in horror as the water turned scarlet.

"No!" Chandra screamed.

She ran from cover and fell to her knees on the riverbank.

She searched the water frantically for signs of Midnight Falcon.

"Midnight Falcon! Please, be alive!" she cried,

aware now of no longer being alone. Little Snow Feather and Shannon had knelt on either side of her, sobbing.

Chandra flinched as a body suddenly bobbed to the surface, lifeless. She recognized Black Rock as his body floated away, no one to claim it now that his people's canoes were all out of sight.

When Midnight Falcon finally surfaced, a wondrous joy filled her soul, and she felt as if heaven had opened its doors and sent a beautiful white light down into her heart. Midnight Falcon came from around the overturned canoe and saw Chandra, his eyes filled with emotion.

"He's all right," Chandra whispered as he swam toward shore.

The girls cheered him on and gave Chandra big hugs, eagerly waiting for Midnight Falcon to reach them.

When Jan-Michael and his men slipped from hiding, still holding their firearms, Chandra's heart sank. She was afraid that her brother would start firing at the Powhatan now that the Pocoughtaonacks had left.

She rushed to her feet and ran toward Jan-Michael and the others.

"Jan-Michael!" Chandra shouted, frantic to make him see reason. "If not for Midnight Falcon and his warriors, you would be dead! They saved your lives!"

She wasn't aware that the Powhatan warriors

had inched out from cover, their arrows aimed at the white men.

Jan-Michael was very aware of the danger, though, as were his friends. Slowly they bent over and laid their weapons at their feet; then all of them held their empty hands up for the warriors to see.

At first, Chandra thought that her brother was giving up his mission voluntarily and had taken her words to heart. But she soon realized by the way he and his men had surrendered their weapons that they had only done so because they felt they couldn't win.

Midnight Falcon came ashore and motioned for his men to come and stand with him. Chandra held her breath as she waited to see what would happen between her brother and the man she loved.

Jan-Michael broke the silence. "Midnight Falcon, I want to thank you and your warriors for savin' our lives," he said. "I . . . I apologize for the wrong I have caused you. I promise never to cause problems for you or your people again."

He looked over at Chandra, standing halfway between him and Midnight Falcon, wide-eyed.

"I will even step aside and say no more about my sister's relationship with you," Jan-Michael said, his voice drawn. He then turned his gaze to Shannon and Little Snow Feather noticing that the two girls were holding hands. "Or about my daughter's friendship with your sister."

Jan-Michael looked at Midnight Falcon again. "I was wrong to interfere in so many lives," he said, then cleared his throat. "I hope that you will allow me and my friends to return home. I have decided to start up my fishin' business again and planned to take them aboard my boat for the first time."

Tears spilled from Chandra's eyes, and badly wanting to believe that her brother was being sincere, she ran and hugged him.

When he wrapped his arms around her and held her close, she heard the thunderous beats of his heart against her cheek and hoped that he no longer held any hatred there.

"Do you mean what you said?" Chandra asked, gazing into his eyes.

"Chandra, I've wasted enough time," Jan-Michael said. He gently swept a fallen lock of her hair back from her eyes. "I'm ready to live again."

"Then you truly won't stand in the way of my relationship with Midnight Falcon, or Shannon's with Little Snow Feather?"

"I'll never like it, but I see now that there's nothin' I can do about it," Jan-Michael said hoarsely. "Each of us has our own life. We each choose how we wish to live it. You have chosen yours. I have chosen mine."

"And Shannon?"

"I see nothin' wrong any longer in her bein' friends with the Indian girl," Jan-Michael said, even though he didn't quite believe it. He did not think he could ever feel comfortable about any of these changes in their lives, but he had decided to try to accept them.

He must, or lose both his sister and daughter to another way of life.

"Thank you," Chandra murmured.

She gave him another hug, then moved to his side when Midnight Falcon approached them. She was very grateful when he held out his hand in friendship to Jan-Michael.

She was amazed that Midnight Falcon forgave so easily, yet she knew that if it were not for her, he would not act this way toward someone whose intention was to kill him.

She also knew that although he offered his friendship, he would never totally trust Jan-Michael. He would always be on guard in case her brother lied as so many whites did to Indians.

"*Tassantasses*, I am finally rid of one enemy today, forevermore," Midnight Falcon said. "I would like to make peace with the other."

When Jan-Michael clasped his hand to Midnight Falcon's, Chandra studied her brother's eyes and looked for any sign of deceit.

She sighed with relief when she saw none.

Yes, perhaps this was one obstacle out of the way of her future happiness with Midnight Falcon.

But she still had to tell him about the baby.

First, she would tell her brother, for that might

be a way to make him not feel so left out of her life and to bring them closer together, the way they once were.

After she told Jan-Michael about the baby, she would tell him about her marriage, praying that she still could plan on that wedding day.

She would not let herself believe that an innocent baby would change the way Midnight Falcon felt about her.

For the moment, she was just so relieved that both her brother and Midnight Falcon were all right, since they could have been killed today.

She would hold on to that thought for now and hope that after she talked to her brother about all of the changes in her life, she would have cause to feel twice blessed.

26

Into her dream he melted, as the rose,
Blendeth its odour with the violet,
Solution sweet.
—JOHN KEATS

The warm, orange glow of a campfire illuminated the walls of the cave. A waterfall just outside the cave entrance splashed rhythmically downward into the river below. A handful of pink roses that Chandra had picked as Midnight Falcon swam in the river were spread out on the rocky floor.

Chandra picked up one of the roses and carefully began removing the thorns from the stem. "I can't stay long," she said.

She had been so glad to get away from the battle scene. It was wonderful to be in the cave behind the waterfall, a place that served two lovers well.

"It seemed fine that Shannon left with Jan-Michael," she continued. "But once he arrives home and begins thinking about what happened, how he suddenly made friends with you, and how he did not object when I told him that I wanted to stay to make sure you were truly all right, he might reconsider everything."

"I cannot trust his behavior now either, when before his prejudice toward all men and women with red skin was so strong inside his heart," Midnight Falcon said, pushing another log into the flames.

He turned to Chandra. "Be wary, my woman, of a person whose mood changes as quickly as a chameleon changes its colors," he said. "My heart was in the right place when our hands came together in friendship. But only time will tell if he was being truthful in his gesture, or if it was a ploy to protect him from my warriors who had saved him from the cannibals."

"Cannibals," Chandra said, a shudder racing through her. She laid the rose aside and pulled close the warm blanket that Midnight Falcon had gently placed around her shoulders when they first arrived.

"Do not fear the Pocoughtaonacks tribe ever again," Midnight Falcon said. He drew his own blanket more comfortably around his bare shoulders. He wore only a breechclout, the river having washed the war paint from his flesh.

He had brought Chandra to the cave where they were assured privacy, for although it seemed that Jan-Michael had accepted their relationship, Midnight Falcon would never truly believe he had done it from his heart. He wouldn't tell Chandra the extent of his doubts about her brother.

He would not rest easily until after the wedding ceremony, which would seal their love forever. He sensed a sort of madness in Jan-Michael's eyes, which suggested he was capable of anything at any time.

Even if Jan-Michael allowed the marriage ceremony to take place, he might decide that he had been wrong and find a way to retaliate.

"Midnight Falcon, you turned your back to me for a moment as you bent to retrieve your breech-clout from the ground after your swim, and I thought I saw a tattoo in the shape of a bird on your skin," Chandra said.

"All people of the Powhatan tribe have tattoos," he said. "It is called 'pouncing,' and each family chooses its own body crest. As far back as my family goes, the cardinal has been ours. It is a bird that brings happiness into the hearts of those who see and hear it. By wearing the tattoo in the shape of a cardinal, my family wears happiness."

Chandra felt uneasy. "You said that all of your people wear tattoos. Does that mean if I . . . when I become your wife, I will also have to be tattooed?"

Midnight Falcon laughed softly. "You say that with much hesitation, my woman," he said, dropping his blanket away from his shoulders. He knelt before her and slowly slid her blanket away from her. "Would you not enjoy wearing the same crest as your husband?"

"Then I will have to be tattooed?" Chandra asked. She trembled with anticipation as he bent closer to her and brushed a kiss across the slender column of her neck.

"You will be the wife of a chief, so, yes, you must." He turned away from her to spread his blanket down before the fire.

"Does it hurt?" Chandra asked, hating that she seemed so cowardly.

First she had to admit that she feared water. And now, tattoos.

She wished that she could be stronger, but she could not help her fears, and he had fallen in love with her despite them.

He began removing her clothes, and the way he touched her sensitive places made her melt with rapture.

"Do you think I would do anything to hurt you?" Midnight Falcon asked. He tossed her garments aside and pulled his breechclout down his muscled thighs.

Chandra was too lost in ecstasy to comprehend what he said or even remember what she had asked him about. He leaned over her until he had blanketed her with the warmth of his flesh.

She moaned as he thrust his heat deeply inside her.

Her breath quickened with yearning, and she swept her arms around his neck.

Exquisite sensations spiraled through her body as he enfolded her with his solid strength and began moving rhythmically inside her.

His mouth was hot and sweet when his lips met hers.

He moved his lips to her ear and breathed her name as though he couldn't live without her.

"Midnight Falcon," she whispered, stroking his back. "Oh, how I love you."

"Each moment I am not with you I am filled with such longing," he said, his eyes hungry with desire.

"If only we never had to say good-bye," Chandra murmured.

He moved a hand between them and cupped her breast within it, his thumb circling the nipple.

Then he leaned away so that he could sweep his tongue around her nipple, drawing a rapturous moan from deep within her.

She closed her eyes and tossed her head from side to side, gasping in pleasure when his fingers found that part of her that was throbbing and aching with want. As he stroked her in rhythm with his continued thrusts, Chandra felt herself growing dizzy, the ecstasy was so sweet.

Feeling her sensual response, his own body on fire with need, Midnight Falcon reeled in drunken pleasure.

Again he kissed her.

Again he moved deep inside her.

Again he teased her nipple with his tongue, occasionally nipping at the tender skin.

Near the point of wondrous release, Chandra framed his face between her hands and led his mouth back to hers, seeking his lips with a wildness that she had never before experienced. She trembled with readiness as he drove more swiftly and urgently.

Midnight Falcon was aware of how close she was; then, soaring with joy, he gathered her into his arms. He groaned as he thrust into her one last time, bringing them both to the height of passion.

Still trembling, Chandra clung to Midnight Falcon. She didn't want to let him go. She felt so close to him and decided not to wait any longer to tell him about the baby. It wouldn't be right to share such a secret with her brother first, she realized, when Midnight Falcon's reaction was all that mattered to her. If he thought she was deceitful for not telling him earlier, she wasn't sure if she would blame him. She knew now that she should have told him as soon as possible after she found out a child was growing inside her.

"You are so quiet," Midnight Falcon said, his eyes hazy in the aftermath of lovemaking.

"I know," Chandra said, swallowing hard.

"I understand." He smiled down at her. "I, too, enjoy the special time after making love with you."

"It was so wonderful," Chandra murmured. She reached up and gently brushed his hair back from his face. "I love you so much. These moments alone with you are so magical."

"But you have to leave, do you not?" Midnight Falcon asked, recalling how she had said that she shouldn't stay long. And he didn't think that she should, either, because of her brother.

Chandra nodded, then pulled him closer to her, hoping that he wouldn't feel the desperation in her hug. She was terribly afraid of what she was about to tell him. If he turned his back on her, how could she bear it?

"I have something to tell you," she said, surprised that she found the courage to do so.

He rolled away from her onto his side, and leaned up on one elbow as she turned to face him.

"Please, please don't hate me for not having told you sooner," she said, her voice breaking. "I . . . I only recently became certain of it myself. Since then so much got in the way of telling you, forcing me to wait. . . ."

As she expected, the words would not come out.

Her courage had that quickly waned!

She looked into his eyes and saw an intense questioning there.

Slowly she sat up. She drew a blanket around her shoulders and stared into the dancing flames of the fire.

Midnight Falcon sat up and placed his hands on her shoulders and turned her to face him, her blanket dropping away from her. Chandra gazed into his eyes and prayed that these next moments would not bring her an unhappiness she would never be able to get over.

"You can tell me anything," Midnight Falcon said. "We are going to be man and wife. There should not be any secrets between us now, or ever."

"I didn't mean to keep this from you," Chandra said, swallowing hard. "Honest. I . . . I . . ."

"Tell me now, for there seems to be nothing stopping you except your lack of courage, and I do not understand why you should feel afraid to talk to me." Midnight Falcon could not hide the hurt in his voice. "Or is it something that you cannot tell me, after all?"

"I just don't want to lose you," Chandra said. Sobbing, she flung herself into his arms, relieved when he wrapped his arms around her.

"You have me forever," Midnight Falcon said. With a finger he lifted her chin so that their eyes met. "I can tell you that whatever it is, I will still love and want you, for there is nothing that can ever make my feelings for you change."

"Even if . . . even if I tell you that I am with child, a child fathered by someone else?" Chandra blurted out. "The child was conceived before my husband died. It is his, although I truly wish it was yours."

Chandra grew pale. Her secret was finally out in the open and Midnight Falcon was suddenly quiet, his eyes filled with surprise.

The waiting was torture, even though it actually was not all that long, for soon he was drawing her into his embrace, his lips warm as he spoke against her cheek.

"The child will be raised as ours," he said

hoarsely. "I love you so much. I will love the child as much, because it is a part of you."

Chandra choked back a sob of joy. He let her know that she didn't have to worry any longer by giving her an all-consuming kiss.

Chandra clung to him, her lips trembling against his. Tears of joy flooded her eyes, for she was happier now than she had ever been in her entire life. Who could ask for more than what this wonderful Powhatan warrior had given to her?

He had, in a sense, given her back her life by accepting her child so readily. Had he rejected her, she would have lost her will to live. Midnight Falcon was her future!

27

Forever wilt thou love, and
she be fair!
—JOHN KEATS

The sun was just shining through the breakfast
room window as Chandra entered. Her pulse
raced when she discovered that Jan-Michael also
had risen early and was sitting at the table sip-
ping tea and reading a book.

She was so proud that she had been able to
teach him how to read since he had not had time
to go to school as a boy because he had to work
to support the family.

Afraid to tell him about the marriage and child,
Chandra barely had been able to sleep the entire
night. She had seen Jan-Michael standing at his
bedroom window watching her return home from
the cave the day before.

When she had returned to the house, he had
not left his room to discuss the events of the day
or to ask why it had taken her so much longer to
return home than he probably had expected.

She had wondered what Jan-Michael would say
about Midnight Falcon, but discovered that he had
retired to his room for the entire evening.

As Chandra and Shannon played chess before

the fire during the evening, Chandra had watched the door for her brother to come and join them. When he hadn't, she could not help but believe that the day had taken its toll on him.

She wasn't sure what sort of mood he would be in this morning, whether he would be polite or angry.

But Chandra didn't want to wait any longer to find out. She had to get everything off her chest, to tell him about the child and her upcoming marriage. She would see then just how sincere he had been about making friends with Midnight Falcon!

Nervously, Chandra cleared her throat to get her brother's attention. She sat down in a chair at the round oak breakfast table opposite her brother.

When he looked up at her, she studied his eyes. She saw no trace of anger or discontent, but instead he seemed rested and relaxed and happy, making her breathe more easily.

"What does your day hold for you?" Chandra asked, pouring herself a cup of tea from the silver teapot. "Are you going to go out on your boat with your new crew?"

"Some of the men need more time," Jan-Michael said, slipping a ribbon between the pages of his book to mark where he would resume reading. His eyes narrowed. "Especially after yesterday. Thank God no one died, but some are still pretty shaken over the incident."

"I'm so glad you are all right," Chandra said.

She watched him over the brim of the cup as she took a sip of tea.

"And of course Midnight Falcon," Jan-Michael said.

"Yes, and also Midnight Falcon," Chandra said, setting her cup on the table.

"Shannon could've been killed," he said. "What on earth did you think you were doin' involvin' her in something so dangerous?"

"If you hadn't taken it upon yourself to try to kill Midnight Falcon, neither your daughter nor your sister would have been anywhere near the Pocoughtaonacks tribe," Chandra said. "When I heard you making plans with those men, I had no choice but to go and warn Midnight Falcon. It just happened that Shannon and Little Snow Feather joined me."

"You listened to me through the door like a spy," Jan-Michael growled. "That's not like you, Chandra."

"You aren't anything like yourself these days. But I hope now that you see how wrong you've been acting, you will once again act like the brother I knew in England."

Chandra glanced over her shoulder at the door, hoping that Shannon would stay in bed until she was able to tell her brother everything. She did not want to pull Shannon into the fray should her brother become enraged.

"Jan-Michael, I have something besides yesterday to discuss," Chandra said softly. She could not help feeling anxious, but she was ready for whatever way he reacted to the news.

"Thank God," Jan-Michael said, sighing. "I'm damn tired of bein' accused of all sorts of ungodly things."

"I never accused you of anything you weren't guilty of doing," Chandra said, her eyes flashing. "Can I get on with what I want to tell you, or are we going to sit here all morning wasting time?"

"Go ahead," Jan-Michael said, combing his fingers through his hair. "Tell it. Say what you've come to say."

"I am with child," Chandra said matter-of-factly. "I got pregnant, perhaps the night before Lawrence's heart attack. I went to the doctor in Jamestown yesterday. He confirmed it."

Jan-Michael's eyes lit up and he broke into a wide grin.

He rushed so quickly from his chair that it tumbled over onto the floor as he came around the table and pulled Chandra into a big hug.

"A child!" he cried.

After a moment, he held her away from him so that he could gaze at her tummy.

His eyes danced as he looked at his sister. "I hope it's a boy," he said. "I'll raise him, Chandra, as though he were my own son. I'll teach him everything I always wanted to teach a son, had I been blessed with one."

Chandra was thrilled over how happy he was about the baby, but hearing his eagerness to be a substitute father left her cold. It made it much harder to tell him that she already had someone who would be a father to her baby—Midnight Falcon.

How was she to say the words that would anger as well as hurt her brother?

She eased away from him, clasping her hands together behind her and smiling nervously. "I have something else to tell you," she said, her voice full of emotion.

Jan-Michael's smile waned. He raised an eyebrow. "And?" he said. He slowly slid his hands into his front pockets and waited. His eyes, which had been so filled with wonder and happiness, were slowly growing dark.

"Please understand and please be happy for me," Chandra said. She saw him flinch, as though he knew what she was about to say.

"You know that I want nothin' but happiness for you," he said. "So tell me. What else is there besides the baby? And why do I sense that it will not make me nearly as happy?"

"I'm going to marry Midnight Falcon," she blurted out. "He's already agreed to take my child into his heart as his own."

Chandra scarcely breathed as she awaited her brother's response. She was truly confused when he seemed to have no reaction whatsoever. She could not even read his mood in his eyes, which usually gave her hints of how he felt.

"Say something," Chandra said, reaching a

hand out for him. "Please tell me that you are all right with this. I do love him, Jan-Michael. And he will make a wonderful husband and father."

"It's your life," Jan-Michael finally said. "You live it."

Stunned, Chandra watched him leave the room. She walked slowly to the door and saw him leave the house.

It was strange how there was no haste in his step. She could see no anger that might be fueling his need to leave the house.

She ran to the window and watched him go to the stable. "He must be angry," she whispered to herself. "Why else would he leave?"

Yet his anger seemed too controlled, almost as if he had taken the news too lightly. He had been so quiet about it all.

Her heart skipped a beat when she saw him ride from the stable, a long, double-barreled gun that she had never seen before thrust into the gunboot at his side. She wondered if he had purposely hidden the gun to use in secret.

"Where are you going?" she shouted, but he didn't hear her.

"Midnight Falcon!" she gasped. He must be going after Midnight Falcon!

That would explain why he had kept his temper in front of her, so that he could leave the house without her suspecting what he was really feeling. If she didn't think he was angry, he would be free to do whatever he felt he must to stop his sister from marrying a redskin.

Chandra saw no choice but to go to Midnight Falcon and warn him once again of her brother's murderous intentions. She knew better than to go after Jan-Michael and try to stop him. He would cleverly deny her accusations.

In desperation, Chandra fled to the stable, saddled White Iris, and left her estate at a hard gallop. She usually arrived at the Indian village on foot, but this time she didn't have a chance to enjoy the outing. She had to get to the village ahead of her brother.

She was fast learning the lay of the land, and surely knew it much better than Jan-Michael, since he had spent more time in the house than out-of-doors since his arrival. She knew a shortcut that would take her to the village before Jan-Michael, even though he had a head start on her.

Her hair blew in the wind and her silk dress fluttered up past her knees. Her fingers were sore from holding on to the reins so tightly.

She worried that riding a horse in such a way today might endanger the baby. But Midnight Falcon was her main concern at this moment. Again she had to take a warning to him that his life was in danger. She hoped this would be the last time for such warnings, and that Jan-Michael would learn a much-needed lesson. She only prayed that he would not be harmed in the process!

Seeing the outskirts of the village a short distance away, Chandra leaned low over the horse and urged it to go even faster.

She didn't even slow its pace when she entered the village, although she felt bad that she almost trampled someone in the way.

"I'm sorry!" Chandra cried over her shoulder.

When she reached Midnight Falcon's lodge, he was already outside watching her approach.

After drawing rein, Chandra slid from the saddle and flung herself into Midnight Falcon's arms.

"Why are you so frantic?" Midnight Falcon asked.

He gently held her away from him so that he could look into her eyes. "In your eyes, I see fear. What has caused it?"

"Not what, who," Chandra said, breathing hard.

She looked at her horse, then nervously glanced toward the edge of the village.

She grabbed White Iris's reins and led the horse to the back of the longhouse, not stopping until it was well hidden in the dark shadows of the forest.

Midnight Falcon followed her and asked her what she was doing.

"My brother," Chandra panted, wiping beads of perspiration from her brow. "I told him about the baby and about our marriage. His reaction was strange. He didn't even object."

"Then why did you see the need to come to me, as though trouble followed right behind you?"

Midnight Falcon asked, his eyes filled with confusion.

"I don't know." Chandra sighed. "I just have a feeling, that's all."

She didn't want to tell him about the firearm, because if she was wrong, she might be causing her brother trouble he didn't deserve.

"Why are you here?" Midnight Falcon asked. "You are not telling me everything."

"I know," Chandra said, her eyes wavering.

Then she blurted out her suspicions to him.

"We will wait him out," Midnight Falcon said softly. "Come. You and I will sit at the edge of the village where we will have a good view of anyone who might approach. Should he come, we will see him first."

"But you have no weapon with you."

"Your brother would not shoot the man you are to marry in your presence," Midnight Falcon said. He took her hand and walked her toward the place where they would wait and watch.

"I'm not sure what to expect of him," Chandra said. "Now or ever. I doubt he will ever again be half the man he once was."

"He has demons inside him that even he would be glad to see gone," Midnight Falcon said. "Do not lose hope for him yet. Did he not shake hands with a Powhatan chief yesterday?"

Chandra nodded, but she did not say how she felt now about that handshake. She thought that it was all pretense on her brother's part.

Chandra knew that the next few minutes, when Jan-Michael would come face-to-face with Midnight Falcon again, would prove her right—or wrong. She was afraid to know the outcome. The love she had for two men lay in balance. She hoped that Jan-Michael did not make her choose.

She stopped and pulled Midnight Falcon into her arms. "Hold me," she said, a sob lodging in her throat. "Please hold me for a moment?"

He held her close, yet he did not drop his guard. He watched for a man he now believed could never be a friend. He listened for the approach of a horse that would be bringing this enemy to him again.

28

She looked at me as she did love,
And made sweet moan.
                    —JOHN KEATS

Jan-Michael urged his steed into a thunderous gallop through the forest on his way to the Powhatan village. The sound of his horse's hooves sent wildlife scattering in all directions. He was exasperated.

"Nothin' will ever be the same for my sister now," he muttered into the wind. "Or our family!"

When he heard about Chandra's pregnancy, he had been so happy for her, but his happiness was just as quickly shattered when she told him that she was going to allow a redskin to raise the child—that she was even going to marry the savage!

"Never!" Jan-Michael shouted to the treetops.

It had been hard enough for him to back down and promise not to interfere if his sister and daughter wanted to be involved with the Powhatan.

Even when he suspected that Chandra might want to marry Chief Midnight Falcon some day, Jan-Michael had tried to accept it.

He had hoped that Chandra was only infatuated with the savage warrior, dazzled because this was the first time she had ever met an Indian, and because he just happened to be a powerful chief. Eventually, she would realize there was nothing to her feelings and regain her senses.

But now it had gone too far, making his blood boil with anger.

Jan-Michael felt that he had no choice but to stop his sister's madness before it went any further, especially now that she was with child. He had decided that the only way to get his sister to stop seeing the Indian chief was to finish what he had started yesterday.

If it weren't for Shannon, Jan-Michael would not even care if he was killed as long as he killed the man who had torn apart his family.

But he hoped to live through this so that he could raise Chandra's child himself.

He would be careful. He would watch Midnight Falcon's comings and goings until there was a chance to ambush him.

An evil glint entered Jan-Michael's eyes as he formulated his plan. Perhaps the Powhatan might think that one of Black Rock's warriors had come, alone, to avenge the death of his chief by killing Midnight Falcon.

That is what *he* would think if he were a Powhatan warrior discovering the body of his chief shortly after the confrontation with the

Pocoughtaonacks. Jan-Michael chuckled at his own cleverness.

Having taken what seemed like a shortcut through the forest to get to the Powhatan village, Jan-Michael calculated that he must be close. Since he wanted no one to see him, he decided that it was best to leave his horse behind and walk the rest of the way on foot. A horse's approach was too risky. What he had to do must be done in total silence!

"Whoa!" Jan-Michael said, drawing his reins tightly. His horse came to a fast stop.

He slid from the saddle, walked the horse over to a low limb, and secured the reins. He yanked his firearm from the gunboot.

His jaw tight, his heart filled with a vengeful hate, he walked onward.

But after only a short distance into the shadows of the forest, he suddenly saw a strange sort of dazzling light up ahead.

He laughed to himself when he realized that it wasn't anything strange after all. It was only a break in the trees where the sun shone down like spirals of gold onto a small pond.

His heart skipped a beat when he heard the sound of water splashing. He thought he even heard a female giggling, as though someone was enjoying a midsummer's swim.

His curiosity turned to anger when he recalled his daughter swimming with Little Snow Feather. He was afraid that he might be hearing Shannon now, possibly having gone for another swim with her friend even though Jan-Michael had forbidden such shameful behavior. He gripped his firearm more tightly and strode toward the pond.

But when he reached a place in the trees where he could not be seen, and took a good look at who *was* swimming there, he stopped with a start. He took a shaky step backwards. It wasn't his daughter or her Indian friend but a vision of loveliness that would forever linger in his mind.

He had never seen anything, anyone, as beautiful in his life!

He was transfixed by a beautiful Indian maiden who was swimming nude in the river.

It was not lust that he felt. He was moved in a different way, by the woman's ethereal beauty and her grace as she swam.

Mesmerized, his heart pounding, his mouth agape, Jan-Michael continued to stare. He had never seen a woman who could look so at peace with herself and so lovely at the same time.

Her long, thick black hair spread out in the water around her like a halo.

She turned slightly so that he could fully see her face, and his breath caught at the sight of her features.

The sun gleaming on her copper face, she closed her eyes for a moment.

Her eyes, framed by thick lashes, were dark and intriguing. He saw a goodness and sweetness in their depths.

It was the peace, the utter peace, that she radiated that spoke to him, something that he had never seen before in anyone except . . .

"Chandra," he gasped. He paled to think that only recently, after having met the Powhatan Indian chief, had his sister taken on such a look of utter joy, a blissfulness that he knew was caused by one thing.

Midnight Falcon had made all the sadness leave his sister's heart, he thought, only now realizing how wrong he was to interfere.

All of his life he had wanted his sister's happiness, and now that she had found it, he was doing everything within his power to take it away from her.

A sudden shame swept through him at the thought of how far he had planned to go to steal this wondrous joy from Chandra.

Until this moment, until he had recognized the same joy that he saw in his sister's eyes and every movement, he had not stopped to think what had caused her happiness.

"If I could have this beautiful Indian maiden, even I could love again," he whispered, stunned by how far his sudden infatuation with this woman had taken him.

And she wasn't just any woman. She was an Indian, one of a people whom he had learned to hate because of how his wife had died.

Only now, under the spell of this beautiful creature, did he understand that not all people with red skin were bad just because some were.

"I have been so wrong," he said aloud.

He inhaled a deep breath. He was amazed by how his emotions had so suddenly and so completely changed. Minutes ago, he had ridden on his horse with hate in his heart. It was gone now, as though he had never experienced it.

The lovely woman stopped swimming and placed her feet on the bottom of the pond, revealing the upper lobes of her full breasts. Jan-Michael turned his back to her with a start. He felt the need to pay this woman a deep respect by not watching her leave the water, nude.

Hoping to find a way to get to know her, he intended to do nothing to make her loathe him. He would wait for her to leave the water and get dressed, and then, only then, would he attempt to meet her.

She was the kind of woman who came only once in a man's lifetime. He had to know her. He had to convince her that he was a friend.

His pulse racing, he found it hard to stand there waiting. He was eager to see her in the white doeskin dress that she had left on the ground, imagining how her long black hair and her copper skin would contrast against the white of her dress, and how the dress would define her shapely figure.

But he had to give her enough time to leave the water and get fully dressed before he stepped out into the open, if even he could. His knees were so weak, they threatened to buckle beneath him.

His heart was racing so hard, he could swear he heard the thundering of its beats.

He prayed that she would not be frightened by his presence, and that she would not think that he had been staring at her while she dressed.

When he felt that enough time had passed and he was not able to stand the waiting any longer, Jan-Michael spun around to step out into the open and speak to her.

His heart sank when he saw no one there. She was not still in the water, but there were no pools of water on the ground to prove that she had been there. She would have been dripping wet from her swim.

And how could she have gotten past him without him at least hearing her footsteps?

It was as though she had disappeared into thin air.

He took an unsteady step closer to where she would have had to stand while dressing. He bent to a knee and looked around for any signs of water but found none. He felt an eerie sensation that perhaps he had been imagining everything.

He moved shakily to his feet and raked his fingers through his hair.

"No, I did not imagine her," he argued to himself.

She had been there. He could have never thought up something so beautiful.

Her disappearance shook him to his very core. He had to find her.

He shuddered again at the thought of what had brought him to this time and place—a plan to murder a man who was probably the chief of this woman's tribe. If he had not seen her, he might still be on the road in search of vengeance. The need for vengeance had grown inside his heart, his very soul, since the death of his wife, and when his daughter and sister became involved with redskins, it spiraled out of control.

But now it was gone from his heart.

A lady with the face and movements of an angel had cleansed his soul and healed his heart. He would never allow himself to hate the Powhatan again. How could he?

Even though he had seen this woman only briefly, it was enough to make him fall deeply in love with her.

His eyes lit up with a plan. He would ask Chandra if she would arrange for him to meet the woman. She had to be from Midnight Falcon's village.

Other tribes were too far away.

"By God, I must find her," he said, breaking into a mad run toward where he had left his horse. "I *will*."

He mounted Thunder to search for the maiden before heading for home to ask for Chandra's help. The vision of the maiden was so vivid that he felt as though she were with him on his horse.

He did feel a presence, as though someone was

embracing him, the faint, sweet smell of perfume filling his senses.

All of a sudden it felt as though lips were pressed against his, dizzying him with an unexpected passion that forced him to rein in his horse.

And then it was over and he felt totally alone, yet flooded with awe. He felt afraid of what he had just experienced, sure that it would be called madness if he were to try to explain it to someone.

Shaken, he resumed his journey home, continually searching for signs of the mystery woman.

"Was she real?" he wondered, beginning to doubt his own sanity.

29

'Tis the past of love,
That fairest joys give most unrest.
—JOHN KEATS

Still in a haze over his experience by the pond,
Jan-Michael almost stumbled up the back steps of
his house. Shannon came to the door, holding it
open for him with a quizzical look in her eyes,
and he forced himself to appear as normal as possible even though he carried a secret inside his
heart.

"Papa, when I came down to breakfast and
found both you and Chandra gone, I was afraid,"
Shannon said. She stepped aside and followed him
down the back corridor.

He, too, had noticed that Chandra's horse was
gone from her stall.

"Where is Chandra?" Shannon asked. "Where
have *you* been?"

"Well, I . . ." Jan-Michael stammered. He did not
yet feel ready to tell anyone what had happened.

And he needed to talk to Chandra first, since
he would need her assistance to find out about
the woman.

Chandra could take Jan-Michael to Midnight
Falcon. Surely Midnight Falcon would know the

maiden by his description of her. Perhaps he would see her the moment he entered the Indian village!

It bothered him that he might look like a fool if no one knew her and he never found her, for all of the Powhatan Indians would know that he had become infatuated with a woman of their skin coloring.

To hell with pride at a time like this! he thought. He did not care what sort of humiliation he had to go through to discover the name of the woman and her whereabouts.

He had not taken to praying much since his wife's death, but he said a silent prayer that he would find the maiden, and that she would not belong to another man.

Just seeing her had been magical in that she had changed his hate to love. He finally felt at peace.

"Papa, this isn't like you," Shannon said, reaching to take his hands. She stared at him in wonder. "You are never one to be speechless. And what has happened to make your hands tremble?"

She stood on tiptoe to try to get a better look at her father's head. "Did you take a spill on Thunder?" she asked, reaching up to run her fingers through his hair to search for a possible lump or two.

Jan-Michael smiled and took her hand from his hair. He lovingly held it.

"No, I didn't take a spill," he said. "I'm fine."

He spun Shannon around and gave her a playful slap on the back. "Now get Scottie and go into the sun room for something to eat." He waited for her to awaken the dog sleeping at the foot of the back steps.

When Scottie was obediently following Shannon, Jan-Michael went with them into the bright room. "A cup of tea is what your father needs," he said, hoping that would help calm him until Chandra came home.

"Katie has prepared a special bread pudding," Shannon said over her shoulder as she pulled a chair away from the oak table. She smiled at Katie as the maid gave her a bowl of leftover stew meat for Scottie, which she quickly placed on the floor before Scottie's sniffing nose.

After the dog began lapping up the food, Shannon looked over at her father. "Look, Papa, Katie even found wild strawberries yesterday. Won't they taste delicious in cream with the bread pudding?"

"Yes, delicious," Jan-Michael said, sitting down at the table opposite Shannon.

He watched her spoon several strawberry slices into her bowl of pudding, then carefully pour cream from the pitcher.

He loved her so much and he felt such guilt for having missed many pleasurable moments with her all because he could not shake the devilish mood that had plagued him since their arrival in America.

He vowed that everything would be different now.

Being in the presence of an angel had done it, had changed him.

Even if he never found the lady, he would still hold on to this peacefulness inside his heart, for which she was responsible.

But he would not allow himself to give up on seeing her without at least going to the Powhatan village to seek her out. If he didn't see her there, where would he look next? Perhaps heavenward, where angels laid their beautiful heads amidst the clouds?

He shook his head to clear his thoughts, realizing just how strange they were.

Why on earth did the Indian maiden always make him think about angels?

"Jan-Michael? Shannon?" Chandra called. As she came into the breakfast room, her brother turned his head to look at her.

She was taken aback by something about Jan-Michael. Normally he would explode immediately, questioning her about where she had gone so early in the morning, alone.

She sat down at the table and waited for his questions, but there were none.

In his eyes, she thought she saw a gentle peace, and also a certain eagerness.

She was relieved that Jan-Michael had not gone to the Indian village as she had expected him to. She had sat with Midnight Falcon until a warrior sought him out and reminded him of a council that was planned for the morning.

By then, they had already decided that Jan-Michael had gone elsewhere on his early-morning ride. He must have only needed time alone, to allow what she had told him to sink in. She hoped that by the time he got home again, he would have accepted things regardless of how he might wish them to be himself.

"Jan-Michael, where did you go this morning after our talk?" Chandra asked, wishing to put to rest her earlier suspicions.

"I could ask you the same question," he said. He immediately regretted snapping back at his sister, remembering his promise to change.

"I'm sorry, Chandra," he said softly. "I didn't mean that."

Chandra raised an eyebrow, and he understood her doubt. From now on she would see the new Jan-Michael, who would try to never make her uneasy over spiteful words or demands he had no right to issue.

"That's all right," Chandra said, still studying her brother. Something had happened to change him, but what?

She was almost afraid to ask for fear that the question might break the spell that her brother seemed to be under.

Jan-Michael nervously toyed with a spoon. He smiled at Katie as she came in with a stack of toast oozing with freshly churned butter and strawberry jam.

He waited until Katie was gone, then gave Shannon a sideways glance. He had decided to talk to Chandra alone about the woman in the pond, but perhaps he should stop treating Shannon like a child. She had proven to him that she was far more grown up than her ten years.

He would take this into consideration from now on when family discussions were needed.

He looked at Chandra, watching the way she delicately picked up a piece of toast and laid it on a saucer before her, then gingerly spread a white linen napkin on her lap.

She did everything with such care.

Since they had arrived in America and moved to this mansion, she had grown used to riches and the comforts of the house. Would she be able to retreat to a life of hardship, which undoubtedly the Indians experienced?

Was she so willing to give it all up for a man?

Even if it meant bringing up her child to face the sorts of difficulties that she and her entire family had in England?

Yes, he concluded, she would be willing to give up everything for the man she loved, and he understood that now more than ever before, because he suspected that he would do the same for the woman in the pond.

His thoughts turned back to the Indian woman, and he found himself blurting out his secret.

"While I was in the forest this morning, I came across a beautiful Indian maiden in a pond," he said.

"Chandra, besides my dearly departed wife, may she rest in peace, I have never been so taken with a woman as I was today."

Shannon's eyes widened as she stared at her father. Stunned by his words, especially since he was talking about an Indian, Shannon scarcely breathed as she listened. But she gasped when he described the woman, his description matching Little Snow Feather's description of Pocahontas!

Could it be? Had her father been lucky enough to see the ghost-spirit of Pocahontas? If so, why?

Shannon's heart pounded as she slid her chair back from the table. She waited just long enough to hear her father describe the woman again, and how he was in awe of her. He said that she must be from the Powhatan village, for the other villages were too far away from the forest for the woman to have walked there for a swim.

While her father was asking Chandra to accompany him to the Powhatan village to look for the maiden, Shannon crept from the room. No one noticed her leave, and she hoped they didn't see her run from the house to the stable.

She wanted to get to the Powhatan village as quickly as possible. She needed to get there before her aunt and father because she had a lot to tell Little Snow Feather. She had to ask her if the maiden that her father had seen could have been the ghost-spirit of Pocahontas, and why the princess would have shown herself to him when she would not even allow Little Snow Feather's very best friend to see her?

"Shannon, where are you going?"

Her father's voice brought Shannon's escape to a quick halt. She was just setting her saddle on her pony's back when her father and Chandra came to the door of the stable.

"I heard what you said about seeing the woman and I wanted to describe her to Little Snow Feather. I was hoping that she could tell me who the woman was."

She didn't tell the full truth.

If her father had witnessed something magical today, Shannon hoped that she would also be offered the same opportunity one day soon!

"Isn't that sweet," Chandra said, hugging her niece. "You wanted to help your father find the woman. How unselfish of you, Shannon. You are such a devoted daughter."

Shannon squeezed her eyes shut, feeling guilty.

She wasn't being unselfish. It only looked that way.

Shannon wanted to go to Little Snow Feather and tell her what had happened. But after it was all said and done, there probably would be a woman in the village who fit the description, and it would have nothing even to do with Pocahontas.

"We shall all three go to the village together,"

Jan-Michael said, putting an arm around each of them. "Come on. Let's saddle our horses. We shall take our first ride together since we've been in America."

Chandra smiled as he stepped away from her and headed for Thunder's stall. It seemed miraculous. Never would she have thought she would see her brother eager to go to any Indian village, much less the Powhatan's. Never would she have thought that she would see him eager to meet an Indian maiden!

She prayed that they would find the woman and that she was single and might learn to care for Jan-Michael. That would make Chandra's new world complete.

To have her brother, as well as Midnight Falcon, in her life was something she had not dared to dream.

But if Jan-Michael couldn't find the woman, would he change back into the kind of person who wore his prejudices on his shirt-sleeve?

She turned and gazed at him.

No. She didn't think that her brother would let that ugly side surface again, at least not any time soon.

What had happened today had seemed to change him. A miracle within a miracle!

"Let's hurry along now with those saddles," Jan-Michael said, already fitting his on his horse. "It's a beautiful day for a ride!"

In his heart he was thinking that it was a beautiful day to meet a beautiful woman.

He prayed that that very thing was only moments away.

30

Love in my bosom like a bee
Doth suck his sweet.
—THOMAS LODGE

On realizing that there was no woman in the
Powhatan village who fit her father's description,
Shannon was more eager than ever to be alone
with Little Snow Feather. They were all sitting in
the Powhatan council house, and the villagers
were filing in, one by one, not only to congratu-
late Midnight Falcon and Chandra on their upcoming marriage, which had just been announced
early that morning, but also to meet Chandra's
brother. Since Shannon was already known by
most of the Powhatan, and she no longer needed
to stay, she happily left the lodge with Little Snow
Feather.

Giggling, they ran into the privacy of Little
Snow Feather's longhouse, where venison stew
was simmering over the cook fire.

Little Snow Feather got two wooden bowls and
spoons and ladled some of the stew into each
bowl. She sat down beside Shannon and they both
gobbled down the delicacy.

Shannon was eager to talk, but knew that it
was polite to accept the offering of food first. The

first time she had seen how this stew was made, with the deer's head and entrails put in the pot intact, she had felt ill to her stomach at the thought of eating it.

But never wanting to disappoint Little Snow Feather, she had forced herself not to think about those things and had eaten the cooked stew with a smile. It turned out the smile was not even forced, for she had discovered that nothing compared with the deliciousness of the stew.

Her stomach now comfortably filled, Shannon set the bowl aside.

She turned to face Little Snow Feather. "Did you hear my father?" she asked. Her excited words were almost too jumbled together for Little Snow Feather to understand. "Did you hear him describe who he saw? Didn't it sound exactly like Pocahontas? Do you think that it was? My father said that he didn't see the woman among those who came into the council lodge. Was there anyone who didn't come who might fit the description? Or do you think he was honored with a visit from Pocahontas's ghost-spirit?"

"I hope that what I am going to say will not hurt your feelings," Little Snow Feather said.

"Nothing you could ever say would hurt me because we are best friends." Shannon swallowed hard. "What is it?"

Little Snow Feather reached over and took Shannon's hands and held them. "Your father *did* see the ghost-spirit of Pocahontas," she said, her voice betraying her own dismay. "I am trying to understand why, because as far as I know, I am the only one who has ever seen her. I have not even shared this with my brother, fearing that he would think I have lost my mind."

"Then why would Pocahontas show herself to my father?" Shannon asked softly.

"It had to be for a good purpose," Little Snow Feather said, drawing her hands away. She faced the slow-burning lodge fire and crossed her legs beneath her. "Pocahontas was in the pond to draw your father's attention," she said.

Shannon thought about this for a moment. "But why?"

Silence fell between the two girls. Little Snow Feather moved back to face Shannon and her eyes widened with wonder. "I know why," she blurted out. "Pocahontas was there to lure your father into wanting her. That is why she allowed him to see her in the pond. Imagine how she must have looked in the water, her beautiful hair spreading about her as she swam. Your father saw her and wanted to be with her. That was the princess's plan. She cast a spell over him in order to make him see how wrong he has been. If he could fall in love with a Powhatan maiden, would not that make him understand how your aunt fell in love with my brother? Would not that make him hunger for peace with my people?"

"But my father had already made peace with your people, and with my aunt and your brother,"

Shannon said. "I am certain he would not have tried to stop their marriage."

"Something must have happened to make Pocahontas appear to him," Little Snow Feather said. "Perhaps your father had only pretended friendship with my people. Perhaps he had planned to harm Midnight Falcon to keep him from marrying Chandra. Maybe Pocahontas came to stop him. Today, he was different. Did you not see his sadness when he did not find the woman from the pond? As he sat with my brother and your aunt, he seemed sincere. He met each of my people, one by one, and I saw no signs of hate in his eyes or his smile."

"Yes, I saw all of that, also. Even if you're right, what happens when my father gets over this woman who was really a spirit? He might again hate all Indians."

"I saw goodness in your father today that seemed to come straight from his heart," Little Snow Feather said. "My people's princess knew how to touch his heart in ways neither you nor I could possibly understand. Let us be happy that this has happened, for now our future will be even better. We do not have to hide our friendship. There is so much to see! To do!"

"What fun we will have!" Shannon said.

Then she grew serious. "Best friend in the world, might I ever see Pocahontas myself?" she asked. "Might I ever get to talk with her as you have? Will she ever show herself to my father again?"

"I doubt that she will ever show herself to you, for there is no need. You are already my people's friend. And if your father has changed the way we think he has, he will never see her again."

She gently squeezed Shannon's hand. "Give me your word that you will never tell anyone about any of this, about who your father truly saw? Promise me?"

With her free hand, Shannon crossed her heart. "I promise," she said.

"Then let us make plans for tomorrow. I would like to take you to a cypress swamp."

"What will we find there?" Shannon asked.

"Rushes and grasses grow in the saltwater marshes, which are used by my people," Little Snow Feather explained. "The marshes are very valuable to my people because of the animal life there. I will show you periwinkles, an emergency food when our winter supplies run low. I will also show you *quahogs*, which are hard-shelled clams that live on the sandy bottoms, and *maninose*, or soft-shelled clams."

"Let's go at the break of dawn tomorrow," Shannon said, her eyes wide with excitement.

"I shall meet you beside the river just past your father's large boat." Little Snow Feather leaned over to push a log into the fire.

"Papa will soon be riding the waves with many

fishermen eager to catch fish," Shannon said, glad that her father's life was turning around.

She would never forget the disappointment in his eyes, though, when he realized that the woman he had seen wasn't at the Powhatan village. She knew that he would always be watching for her everywhere.

It did not seem fair that Shannon could not tell him the truth to prevent him from searching for the woman in vain, but when she gave a promise to anyone, it was forever.

"It is so good to share things with you," Little Snow Feather said, reaching over to hug Shannon. "Tomorrow will be such fun!"

"Is it dangerous in the swamp?" Shannon asked.

"Only if you get lost in it," Little Snow Feather said. She laughed when she saw Shannon's horrified reaction. "I did not mean it. I know my way around the swamps. We could never get lost."

31

And I will make thee beds of roses
And a thousand fragrant posies.
—CHRISTOPHER MARLOWE

Chandra sat with Midnight Falcon on thick, plush pelts beside his lodge fire. Alone with the man she loved, she felt serenely content.

"This is the first time we have been alone in your lodge for any amount of time."

"Little Snow Feather and Shannon are out on your niece's pony," Midnight Falcon said. "Shannon is teaching my sister how to ride, and my sister said that she, in turn, will be showing your niece things that are new to her. She is enjoying teaching Shannon things of our people."

"Shannon could hardly eat her breakfast fast enough this morning," Chandra said. "She even got up earlier than my brother and I. I saw her ride from the stable on her pony with such excitement in her eyes."

"A lot of that is because she is now free to be with my sister without her father's interference."

"My brother has his own life back, so he will not concentrate so much on mine and Shannon's." That morning Chandra had seen Jan-Michael float away in his boat. Her heart filled with joy as she watched the sails fill with wind, his crew preparing for a day of fishing.

"Shannon is with my sister and Jan-Michael is on his fishing vessel and you are with me," Midnight Falcon said. "And my enemy is no more. Is not it a perfect world? Will not it even be more perfect when we are man and wife?"

"And when will the marriage ceremony take place?"

"Soon. There is one important ceremony before ours. The *huskanaw* ritual, which is a test of endurance for the youths of my village."

"When will that be?"

"Very soon, but let us not linger on talk of the *huskanaw*," Midnight Falcon said.

When he pulled buckskin and doeskin dresses from a trunk made of wicker, Chandra gasped in awe over their loveliness. Each was decorated in its own way, some with colorful beads or tiny seashells. One even had the design of a heart on the bosom made of the rare purple pearls that she had heard so much about.

"This one is the prettiest of them all," she said of the soft white doeskin dress as she slowly ran her fingers over the pearls.

"Of all the dresses that were my mother's, this was also her favorite," Midnight Falcon said, his voice low with melancholy. "She wore it many years ago, on the day of her wedding to my father."

He laid the dress across Chandra's lap. "I would like you to wear it on our wedding day," he said.

"My mother would want her son's bride to wear it."

Chandra's face flushed with excitement over the talk of their upcoming marriage. She was touched that he offered her such a beautiful dress to wear for the ceremony, but she remembered what he had said earlier when he had taken this trunk out of storage. "I thought these dresses were being kept for Little Snow Feather, to wear when she grew to the right size," she said. She could not take her eyes off the dress, marveling over its beauty and how it had retained its white color through the years.

She gazed up at Midnight Falcon. "Shouldn't you save this dress for your sister's wedding?"

"She, too, can wear the dress," Midnight Falcon said, reaching to run his fingers over the pearls. "Mother would be twice blessed were her son's bride to wear it as well as her daughter."

When Chandra didn't speak up right away, Midnight Falcon placed a hand on her cheek. "Do you not wish to share with my sister?" he asked.

Overcome by emotion, Chandra nodded. "I do wish to share it with your sister," she murmured. "I will be honored."

She looked at the other dresses, and then back at Midnight Falcon. "But I don't believe it is right of me to take any more of the clothes that you have saved for your sister," she said.

"She is already skilled at making her own dresses." Midnight Falcon leaned over to move the items he had taken from the trunk into a pile. "These that I have chosen from the trunk are now yours, forever."

He gingerly lifted the wedding dress from Chandra's lap and placed it atop the others.

"You are going to keep them here in your lodge, aren't you, until my wedding day?" Chandra asked. A part of her wanted to take them home to try them on over and over again in front of her full-length mirror, but she felt that they belonged here, not in the white world she soon would be leaving behind.

"Yes, they will be here for you," Midnight Falcon said.

He moved to his knees before Chandra. His hands went around to the back of her dress and started undoing it.

"Would you also like to leave this dress here?" he said, his eyes gleaming.

Chandra giggled as he pulled the dress over her head. She raised her arms straight up to help him.

He removed his breechclout, then lowered her down onto the bed of pelts. "I wish to make love with my future wife beside my lodge fire," he said, his voice husky. "I wish to think back to this moment when we are sitting with others beside the fire, entertaining with food or stories. While everyone listens and eats, you and I will have this beautiful secret. I will see the quiet laughter in your eyes as you smile at me and remember. I shall smile back at you, so that you will know that I, too, am thinking about today."

"I will truly enjoy entertaining as your wife," Chandra murmured.

Midnight Falcon placed his hands gently on her tummy and slowly caressed it. "Beneath my hands, in your belly, a baby awaits to be born," he said wonderingly.

He reached for one of her hands and placed it there, as well. "Soon, when you lay your hand there, you will be able to feel the child kicking." He smiled at her as she gazed up at him. "When my mother was carrying my sister, she allowed me to feel the baby move."

"I can hardly wait to experience that," Chandra said, tears coming to her eyes as she saw this tender side of her lover. "We shall, together."

"I love children so," Midnight Falcon said. "My mother had only two children, although she wished for many more. When she became pregnant with Little Snow Feather, she had been trying for many years, and we all rejoiced over this miracle. And when my sister was born, I could have never loved anyone at that moment as I loved her."

He reached up to place his hands on either side of Chandra's waist. "My woman, I shall cherish this child inside your belly as though it were my own," he said, holding her tightly as she threw her arms around him. "It will be raised with much love from both its mother and father. The child will be ours, in all ways that matter."

"How can you be so good to me?" Chandra cried. "I am so fortunate to have your love. Your people are so fortunate to have you as their leader."

"I am the fortunate one," Midnight Falcon said. "I have your love, and soon a child born of your body. I have my sister, and I have my people whom I cherish as though each of them were my children." He chuckled. "Even those who are too old to walk I think of as my children."

"Both my grandfather and grandmother became like children again just before they died," Chandra said, lying back down. She looked up at Midnight Falcon as he moved over her again, their bodies touching. "It was sad, but they were never without the love they needed before leaving this earth."

"We are still very much a part of this earth, and the living," he whispered against her lips. "Let us make love. My body aches for you, Chandra."

"I never knew that love could be so beautiful," Chandra whispered back to him.

And then his mouth covered hers in a thrilling kiss that was filled with passion. Chandra felt more alive with his every touch. She moaned in ecstasy and with one quick movement he was inside her, filling her with his heat.

Her body moved rhythmically with his as he surrounded her with his hard, strong arms.

They clung to one another, whispering each other's names as their hands explored.

"I yearn for you when we are apart," Chandra whispered into his ear, her mind swirling with hot desire. She trembled as he began moving inside her more urgently.

"Soon nothing will ever part us again." He kissed her, his hands caressing her breasts. "My wife. It will be so good to be able to finally call you my wife."

"My husband."

Again they kissed.

Chandra writhed in response and Midnight Falcon gave himself up to the rapture.

He held her tightly against him as they reached a feverish, passionate climax.

Their bodies still intertwined, they lay breathlessly together for a few minutes before Chandra spoke.

"Will your duties as chief call you away from me this morning?" she asked. Her eyes searched his as he leaned over her again.

"Today my duty is only to you."

Again he swept his arms around her and drew her tightly against him, thrusting inside her as her body opened to him.

"I wish for today never to end," Chandra whispered. She sighed contentedly, feeling as though her insides were melting with every hot, sweet kiss.

32

The power of one fair face makes
My love sublime, for it
Weaned my heart from low desire.
—MICHELANGELO

Shannon had made sure Scottie was back home and safely in her bedroom, closing the door so that her dog could not follow her. She had left her pony tethered on the edge of the swamp some time ago, and now she was walking with Little Snow Feather along the marsh.

The water rippled with life.

Ospreys circled overhead, and cormorants and herons were sunbathing on the banks. Rushes and grasses grew from the marshy water, and bald cypress trunks were thick near the water level. Shannon had already seen the periwinkles that Little Snow Feather had earlier described as the Powhatan's emergency food. Clams were everywhere.

"I keep hearing bird calls," Shannon said, marveling at how they echoed around her.

"The swampy marshes are full of wildlife because they are rarely disturbed by humans," Little Snow Feather said.

"The swamps are so beautiful in some places, and so ugly in others," Shannon said. She gazed at the breathtaking sight of flowering vines, some of which climbed the tree trunks, while others hung from branch to branch.

She sighed in pleasure as she saw yellow and blue jessamine, supplejack, and many other strange plants.

"Spanish moss lives on the cypress branches and so does mistletoe, which you also can see in the branches of the water gums and red maples," Little Snow Feather said, pointing out the mistletoe to Shannon. "We use that plant to cure toothache."

Shannon giggled and told her, "In England, if one holds the mistletoe plant above a lover's head, it is the custom to kiss the one who is beneath the plant."

"That is interesting," Little Snow Feather said, looking up at the shiny plants that grew in clusters even on the cypress.

Shannon tried to absorb everything as they continued to walk through the marshland, the forest thickening on one side of them.

"The Powhatan prefer the mixed forest," Little Snow Feather said. "These forests are rich in nuts and berries. And so many acorns bring lots of animals, which my people depend on for food."

The water became increasingly swampy, and the sun began to sink lower in the sky. Shannon felt uneasy. They had been weaving in and out of the trees, confusing her as to where they had been, or were going.

She looked over her shoulder, concerned. "We won't get lost, will we?" she asked. "You have been here before? You know how to get back to where we left my pony?"

"Yes, I have been here often," Little Snow Feather said, reaching over to take one of Shannon's hands. "We will go a little farther and then turn back. I don't want you to become too frightened ever to come here with me again."

"I'm hungry, not frightened," Shannon said, even though she knew that her voice had given her away. She was worried about how far they had gone, and how night soon would be falling all around them.

She wanted to get back to her pony and get home before it got dark.

"Then we shall stop and eat before going home," Little Snow Feather said, breaking away from Shannon and running on ahead of her. "Come. We will have a feast!"

Shannon winced at the thought of what her friend might consider a feast. She had seen nothing desirable to eat. Yet she knew that she should welcome anything that Little Snow Feather wanted to show her. It was even more important to learn about the Powhatan now that Chandra had announced she was going to marry Midnight Falcon. Shannon would be spending a lot of time in the Powhatan village with her aunt. She didn't want to look ignorant by not knowing as much as she could about their customs.

"Over here!" Little Snow Feather shouted, waving to Shannon, who had fallen behind. Little Snow Feather had spotted something for their snack.

"What is it?" Shannon said, running up to her. "I don't see anything to eat."

Little Snow Feather began plucking young shoots from a group of cattail plants.

"Those?" Shannon said, shivering at the thought of eating the wild plant that Little Snow Feather handed her.

"Although my people use the leaves of cattails for mats, we also eat the young shoots," Little Snow Feather said. "Taste it. You will see that it is not only good for you, but it also tastes good."

Shannon hesitantly bit into the tender, tiny stalk. She was surprised to discover that it *was* good. It was sweet and juicy. She ate another one, and then another.

Suddenly they heard something that sounded like someone splashing in the water. They both turned toward the noise and were shocked to see a man aiming an arrow at them.

"I thought you were dead!" Little Snow Feather said, gaping at Chief Black Rock.

There was an obvious wound on his chest, which seemed to be healing. Little Snow Feather stared at it, knowing her brother must have caused it. Everyone had thought the Pocoughtaonacks chief was mortally wounded.

She herself had seen Chief Black Rock floating

away, his face downward in the water, his life's blood surrounding him.

"I do not die easily," Chief Black Rock said, in a good enough approximation of English for both of the girls to understand. "I have been surviving on plants in these marshes. I am well enough to return to my people, but I need transportation."

He looked quickly in the direction from which they traveled.

He glowered at Little Snow Feather. "Where is your canoe?" he said, his voice low and threatening. "I will take it. You can return to your village on foot."

Then he laughed. "No, that is not how you will return. You will not return at all! Once you have taken me to your canoe, I will have no further use for you. I will kill you as I should have killed Chief Midnight Falcon."

Trembling, now holding hands, Shannon and Little Snow Feather exchanged frightened looks.

"Canoe?" Little Snow Feather said, gazing at the evil cannibal chief.

She had to think fast and be clever.

She couldn't let this man know there was no canoe, that they had arrived by pony, an animal that would be of no interest to him. He, too, depended on canoes for travel, not horses.

She prayed that Pocahontas's ghost-spirit might be near to offer help at a time when she needed it the most!

"Do not pretend you do not know what I am

talking about," Chief Black Rock said. He motioned with his notched arrow toward Shannon. "I will kill your friend if that is what it takes to get you to cooperate. I want to return home to my people, who thought I was killed by your chief. I have lived off periwinkles and cattail sprouts long enough. I am well enough now to leave the swamp."

"We have walked far since we left the canoe," Little Snow Feather said. She tensed, waiting to see if Shannon would give them away.

She was relieved when Shannon showed no signs of revealing the truth to Black Rock. Leading him on with a lie was the only way they both might survive this ordeal.

Little Snow Feather hoped that if they could stall long enough, someone would realize they should have returned home already. They had been gone longer than they had planned. The sun was lowering in the sky behind the tall trees.

Their absence would soon be noticed. She hoped the search would lead her brother to the edge of the swamp, where he would find the pony patiently awaiting the return of its mistress and friend.

Little Snow Feather decided to go back the way they came, but this time she'd weave farther into the forest in order to make their trek back take twice as long.

She prayed that before they reached the tethered pony, many Powhatan warriors, led by their chief, would have discovered the girls' plight. They would kill Chief Black Rock this time, for certain.

"I have to take the exact path that got me and my friend here, or I will get lost," Little Snow Feather said, forcing herself to look steadily into the evil chief's eyes, even though she felt anything but steady.

Her knees were trembling and her heart was thudding like a drum inside her chest.

As she held on to Shannon's hand, she could feel it shake.

She felt guilty for having led her friend into such a dangerous situation. But who could have known that Black Rock could possibly be alive to exact revenge?

"I will follow close behind you," Chief Black Rock said. He motioned with his arrow again. "Remember, I will kill your friend if you try to trick me in any way."

Shannon swallowed hard as she caught Little Snow Feather's glance.

"It'll be all right," Shannon said. "Just do as he says. Maybe he will have mercy on us after we help him."

"Perhaps I will have mercy enough not to kill you, but I will make sure that you cannot return home soon to warn Midnight Falcon that I am alive," Chief Black Rock said. "I will be way on my way home before you are found."

"Thank you for even considering sparing our lives," Shannon said, her voice filled with fear.

Chief Black Rock snickered, then nodded at Little Snow Feather. "Go!" he shouted. "Darkness is near."

Still holding hands, Shannon and Little Snow Feather began to walk through the forest, and then alongside the swamp, and through the trees again.

Shannon kept glancing at the sky, worried by the first streaks of black, which meant that soon all of the sky would turn that ugly color. Being in the swampy marshes at night would be frightening enough.

But now? With Black Rock as a threat?

She wondered if she and her best friend could possibly survive.

She prayed that someone, anyone, would find them and save them.

Praying gave her some hope that the ghost-spirit of Pocahontas was there with them, watching over them.

Surely she would never allow such a man to take the life of Pocahontas's namesake, or her friend.

If ever Shannon was to truly believe in ghosts, now would be the time. She hoped that she would soon get proof!

33

Oh, Thou art fairer than the evening air,
Clad in the beauty of a thousand stars.
—CHRISTOPHER MARLOWE

Chandra walked her horse to its stall in the stable and stopped with alarm. She stared at the
empty stall where she would have expected Shannon's pony to be. Shannon hadn't returned home.

She hadn't been at the Powhatan village, either.
Chandra could sense that something was awry.

She hadn't thought anything about Shannon's
whereabouts when she had said good-bye to Midnight Falcon. She had just taken it for granted that,
as late as it was in the afternoon, Shannon would
have been safely home by now.

Chandra groaned. Little Snow Feather hadn't
been anywhere in sight either when Chandra had
left Midnight Falcon's lodge.

But Chandra figured that Little Snow Feather
must have returned. When the girl saw that Chandra's horse was still tethered outside Midnight
Falcon's lodge, she must have decided not to
bother her brother and his betrothed and had gone
elsewhere in the village until she knew that it was
appropriate for her to return home.

"Chandra, where in God's name is Shannon?"

The alarm in her brother's voice made Chandra jump. Jan-Michael entered the stable with wide, determined strides.

"I don't know," Chandra said, swallowing hard. "I only now noticed that she wasn't home."

"I thought that she would return when you returned," Jan-Michael said, going to stand before the empty stall. He nervously raked his fingers through his thick crop of red hair.

"Where is she?" he asked, turning to face Chandra. "When did you last see her?"

"Probably when you last saw her." Chandra felt a cold chill of fear circling her heart. "When I arrived at the Powhatan village, Shannon and Little Snow Feather were already gone. Midnight Falcon said that Little Snow Feather was on Shannon's pony with her. It was something they had wanted to do for a long time, but while they had you to worry about, they didn't dare go horseback riding together."

"Damn it, Chandra, don't start blamin' me for what might be wrong now," Jan-Michael said.

Chandra led her horse into its stall, secured the gate, then went to Jan-Michael. She hugged him. "I'm not blaming you," she said, stepping away to look up into his troubled eyes. "If anyone is to blame, it should be I. I should have been more attentive before leaving the village, and realized the girls weren't back from their outing."

"An outing that took them all day," Jan-Michael added. "Had I not been so preoccupied on my boat, I would've noticed much earlier just how long Shannon had been gone."

"Let's both stop trying to find blame," Chandra said. "What we should be doing is going to the village to see if Little Snow Feather has returned. If so, Shannon is probably with her, or well on her way home by now."

"Ay, that's what we should do," Jan-Michael said, hurrying to his horse's stall.

Chandra quickly saddled White Iris again as Jan-Michael prepared his steed for riding.

They rode from the stable together and headed toward the Indian village.

"I don't like this at all," Jan-Michael shouted. "All sorts of things could happen to two innocent girls." He glared at Chandra as she looked over at him. "I told you that Shannon shouldn't be allowed to run around so carefree on land that is new to us all. Lord, what if those cannibals decided to come back and avenge their chief's death? Wouldn't they love to take the Powhatan chief's sister away, as well as her friend?"

His face grew pale. "For God's sake, Chandra, those Pocoughtaonacks are cannibals," he said, his voice breaking.

"Don't think such a thing," Chandra said, fear flooding her like ice water through her veins.

They grew quiet, alone in their private thoughts as they rode hard toward the Powhatan village.

Chandra broke away from Jan-Michael and pushed her horse even harder when she caught sight of the village in the dusky light of early evening.

Overhead the moon already hung like a cradle in the sky. The earliest evening star sparkled close by the moon.

"Soon it will be dark, and Shannon might be lost somewhere out there," Chandra whispered to herself.

She was so relieved when she saw Midnight Falcon, until she realized where he was headed.

To the river.

She looked toward the river and saw many canoes filled with warriors. The men waited for their chief, his canoe already manned by three of his favored warriors.

"Midnight Falcon!" Chandra cried as she turned her horse in his direction. "Wait!"

Midnight Falcon heard the approach of the horse, and then Chandra's frightened cry.

He stopped and waited for her to rein in beside him.

"You are here because of your niece?" Midnight Falcon said as Chandra slid quickly from her saddle.

He looked past her and saw Jan-Michael quickly approaching.

"Yes, she should have returned home by now."

"As my sister should have returned home, but she has not," Midnight Falcon said. He gently placed a hand on Chandra's shoulder. "They both are out there, surely lost."

"But I thought your sister knew the lay of the land so well," Chandra said, her voice breaking. She turned to gaze at the waiting canoes. "Why are the canoes readied for traveling?" she asked, feeling desperate. "The girls didn't leave in a canoe. They were on Shannon's pony."

"I know where they were headed and traveling by canoe will get us there faster than by foot." Midnight Falcon barely nodded at Jan-Michael as he dismounted and stepped up beside Chandra.

"Where were they going?" Chandra asked. "I thought they were enjoying a pony ride. Did they have some place they wanted to go to?"

"The marshes," Midnight Falcon said. "The swamp. My sister told a friend that she was taking your niece there today to teach her more about the ways of our people."

"Had she been there enough times not to get lost?" Jan-Michael asked.

"Many," Midnight Falcon said.

"Then maybe something else happened instead," Chandra said, the thought making her heart sink.

"We will not think the worst," Midnight Falcon said. "We must go now." He gave Jan-Michael a steady stare. "You will go with us in our canoes? You are welcome to."

"Yes, I wish to be a part of the search. I will do what you think is best," Jan-Michael said, nodding eagerly.

"We will work as a team and find them," Midnight Falcon said, extending a hand to Jan-Michael. "I welcome you, Jan-Michael, as a part of our search team."

Jan-Michael didn't hesitate to clasp Midnight Falcon's hand. After securing the horses, the three of them hurried toward the canoes.

When they arrived there, Chandra saw the unlit torches at the bottom of Midnight Falcon's canoe. She gave him a questioning look.

"Night is near," Midnight Falcon said, reaching a hand to Chandra's cheek. "Torches will be the only way to find them once we arrive at the marsh."

Feeling as though she had entered some sort of nightmare, Chandra flung herself into Midnight Falcon's arms and clung to him, only scarcely aware of her brother's stare.

Chandra was only concerned about one thing now—finding the children!

"We must go," Midnight Falcon said as he eased Chandra from his arms.

Chandra nodded, then followed the two men into Midnight Falcon's canoe.

Sitting at the far back, away from the warriors in charge of the paddles, Chandra welcomed Jan-Michael's arm around her shoulders.

"We will find her," he said.

The canoes swept out to the center of the river and began racing toward the marshes.

Every draw of Midnight Falcon's paddle seemed to be an extension of Chandra's own heartbeat. She watched the shoreline for any signs of the girls, but so far, she had seen nothing besides wildlife. Even the animals seemed intent on finding their nests before night fell.

She looked at Midnight Falcon with confidence, trusting with her whole heart this man who knew the land better than anyone.

34

If you press me to say why I loved him,
I can say no more than it was because
he was he and I was I.
        —Michel de Montaigne

There was only enough light left now for Shannon to make out where the land and the water met. She gave Little Snow Feather a worried glance, then walked onward.

Her heart raced with fear to know that they were almost to the pony.

The moment that Black Rock realized he had been duped, he would not hesitate to kill them both.

Shannon knew that Little Snow Feather held out hope for her brother to come looking for them. But soon it would be too late.

"I'm so afraid," Shannon whispered. "We've almost run out of time."

"I never give up hope, ever," Little Snow Feather whispered back.

Black Rock ordered them apart and shouted at them to be quiet. He came up closer behind the girls. "Where is your canoe?"

Shannon felt the sharp point of the arrow through her dress and stifled a scream.

"Have you purposely led me elsewhere?" Black

Rock said. "Do you not know what will happen to you if you have lied to me?"

"You plan to kill us anyway," Little Snow Feather said, her pulse racing. She saw how he stood close behind Shannon, the arrow shaft against her back. With only one shove he could kill her friend.

"So you have not planned to lead me to your canoe after all?" Black Rock glared at Little Snow Feather. "Have you led me in circles?"

"Wouldn't you have, if you were in our place?" Little Snow Feather said, bravely lifting her chin. "You are my brother's worst enemy. You are the one who is responsible for my mother's and father's deaths, and for the deaths of so many more whom I loved."

Shannon's fear mounted. Why had Little Snow Feather chosen such a moment to be courageous? Surely she knew that talking to the chief in such a way would only hasten their deaths. Shannon believed that she was at this very moment inhaling the last breaths of her life.

But then Shannon saw how Chief Black Rock suddenly seemed uninterested in what Little Snow Feather was saying, and he looked past them both. Whatever he saw caused him to slowly lower his bow and arrow. A smile was even tugging at his lips!

"What are you looking at?" Little Snow Feather asked. She, too, had noticed how he seemed transfixed by something that obviously pleased him. He no longer seemed intent on killing Shannon.

"You told the truth," Chief Black Rock said, already walking past the girls.

They turned to see what was causing his changed behavior and stared in wonder. A lone canoe rocked and swayed in the water only a few feet away where the swamp left off and the river began.

From this point a person easily could paddle out to the middle of the James River and soon make a quick escape.

Chief Black Rock was now running toward the canoe, having dropped his bow and arrow to the ground, and Shannon and Little Snow Feather knew that he was no longer thinking of them. Returning home to his people seemed to be more important.

Shannon and Little Snow Feather inched closer to the shoreline. They held hands, eyes wide, as Chief Black Rock boarded the canoe, lifted a paddle, then smiled at them.

"Go home, young maidens, as I will hurry onward to mine," he said.

Shannon was too curious not to keep quiet. "You never planned to kill us once we took you to a canoe?" she asked.

"I am not a child killer," Chief Black Rock shouted as he headed away from the swampy marsh. "I have daughters and even a granddaughter. In you I have seen them. They are as brave!"

They said nothing more to Black Rock, but watched him paddle farther and farther away from them, soon reaching the middle of the river.

"Little Snow Feather, whose canoe is that?" Shannon asked. She heard her pony whinnying in the distance and realized they were only moments away from having reached him. "Surely we would have seen the canoe when we were here earlier."

"I would have thought so." Little Snow Feather looked back at the escaping Pocoughtaonacks chief. "That can only mean . . ."

She didn't get a chance to finish what she was going to say. She gripped Shannon's hand more tightly as she suddenly saw another canoe out in the water. Yet she knew that it wasn't truly real. It was made of the snowy white down of swan feathers, and it was not traveling through the water at all.

Instead, it was floating just above the water line.

And there was only one person in this canoe— an Indian maiden!

Shannon gasped at the loveliness of the woman. She was ravishingly beautiful, slim, and amber-skinned, and she wore a mantle of blue feathers that were so thickly sewn, they seemed like satin. She had dark eyes like Little Snow Feather, and her long black hair streamed down her back in shimmering waves.

Shannon knew that this was Pocahontas.

Shannon saw Chief Black Rock drop his paddle as Pocachontas's canoe moved closer and closer to the cannibal chief.

She saw how he moved slowly and shakily to his feet, his eyes glued to the mysterious sight.

He was standing in the canoe now, his knees trembling, his eyes wide. He tried to scream but his throat was too dry.

Shannon covered her mouth with her hands in disbelief. She watched the chief's canoe begin to rock back and forth in the water, and then he suddenly fell over the side. He was soon lost in the murky water.

Darkness had now fallen all around them, yet the moon was bright enough so that its silver rays reflected on the water. They could see a sort of whirlpool swirling at the very spot where the chief had fallen into the river.

Amidst those whirling rivulets were bubbles, which both girls assumed were the last signs of the chief's life. Soon they, too, were gone, as was his canoe, and even the whirlpool had disappeared. The water was calm.

Trembling, Shannon looked around her, first in the water, and then along the shore, and she realized that the lovely maiden in the beautiful canoe made of swan feathers was also gone.

But it thrilled her to know that Pocahontas had allowed her at least that one glimpse of her. Shannon would never forget it, how mystical and mag-

ical it was, and how a man whose life was guided
by evil finally got what he deserved.

"She was so beautiful," Shannon murmured,
turning to smile at Little Snow Feather. "I shall
never forget her." She gazed at her friend for a
moment. "There is such a resemblance," she said.
"You both are so beautiful."

"I am glad that she showed herself to you, at
least this once," Little Snow Feather said, drawing Shannon into a hug.

"She had to have placed that canoe in the water
for the chief to find," Shannon said. She moved
away to look back at the water, still marveling
over all that she had just witnessed. "But why did
she wait so long to come to our rescue?"

"She knew that my brother and your father
were near," Little Snow Feather said, just now seeing torches in the distance heading toward them.
"She gave your brother and my father more time
to bond as friends while they searched together
for you and me. When she knew they were near
enough to find us, she chose to take away the life
of a man who had senselessly murdered her own
people."

"But he spared our lives," Shannon said, staring at the spot where she had last seen the chief.

"Yes, that is a thing of amazement to me, as
well," Little Snow Feather said, nodding. She
turned to Shannon and took both of her hands.
"Never tell what you saw here today, how Pocahontas's ghost-spirit came to our rescue. Never

ever mention anything about Chief Black Rock being here. It is best to keep that secret between us. Perhaps if we do not speak of the miracle of what we saw, Pocahontas will visit us again while we are together, so that we three can talk and laugh, as she and I have so often." She sighed. "The most important thing of all is that the evil chief is gone—this time, forever."

"Do you truly think Pocahontas will trust me enough to come again in my presence?" Shannon asked, her eyes filled with excitement at the possibility.

"I hope so, but one never knows."

They didn't get the chance to talk anymore of the day's miracles. The Powhatan warriors were moving rapidly closer in their canoes, their way lighted by torches. At the lead was Midnight Falcon's canoe, in which Shannon recognized not only her aunt, but also her father.

Yes! Pocahontas *had* known they were together, searching for their loved ones.

Shannon saw that, as well, as a miracle.

She ran with Little Snow Feather along the shore toward where the warriors were beaching their canoes.

Little Snow Feather ran into Midnight Falcon's arms as he left his canoe.

Shannon ran into her father's.

Chandra stood aside and watched, tears of joy spilling from her eyes. She had just begun to believe she would never see either girl again, doubt-

ing that they could find their way out of the
swamp once darkness fell.

The soft whinny of Shannon's pony drew Chandra's attention. She followed the sound and found
the pony tethered to a low limb. She patted the
horse, then untied its reins and walked it over to
Shannon and Little Snow Feather. The girls were
chattering to everyone like magpies, telling of their
day's adventure, of how they had gone farther
than they had planned. But they left out the most
important event of all, which would never be spoken of again.

Chandra and Shannon's eyes met. When Shannon smiled meekly, then looked quickly away,
Chandra could not help but think that there was
more to the truth than what was being said. She
had to wonder what the girls had experienced that
they were keeping to themselves.

She felt a strange presence behind her and
turned toward a darker part of the swamp.

She gasped when she thought she saw a canoe
drifting away into the moonlight. No, it couldn't
be a canoe. Even though it was in the shape of a
canoe, it seemed made of white feathers.

For a brief moment she even thought that a
woman looked back at her from the feathered boat.
She shook her head to clear her thoughts and
looked again. It was dark and she saw nothing.

"Chandra?"

Midnight Falcon's voice brought her out of her
daze. She turned and forced a smile. She would

never tell anyone what she had just imagined seeing, for they would think that she was daft.

"One of my warriors will lead Shannon's pony home," he said, taking her hands lovingly. "The girls will ride with us. You and your family will be taken safely home, but I do want you all, even Jan-Michael, to join my people tomorrow in the rites that initiate young Powhatan into manhood."

"The *huskanaw* rites?" Chandra said, remembering that once that ritual was over, her marriage ceremony would be next!

"Yes, and I believe it is a good time for your family to strengthen your bonds with my people. Will you all come?"

"I doubt that my brother will." Chandra glanced past Midnight Falcon at Jan-Michael, who was kneeling before the two children, smiling and talking. It was so good to see her brother behave as he once had.

And tonight, seeing that his daughter was alive and well, seemed to make his transformation complete.

When he hadn't flown into a fit of rage, accusing Little Snow Feather of almost causing his daughter's death by getting her lost in the swamp, Chandra knew that, for the most part, his dark moods were a thing of his past.

But to actually join in with the Powhatan as they performed their rituals?

No.

She knew that would be stretching things too

far, too soon, when he had only just begun to put his ill feelings toward Indians behind him.

"I shall be there with Shannon," Chandra said, smiling up at Midnight Falcon. "But my brother has only just returned to fishing. His crew will be waiting for him on his boat at dawn. He is eager to join them."

"I understand," Midnight Falcon said. He watched Jan-Michael reach out for Little Snow Feather and place one arm around her and his other around his daughter. "To see him as he is now with my sister is enough."

"Yes, isn't it beautiful?" Chandra said, walking with him hand in hand toward the waiting canoes.

She turned only long enough to see one of the warriors on foot, leading the pony back in the direction of her home.

It was wonderful how they were all becoming friends.

She could not help but wish tomorrow was over so that she could concentrate on their wedding day.

Nothing could stand in the way now of her marrying the man she would love forever!

35

So dear I love him, that with him all deaths
I could endure, without him live no life.
—JOHN MILTON

Chandra sat beside Midnight Falcon on a slightly
raised platform in the huge council house away
from everyone else crowded into the lodge. The
center remained open for the *huskanaw* ritual.

Chandra had been there since dawn with Midnight Falcon, while Shannon sat with the other
girls her same age and with those boys who were
not participating in the rites.

Chandra's brother had declined her offer to attend, and she understood. But she did expect him
to attend her marriage ceremony.

Trying to focus only on the rites, she pushed
thoughts of her brother from her mind and gazed
at the boys who were involved in the ceremony.
Only the most promising young men between the
ages of ten and fifteen were being publicly recognized by being initiated.

She frowned as Midnight Falcon explained that
this was a rigorous test of endurance in which a
few youths would not survive.

She had been relaxed until then, even eager to
be a part of this exciting day with the man she

loved. Now that he had told her some of the young men might not survive, Chandra's mood turned somber. She no longer wished to be there, but she had to, since it was something expected of the future wife of a Powhatan chief.

But she was not sure now if she could be a part of a culture that took their children's lives so lightly. How could she sit here and wait for that moment when perhaps one or more of the young men would die? How could anyone force their children to participate in rituals that might claim their lives?

She looked around the room and saw the anxious expressions on the faces of most mothers. How could any mother just sit there knowing that her child might not be alive tomorrow?

The proceedings had begun early in the day with a feast in the huge council house, in which the entire village had participated.

There had been so much food. There had been baked maize cakes, fish broiled over outdoor fires, roasted joints of venison, wild fowls on spits, and fresh oysters baked in their shells.

And then had come the dancing. She saw it again now, still in awe of the beauty of the ceremony. People dressed in their very best had formed two large dance circles around an outdoor fire.

Watching and learning, she wanted to be among the dancers after she became Midnight Falcon's wife. She had enjoyed how gracefully the dancers, both men and women, had moved, one circle going clockwise and the other counter-clockwise.

But suddenly the dancing had changed. The men and women, painted, feathered, and beaded, became frenzied. Their dancing was accompanied by shrieks of *yah-ha-ha*, *whe-whe*, *tewittowah*, and other mocking cries.

After they had almost exhausted themselves, the dancing had ceased and everyone had returned to the large council house to further the proceedings that were meant to make men of boys.

At this very moment, as Chandra was wishing that she had not agreed to come, the boys in question entered the lodge, attired only in breechclouts, their bodies painted white.

The boys were led to the very center of the lodge, and those adults who had not danced outside now came forward to form a wide circle around them. They began dancing and singing.

Chandra looked past the circle of dancers and tried to read the expressions on the boys' faces. She was not at all surprised when she saw no fear in any of their eyes. They must have been prepared for this special day since they were old enough to be told about the *huskanaw*, and about the importance of it in their lives. Midnight Falcon said that Powhatan boys readied themselves by playing games of endurance from the time they were small.

Suddenly the dancers stopped. They left the lodge, soon followed by all of the other spectators.

Chandra followed Midnight Falcon out of the lodge, as well. She looked anxiously for Shannon, sighing with relief when she found her walking with Little Snow Feather.

Of course, Chandra had nothing to fear as far as her niece was concerned, for she and the rest of the girls were only spectators today. Chandra had been told that no such rituals were required of the young maidens. Their future was charted out from the day of their birth, to be wives to those boys who would become men today.

It was only the young men who had to prove themselves in order to be worthy of a wife and family.

Midnight Falcon said that today was the worst of the many tests that still lay ahead of them. If they came to the end of the day, having passed this test of endurance, they would have the courage to face the future rituals, for none of them were as important, or as dangerous, as today's.

"Come with me, for the rest of the ceremony is performed away from the council house," Midnight Falcon said, offering Chandra a hand as they walked farther away from the lodge.

She was afraid of what these boys had yet to do, and the ceremony seemed ominous to her now. Chandra gave Midnight Falcon a pensive look and did not take his hand right away.

He seemed puzzled by her behavior. She did not want to disappoint him, even though she was having doubts about whether she was the right sort of person to be his wife. If she could not with-stand the image of boys dying in order to prove their worth to their people, maybe she did not be-long here.

Shakily she lifted her hand to his. When the warmth of his fingers circled hers, and he drew her next to him, she forced a smile.

"You will be all right?" Midnight Falcon asked, his eyes searching hers.

He could not understand her change of attitude. Surely it had nothing to do with the ritual at hand. To him, it was touching how the young boys were so eager to become men. But he had to remember that this was all very new to Chandra. It was up to him to make sure she understood every aspect of it.

"Yes, I'll be all right," Chandra said. "What hap-pens now?"

"The most important part of the ritual is about to occur," Midnight Falcon said.

He swept an arm around her waist and ushered her onward. Everyone was walking in haste to-ward the forest, where the dancing had taken place earlier. Many trees had been felled to make room for the large fire.

"Is this the dangerous part?" Chandra asked as they caught up with the crowd. The Powhatan sat down in a wide circle around a huge cypress tree, the fire now behind them.

"Yes, this is where the abductions take place," Midnight Falcon said matter-of-factly. He was surprised to hear Chandra gasp and see her grow pale.

He stopped, placed his hands gently on her shoulders, then turned her to face him. "You still do not understand the ritual, and where it is leading," he said. "I should have told you more about it before it began. But now I do not have the time to tell it all to you. Just trust me that in the end, all will be well among our people."

"Our people?" Chandra asked, her eyes wide. "You say that as though . . . as though I am already a part of your people."

"You are," Midnight Falcon said, leaning to brush a kiss across her lips. "Tomorrow we become man and wife. Do not our hearts beat for each other the same today as they will tomorrow?"

Chandra looked deep into his eyes, almost wishing that she could look away. She was afraid that he could look into her soul and see her doubts.

"Yes, my love for you today is as strong as it will be tomorrow when we become man and wife," she said, but she no longer felt as eager about their wedding.

She would not reveal this to Midnight Falcon now, not while he was proudly presiding over something that his people saw as so important.

"I do not have time to explain what will happen next," Midnight Falcon said, taking her by a hand again and leading her past those who were sitting to another platform, which had been placed so that he could get the best view. "Just watch. Be as proud as my people are of the young boys who will do what is required of them to become men."

Chandra still could not erase from her mind the fact that some of those proud boys might not see another day.

Should any of them die, Chandra knew that she would not be able to stay another moment in the Powhatan village. She would grab Shannon's hand, and they would leave. Chandra would never return, nor would she allow Shannon to come back.

She sat down beside Midnight Falcon and held his hand. Her other hand circled into a tight fist. Her heart pounded inside her chest as she watched the proceedings continue.

The boys, ten in all, were led to a tree and made to sit down next to it. Several warriors, armed with reed bundles, came and stood before the boys, looking as though they were there to guard them. The warriors stepped away from the boys and formed a line.

Ten older boys, perhaps in their late teens, came and urged the initiates to their feet. They grabbed them by the arms and led them down the line of older men, who suddenly seemed furious with the younger boys.

The warriors began whipping the initiates with their reed bundles. Chandra grabbed her hand away from Midnight Falcon and stifled a gasp behind her hands.

Midnight Falcon leaned closer to Chandra. "What you see is an abduction being acted out," he whispered. "Notice that the reeds do not leave marks, which proves the warriors are barely grazing the initiates' flesh."

"But surely it hurts," Chandra whispered back. Stunned, she watched the same ritual being repeated, not once, but two more times. Then the initiates sat beside the tree again, with no sign whatsoever of having been beaten with the reeds.

Suddenly the warriors dropped the reeds and went to the tree. They tore off small, pliable limbs and quickly fashioned wreaths for the boys and placed them atop their heads.

During this part of the ritual, Chandra's attention was diverted by the women of the village, many of whom had begun to moan loudly, while others wept and cried passionately.

A shiver ran down Chandra's spine. As the villagers started to sing, she thought she recognized the Powhatan words for death and sacrifice.

Her heart sank as she watched women bringing mats, skins, dry weeds, and moss to those who seemed to be mourning. Chandra knew that these were things used for preparing the dead for burial.

Chandra believed that these women were planning for some of the boys to die. They were even ready to prepare the dead for their graves!

Her fears seemed confirmed when the initiates were ordered to their feet and were led to a ravine that had been dug nearby.

Horrified, Chandra watched the boys, one by one, walk into the ravine. They stood stiffly, as the same warriors who had beaten them earlier began thrashing them with the reeds, and this time she could see marks being left on their copper flesh.

One of the boys crumpled to the ground, his eyes closed, and a warrior stood over him and drew a knife from his sheath.

Chandra could not stand watching any longer!

She knew better than to try to interfere and stop the ceremony. All she could think about was fleeing and putting this horrible thing behind her.

And Shannon!

She stumbled down off the platform and ran to Shannon. She grabbed her from beside Little Snow Feather and half dragged her away while Shannon complained loudly.

"Be still, Shannon!" Chandra cried, not easing her hold on her niece's hand as they headed for home. "I've had enough. You should, too!" Sobs tore through her. "How could they? It's so barbaric!"

She heard Midnight Falcon calling her name and knew that he was running hard and would soon catch up with them. Chandra was glad when they reached the river, where many canoes were moored.

"Get in!" she yelled. "We need to get away from this place."

She grunted as she tried to shove the canoe into the water, but found it difficult since it was so large.

She looked desperately from side to side for a smaller canoe.

Then she pleaded with Shannon. "Please, Shannon, help me get this canoe in the water."

"I don't understand why you are so upset," Shannon said, refusing to help. She placed her fists on her hips. "What happened?"

Chandra wiped tears from her eyes just as Midnight Falcon reached them. He spun her around to face him.

"Why did you run away?" he asked, a keen puzzlement in his eyes.

"How can you even ask that?" Chandra tried to ignore the Powhatan people who had followed Midnight Falcon and now stopped to stare and listen. "That boy passed out. And then . . . then the warrior drew his knife. Had I stayed, I would have been witness to a sacrifice to one of your gods."

She pummeled his chest with her fists. "Tell me I am wrong!" she cried. "Tell me I only imagined what I saw. Tell me no boys were to die today. Tell me!"

She didn't give him a chance to answer. She was too filled with horror.

"Midnight Falcon, were I to marry you and we had a son, would you be so insensitive toward him?" she sobbed. "What if our son couldn't pass the test? Would you allow him to die?"

"No boys will die today, or ever, especially not a son born of our love," Midnight Falcon said, grabbing her wrists to stop her assault. "The *huskanaw* ritual is not what you think."

"I saw how the boys were being beaten with the reeds!" Chandra whimpered. She was glad when the Powhatan people went back to the ritual, leaving her and Shannon alone with their chief. "Tell me I only imagined that."

"You did see that, but the wounds you saw are only superficial," Midnight Falcon said. "By tonight, after my people's Shaman medicates them with special herbs, there will be no signs of what happened."

"But the songs your women sang about death and the burial preparations were all real enough." Chandra continued to sob. "How can that be explained away?"

"The deaths spoken about in the songs are symbolic rather than real," Midnight Falcon said, gently drawing her into his arms. He was upset with himself now that he had not taken the time to explain the ritual in detail to her before it began. "Boys pretend to die so they can be reborn as real men. It is not an actual sacrifice, just a ceremonial one."

"The knife?" Chandra asked halfheartedly, realizing how wrong she had been not to have more faith in Midnight Falcon. She was filled with shame and embarrassment.

She had interrupted the ceremony. Would the Powhatan people ever forgive her? Would they be able to accept her now as Midnight Falcon's wife?

For she still did want to be his wife so badly.
She would never doubt his goodness again!

Tonight had shown her not to jump to conclusions so quickly.

"The knife was only supposed to make it look real," Midnight Falcon said. He placed a finger beneath Chandra's chin and lifted it so that he could look into her eyes. "The warriors plunge the knives close to the fallen boys, but never make contact with them. It is dangerous, but no one has ever gotten hurt. It is a part of the ritual, which is required for the boys to become men."

"Was it always this way, or were young men sacrificed among your ancestors?" Chandra asked warily. She scarcely had noticed that Little Snow Feather had come to take Shannon back to the ceremony, which was now proceeding even without the Powhatan chief.

"Long ago, yes, sacrifices were made, but that was a long, long time ago, and things were very different then." Midnight Falcon smiled at her. "Will you return with me to see the rest of the ritual and watch each boy become a man in his own right?"

Feeling foolish, and immensely relieved, Chandra sighed heavily and apologized.

Midnight Falcon accepted her apology heartily. They walked hand in hand back to the platform.

She watched as more boys pretended to die and listened to the funeral songs of their mothers, aunts, and grandmothers.

Even when the boys were laid out on the ground, pretending to be clinging to life, and were given a supposedly poisonous concoction of some kind, Chandra watched, content. Everything looked different now, and she could hardly believe how wrong she had been. She understood that she was witnessing boys who would one day be powerful warriors like Midnight Falcon.

In her mind's eye, she imagined a son of her own becoming a man one day in his father's mighty image!

She could only smile at such a thought. She slid a hand over her tummy. She could hardly wait to know if she was carrying a son or a daughter. No matter which, it would be loved and cherished.

But tomorrow came the second most important day in her life after the one that would bring her first child into the world.

Her wedding!

Yes, she was going to marry Midnight Falcon tomorrow, all doubts now cast into the wind, forever!

Epilogue

There's nothing half so sweet in life
As love's young dream.
—THOMAS MOORE

Some Years Later—Taquitock, Autumn

After a full day of celebrating the harvest with dancing and feasting, Chandra was snuggled beside Midnight Falcon in their bed of soft pelts and blankets. A lone candle beside the bed gave off enough light to see by.

At times like this, she often thought back to her wedding day. The ceremony had been so simple and quick and beautiful.

The Powhatan priest, Limping Fox, had held Midnight Falcon's and Chandra's hands together in the presence of the entire village and Chandra's family.

Midnight Falcon's best friend, Feathered Hawk, had brought a long string of shell beads and broke it over the couple's heads.

The priest had announced then that the couple was married!

Afterward, Midnight Falcon had surprised her by telling her that she was now a queen—his and his people's.

Chandra would never forget how it felt to wear the lovely wedding dress that had been Midnight Falcon's mother's, or how the maidens of the village had prepared her face for the ceremony. She had worn walnut oil and blue clay sprinkled with particles of silver ore on her cheeks and forehead. She had learned that when the Powhatan dressed up for an occasion, they did not wear special clothes but added more ornaments to their everyday attire. They wore necklaces and, depending on their rank, feathers, beads, and other decorations. A chief's wife decorated herself with many strands of pearls, interspersed with copper.

"Today was a good day," Chandra murmured, melting as Midnight Falcon ran a hand down her back. He swept it around and gently cupped one of her breasts, which was swollen with milk for their third child, due any day now.

Midnight Falcon had taken their first-born into his heart as his own, and they had named the boy Two Hawks.

There had been another baby a year after Two Hawks's birth, but it had not survived.

After the loss, Chandra had become determined to learn all about the plants that could be used for childbirth difficulties. She now knew that white trillium might have saved her second-born. She even knew that partridgeberry could be used for speeding childbirth, but she was not ready to risk that. She would let nature take its course, and be sure to have white trillium always at hand just in case.

"The harvest was good, which made the feasting even better," Midnight Falcon said, drawing a patchwork quilt that she had sewn up over them both to ward off the chill that came with being in a room away from the lodge fire. If that did not warm them enough, he would use his new fur cloak, called a match coat, which was spread out at the foot of the bed.

"And our people enjoyed the fish that my brother brought for the feast," Chandra said, snuggling closer to Midnight Falcon to draw the warmth from his naked body.

She smiled as he gazed down at her.

"And isn't my brother's wife, Priscilla, sweet, especially now, when she is so big with child?" Chandra said. "Priscilla enjoyed today's activities. She feels comfortable among our people."

"It is good that Jan-Michael gave up searching for the woman he saw in the pond," Midnight Falcon said. Although he had never said anything, he knew who it had been. He knew of only one woman whose description fit—Pocahontas.

She had been as hauntingly beautiful as Jan-Michael described.

Midnight Falcon had seen her for himself. He had not shared those visits with anyone, not even his wife.

It had happened many years ago, when he was a child lost in the forest. Pocahontas's spirit had come to him and held his hand and led him to safety. She had come to him after that, from time to time, on occasions when his spirits needed lifting.

It was a secret that he would one day share with Chandra. When the time was right he might even beckon Pocahontas to him so that his wife would also know her. Secrets were not good between a man and a wife, even if it was something that he had held close to his heart like a wonderful, sweet elixir through the years.

And should not such elixirs be shared between a man and a wife? Yes, he *would* tell her. Tonight!

"It's wonderful how Jan-Michael and Priscilla met," Chandra said, "in the James City Parish Church, where my first husband was the rector. I'm glad that he began attending church each Sunday. Priscilla and the church have brought such peace to my brother's heart."

She paused. "And to Shannon's," she said. "She loves Priscilla and is even enjoying learning how to knit and embroider, instead of spending all of her time out of doors."

"My sister, even, likes to stay inside now some of the time." Midnight Falcon said, laughing softly. "Little Snow Feather not only knows how to sew with pearls and beads, she now knows how to knit with yarn."

"The bracelet that Little Snow Feather made for Shannon out of those precious purple pearls is so beautiful," Chandra said.

"Your mother should be arriving from England soon. It is good that she will no longer be there alone, without family."

"Yes, I'm so glad that she has decided to start anew in America. She will live with Jan-Michael and his wife in the mansion I gave them as a wedding gift."

Tears filled her eyes at the memory of how much she had wanted her mother there for the birth of her first child. If luck and the weather held, her mother would be there to witness the birth of her next grandchild.

Chandra raised herself up on an elbow when she heard the patter of little feet enter the room.

"Little Two Hawks," Chandra said, turning to face her five-year-old son as he climbed onto the bed beside her. The candle's glow created a beautiful picture. Her son was as handsome as his father, Lawrence, had been. Yet he had the Neal family's reddish hair and golden-brown eyes, along with a few freckles across his slightly up-turned nose.

Chandra had made him warm pajamas out of soft doeskin, which hugged his body from head to foot.

"Did you miss your mommy and daddy?" Chandra asked, as Two Hawks climbed over her to lie down between her and Midnight Falcon.

"I want to snuggle, too," Two Hawks said, giggling when his father tousled his hair. He gazed into Midnight Falcon's dark, warm eyes. "Papa, I want a story. Tell me the one again about how the Powhatan people were made?"

Chandra made sure that her son was well covered, then reached for Midnight Falcon's hand. She squeezed it lovingly as her husband began the child's tale that their son never tired of, about how the Powhatan had been created by a giant hare, who had kept them in a huge bag in a far-distant land, where they were constantly attacked by a group of aged women. . . .

She smiled wickedly as Midnight Falcon moved his free hand slowly up the inside of Chandra's gown while he continued his tale. He rested his hand on her left hip. A tiny red cardinal, her husband's family crest, had been tattooed there by the Powhatan's shaman on the very eve of her marriage.

Even Two Hawks bore the same crest, placed on the inner thigh of his right leg only one day after he had entered this world.

"And, finally, growing weary of the attacks, the hare released the prisoners, who then became earth dwellers," Midnight Falcon said.

Two Hawks giggled and settled down between his mother and father. "I like that story more than all the others you have told me, Papa. But now I'm so sleepy. Can I stay here and sleep with you?"

"Yes," Midnight Falcon said, brushing a kiss across his cheek.

Chandra was so content, it sometimes frightened her. She took each day as a blessing and smiled on it with goodness, eager to do anything she could to help her family and all Powhatan. With Midnight Falcon's love, she knew that all things were possible.

She slid a hand down to her swollen belly, smiling as she thought about this child who she prayed would be her husband's exact image!

Midnight Falcon looked at Two Hawks with pride. "One day you will follow my footsteps and be a great leader." He slid his son closer to him. "Now sleep well, my son. Tomorrow brings many hours of play for you and your friends."

Chandra was touched deeply by how Midnight Falcon accepted her son so readily, already teaching him the ways of a powerful Powhatan chief. She could never be more proud of both her husband and her son as she was at this moment. And she was so proud, herself, to be called Powhatan!

She gazed down at Two Hawks, who was fast asleep, his lips quivering into a smile.

"He's so adorable," she said, stroking his cheek.

"Wife, there is something that I want to tell you," Midnight Falcon said as softly as possible so that he would not awaken his son. "It is about a ghost-spirit that has come to me through the years."

Filled with awe, Chandra gazed intensely into Midnight Falcon's eyes and listened as he confided in her.

Somewhere in the distance, Pocahontas smiled.

Dear Reader:

I hope you enjoyed reading *Midnight Falcon*. The next book in my Signet Indian chief series that I am writing exclusively for NAL is *Fire Cloud*, about the Lakota and Chippewa Indians. *Fire Cloud* is filled with much excitement, romance, and adventure.

Those of you who are collecting all the novels, and want to hear more about the series and my entire backlist of Indian books, can send for my latest newsletter, bookmark, and autographed photograph. For a prompt reply, please send a stamped, self-addressed, legal-sized envelope to:

Cassie Edwards
6709 North Country Club Road
Mattoon, Illinois 61938

You can also visit my Web site at:

www: cassieedwards.com

Thank you for your support of my Indian series. I love researching and writing about our country's beloved Native Americans—our country's first people!

Always,

Cassie Edwards